THE IRON RING

A LIZZY BALLARD THRILLER

MATTY DALRYMPLE

WILLIAM KINGSFIELD PUBLISHERS

*With love to my partner in the dance of life, Wade Walton,
and to all the authors who showed me what was possible.*

1

———

Lizzy Ballard tried to sort through the voices—some clear, some faint—coming from just outside. As she strained against the tape that bound her ankles and wrists to the arms and legs of the decrepit chair, her eyes tried to find a gap at the edges of the dirty blindfold. The shaking in her body was no longer caused only by the frigid air of the room, but by her terror.

"You said you wouldn't hurt her."

"Sure, but I didn't bank on her being such a goddamned pain in the ass. I'm having second thoughts."

"Leave him alone!" Lizzy yelled.

"Be quiet!" one of the voices shouted back in reply.

"I won't be quiet!" She began rocking the chair on which she sat, the legs thumping onto the concrete floor. "Let me go!"

"Little hellcat, ain't she?"

Now she could hear the third voice more clearly. It was a voice she would have known anywhere, in any circumstances. It was close. Right outside the freezing shack.

"You're a bully!" she screamed. "You're a bastard! You're a miserable excuse for a human being!"

"That's it. All bets are off. You expect me to just ignore such insults?" The tone suggested the speaker was only too happy to have an excuse to renege on his promise.

"Now!" Lizzy screamed. "Do it now!"

From outside the shack came the sounds of bodies colliding —of grunting and swearing. She could see it like a movie playing in her brain—hands grappling for a weapon amid a confusion of rage and terror. It seemed to go on forever, although perhaps it was no more than half a minute.

Then there was a cry from one of the combatants, another stomach-churning pause, and then that voice.

"My God, what did he do to you?"

2

____

Two Weeks Earlier

Lizzy sat in a chair next to the hospital bed where her godfather, Owen McNally, lay. He stirred and gave a snuffling snort, then a muffled yelp. She stood and squeezed his big hand where it lay on top of the blankets.

"Uncle Owen?"

He woke with a start, and after a few seconds his eyes focused on her face.

"Hey, Pumpkin," he croaked.

"You okay?"

"Bad dream."

"I'm right here. I won't let anything happen to you."

He gave her a weak smile. "I'm in good hands."

"Go back to sleep."

He nodded, his eyelids already drooping. "Yes, I think ..." He settled and, a minute later, resumed his snoring.

Lizzy stroked the back of his hand for a moment, then sat down. She winced as the scrapes on her shoulder blades—mementos of her escape from the basement of Louise

Mortensen's Pocopson mansion—hit the back of the chair, and she shifted into a more comfortable position.

What could be the subject of Uncle Owen's nightmare? There were all too many possibilities. And if Uncle Owen had been a different kind of person, he might have laughed at her assurance that she wouldn't let anything happen to him. If it hadn't been for her, none of them would be in the situation they were in.

She jumped when a figure filled the hospital room door, but relaxed when she saw who it was. Like his brother, Andy McNally was several inches over six feet, red-haired, and fair-skinned, although Andy's complexion was more fair than pasty. A mustache and recently grown beard were other similarities, although Andy's were shorter and fuller than Owen's somewhat scraggly versions.

The primary characteristic that set him apart from his older brother was that he was missing about a hundred pounds of Owen's heft—although Lizzy realized that with the stress Uncle Owen had been under during the previous few months, the weight difference was probably not quite as much as it had once been.

"Hey, Andy," she whispered.

"Hey," he whispered back. "I talked with the doc—he says Owen's still coming along well."

Lizzy's throat tightened. "That's good. That's really good."

"Yeah."

"How are you doing?" Lizzy asked.

"Livin' the life," he replied with a bleak smile.

"You look like you could use a nap," she said. "Maybe there's some kind of doctors' lounge you could use. I can keep an eye on Uncle Owen."

He shook his head. "No, I'm fine. I should probably go check on Philip."

She stood. "Can I come?"

"Hey, I thought you were going to keep an eye on the patient," he said in a tired version of his usual teasing manner. Before she could reply, he continued. "There's really no point in you visiting Philip until he's alert enough to appreciate it. In the meantime, if you're willing to tear yourself away from Sleeping Beauty, the room at the hotel is all ready when *you* feel like taking a nap somewhere more comfortable than a hospital guest chair."

"That's okay. I think I'll stay here a little longer."

"Okay. I'll be back as soon as I can, and then I can walk you to the hotel and you can get some rest."

"Will you call me when you find out how Philip's doing?"

"Sure thing."

"Thanks, Andy."

She heard his normally light tread recede heavily down the hall, on his way to yet another visit to yet another victim of the situation she had gotten them all into. She hated the fact that Uncle Owen and Philip had been injured, but, she thought bitterly, they were probably safer in their hospital rooms than they had been at any time since the three of them had joined forces back in Sedona.

She pulled the chair closer to the bed and rested her hand on Uncle Owen's. So far, her power had brought them more suffering than safety, but she would find a way to keep them all safe.

She couldn't imagine how, but she'd find a way.

3

———

Louise Mortensen had driven away from her burning home—and the burning outbuilding behind which she assumed Mitchell Pieda lay—in Owen McNally's SUV. When she passed Pieda, Elizabeth Ballard, and the injured Philip Castillo on the rural road behind her Pocopson property, she didn't fool herself that they wouldn't recognize the vehicle.

As she drove west, she placed a call from a cell phone she had been assured was untraceable and, as instructed, set her GPS to a twenty-four hour diner outside Harrisburg. The gray gloom was lightening grudgingly to a weak March dawn when a limo pulled up in front of the diner. She gathered up her coat and handbag and, having already settled the check for the coffee she had ordered but not drunk, worked her way off the sticky vinyl of the booth and stepped outside. A young blond man in a chauffeur's uniform got out of the limo. A heavyset man, not in uniform , got out on the passenger side.

"Good morning, Dr. Mortensen," he said in a heavy Scandinavian accent. "If you'd like to give me the keys of the vehicle you drove here, I'll make sure that it's taken care of."

Louise nodded. "Toyota SUV," she said, and gestured toward where the vehicle was parked. She handed over the keys.

The man nodded and strode off.

The chauffeur opened the back door of the limo and she climbed in. He pressed the door shut behind her, got back behind the wheel, and rolled out of the diner parking lot, headed south.

An hour later, the limo pulled off a wooded country road onto a wide paved drive. Like her own home in Pocopson—her former home, she reminded herself—the drive was blocked by a gate, but rather than the decorative metal gate of her drive, this one was substantial, with an eight-foot-high metal fence running out of sight into the woods on either side. The gate and the fence were set back from the road, so neither would be visible to a casual passerby.

The road wound through wooded hills, for about half a mile, then, with little warning, ended in a circular drive. Louise recalled that on her first trip to the house, almost twenty years before, she had been momentarily confused about where the drive led, until she'd noticed the house. It was all mirrored windows and brushed metal, built low to the ground and blending seamlessly into the western Maryland landscape.

Even on her previous trips, made under less dire circumstances, she had arrived in a limousine sent by her host—he was not a man to give out directions to his home. And even having watched the scenery pass during the drive, even having tried to note road signs and landmarks, she would have been hard pressed to get to the house on her own. She suspected that the chauffeur took a circuitous route for just that reason.

She recalled her conversation with Gerard the one time he had accompanied her to the compound.

"He has to control every little thing," Gerard had complained over dinner when they returned home to Pocopson. "If I go away for the weekend and decide I don't like the company, I want to be able to get into my own car and drive away."

"But look what he's been able to accomplish by controlling every little thing," she replied.

"If becoming a recluse in the wilds of western Maryland is the price one has to pay for those accomplishments," grumbled Gerard, "I think I'll take my own humble achievements."

Louise smiled indulgently. "Gerard, are you fishing for a compliment?"

He flashed her that wonderful smile. "Why not?"

The limo glided to a stop at the entrance and the chauffeur jumped out and opened her door. She climbed out, expecting to be greeted by a butler or other majordomo as she had been on her previous visits. Instead, her host himself stepped out of the house and crossed the flagstone terrace, hand extended.

"Louise, I'm so glad to be able to welcome you back," said Theo Viklund with a slight Swedish accent, "although I wish it could have been in happier circumstances." He was of medium height and slender, with short gray hair cut with military precision, and assessing gray eyes.

She shook his hand. "Theo, I can't tell you how much I appreciate you providing me with a refuge."

Theo waved her ahead of him through the front door. "It is entirely my pleasure."

Inside, they were greeted by a grave-faced woman whom Louise recognized from previous visits.

"Maja can take your coat," said Theo.

The woman eased Louise's coat from her shoulders, then handed it to a man standing to one side of the door whom Louise had not noticed. He disappeared down a wide hallway leading back from the entrance hall.

"I can only imagine how tired you must be," continued Theo, "and I would not ask you to tell me your story before you have rested. Maja can show you to your suite. I'll have some food sent to you. Then, once you are refreshed, we can talk."

"I would appreciate that, thank you very much."

During her previous visits, Louise had stayed in one of the guest rooms off the hallway that ran straight back from the entrance hall, but Maja gestured to the right. "If you would like to follow me, Dr. Mortensen," she said, and led Louise to an unobtrusive corridor leading off the entrance hall.

Louise was struck, even more strongly than she had been during her previous visits, by the impression that Theo Viklund's compound was more like a spaceship than a house. The corridor curved slightly to the right, with a wall of windows on the left side giving a view across the wooded grounds. Louise glanced back just before the curve of the corridor took the entrance hall out of view. Theo stood in the hall, his hands clasped behind his back, gazing benignly after them.

After some distance, the corridor descended a short flight of steps, then ended at a door. Maja opened it, then stood aside to let Louise enter.

She stepped into an expansive suite, floor-to-ceiling windows on the left hand and far walls giving views of the surrounding woods. The furnishings were minimalist and elegant, in tones of ivory, cream, and gray. A large geometric painting in white, gray, and black, with touches of amethyst purple and emerald green, hung over a gas fireplace. With the slope of the land, Louise surmised that the right-hand side of the suite was actually built into the ground. A hideaway indeed.

Maja gestured toward the right side of the room. "Kitchen, bath, and bedroom. I regret we have no clothes for you to change into at the moment, but if you would like to put on the robe that you'll find in the bathroom, I'll have your clothes cleaned so they'll be ready for you after you've rested. There are pajamas on the bed, and we will be able to provide you with other clothes later today."

"Thank you."

"Just leave your clothes in the closet in the bathroom and I'll get them."

There was a knock at the door and Maja opened it. Outside was a young man holding a tray, and Maja indicated with a gesture for him to set up the meal at a table near the windows.

She removed a mobile phone from her pocket and handed it to Louise. "When you have rested and would like to be taken to Herr Viklund, just press zero and I'll come and get you. Is there anything else we can get for you, Dr. Mortensen?"

"No, thank you. You have all been most accommodating."

Maja and the young man stepped out of the room, each making a slight bow to Louise before they departed, and Maja closed the door of the suite soundlessly behind her.

Louise crossed the main room to the bathroom, which was walled with white marble seamed with gray, and found a brilliantly white terrycloth robe hanging on the back of the door. She removed her clothes—a tailored dress that had been crisp and neat a dozen hours before and low-heeled Christian Louboutin pumps—and put these, along with her handbag, in the closet.

She returned to the main room and went to the window. The trees were tall, the canopy twenty or thirty feet above ground strewn with moldering leaves, the view broken only occasionally by lower undergrowth. From this vantage point, with the contours of the ground and no doubt because of the curve of the hallway leading to the suite, no other part of the complex was visible.

She went to the table where the young man had set out the

food. She had not expected to be hungry, but it was so appealingly presented that she sat down to have a few bites.

The toast in its silver rack was the ideal shade of gold, the butter in its small glass dish seemingly freshly churned, each piece of fruit in its porcelain bowl unmarred and sweet. Juana had always wanted to fix Louise an omelet or French toast or eggs Benedict for breakfast—this simple but perfect food was more to her liking. She poured herself a cup of tea from an elegant art deco teapot and smiled slightly. Before this morning, she would have never thought that her life would seem decadent in comparison to another's.

She ate the toast and fruit and poured herself another cup of tea, but her eyelids were heavy. She pushed back from the table.

She went to the bathroom to remove her contact lenses, which felt glued to her eyes. Not bothering to turn on the light, she opened the closet door. Her handbag still sat on the floor of the closet where she had put it, but her clothes and shoes were gone. She had a disorienting moment of wondering if she had fallen asleep while sitting at the breakfast table, and Maja had come into the suite to get the clothes, but then saw a tiny sliver of light at the back of the closet. She realized that the closet must have a door that opened onto another room or a service hallway for the staff to discreetly remove dirty laundry or restock towels.

She almost reached out to tap the back of the closet but stopped herself. What would she do if the door opened and Maja stood there, asking if there was anything she needed? She smiled again, a bit ruefully. Was Theo going to show her up even in the degree of discretion and consideration with which he took care of his houseguests?

In the bedroom, she found a gray silk pajama top and pants arranged artfully on the bed. She removed the robe, donned the pajamas, and slipped between the fine white cotton sheets. A melancholy thought drifted into her head: there was nothing of her former life left. Mitchell, whom she had at one time considered her ally, had evidently thrown in his lot with Ballard. Her house was gone, George was gone. Gerard was dead. But before the melancholy could take firm hold, she was asleep.

4

———————

When the ride share car that Mitchell Pieda had taken from Kennett Square pulled up in front of his aunt's rancher in Jenkintown, he groaned inwardly at the sight of her car parked on the street. He had assumed she would be at work. He climbed out of the back seat and slammed the door on the driver's request that Mitchell have a nice day and consider giving him a five-star review.

His aunt was lying on the couch in her housecoat, watching a soap opera, a box of tissues in her lap.

"Mitch, what are you doing home?" she asked in a nasal honk, struggling to pull herself up on the couch, whose rust-colored plaid was topped with a slippery plastic cover.

"What are *you* doing home?" he replied.

She waved the box of tissues at him. "Cold." She spotted the dirt on his sleeve, which was hiding a smear of Philip Castillo's blood. "What happened to you?"

"Tripped."

"You okay?"

He brushed at his sleeve. "Yeah."

She blew her nose and stuffed the tissue in her pocket. "Let me see if I can get it out—save you a trip to the dry cleaner."

He stepped back. "No, that's okay, I can take care of it."

She looked at him skeptically. "Okay." She extracted the tissue from her pocket, blew her nose again, then headed for the kitchen. "I'm going to make some Jell-O."

He glared at the television, considering turning it off, but she'd just turn it back on when she got back from the kitchen.

He showered and changed into clean clothes: a shirt and pants from Boyd's that had been favorites until he had experienced the clothes Louise had provided while he was living in Pocopson. When he got back to the living room, his aunt was back on the couch, sucking on a Popsicle and trying unsuccessfully to catch the drips in a paper towel. The TV was now tuned to a game show.

"My throat's killing me," she said.

"Tea with honey is good for a sore throat."

"I'd rather have a shot of Jaeger," she said with a raspy laugh that turned into a hacking cough.

With a shudder, Mitchell asked, "Want me to get you that?"

"I think we're out."

As the game show segued with a burst of applause into a commercial for life insurance, Mitchell went to the kitchen and scanned the refrigerator for options. He found the ingredients for an omelet—he had become partial to the omelets Juana had prepared for him and Louise.

As he sprinkled cheese over the omelet, his aunt shuffled in and tossed the Popsicle stick in the trash can under the sink, then used the sponge to wipe ineffectually at a few cherry-red spots on her housecoat.

"What *are* you doing home?" she asked. "Shouldn't you be at work?"

Mitchell hadn't been at work for months. "There was a power outage, they sent everyone home."

She glanced at the Kit-Cat clock on the kitchen wall, whose bug eyes and waving tail Mitchell had disliked even as a child. "Kind of early in the day. They didn't want to wait to see if it came back on?"

Mitchell shrugged. "I guess not."

"How's it working out with that buddy you're sharing the apartment with?" she asked.

It was the story Mitchell had given her when he moved into Louise's house. "He got transferred, so I'll be moving back here. If that's okay."

She shrugged. "Sure, no problem."

He slid the omelet out of the pan onto a plate and took it and a glass of orange juice to the Formica table.

His aunt opened the refrigerator door, jiggled the tray of Jell-O hopefully, then shook her head and got another Popsicle out of the freezer. She lowered herself stiffly onto the chair next to Mitchell.

He scanned her thoughts to see if she was suspicious of his story, but there was nothing there to cause him concern. In fact, as usual, there was very little there at all—it was probably the reason he had been able to live amicably with her since his mother died when he was fifteen.

They sat in silence as she finished the second Popsicle and Mitchell ate the omelet. Then she stood and dropped the second stick into the trash.

"I'm going back to bed. If you're out, can you pick me up some NyQuil?"

"Sure."

She extracted a ten-dollar bill from the purse hanging on the back of one of the kitchen chairs and held it out to Mitchell. He took it by the corner and slipped it into his wallet as she shuffled off to her bedroom, leaving the game show squawking in the next room.

He went to the living room and turned off the TV, then returned to the kitchen. He was still hungry, so he put two pieces of bread in the ancient toaster oven. While the toaster ticked away, he looked around the kitchen, unchanged in the decade he had lived there. Magnets—souvenirs from his aunt's vacations—held a ragged mane of coupons to the harvest gold refrigerator. The clock on the cheap white stove permanently displayed 12:37. The knotty pine cupboards showed the scratches and scars of his aunt's late Bassett Hound's continual search for snacks.

He thought back to the kitchen in Pocopson—the Sub-Zero refrigerator, the Viking range, the marble island that was bigger than his bed. He thought of the supple leather of the chairs flanking the fireplace in the library, the deep pile of the Persian rugs underfoot, the glint of light on the cut crystal decanter at the discreet bar in the corner.

If only the hostess had been as gracious as the decor, he thought bitterly.

At least he was done with Louise Mortensen. She had driven away in Owen McNally's SUV, and he couldn't imagine her coming back. There wasn't anything left for her to come back to.

5

———

Philip Castillo opened his eyes to a sterile whiteness that could only be a hospital ICU. Details swam in and out of focus—the too-bright lights, the buzz of voices and bustle of activity outside the cubicle in which he lay, the monotonous beep of a monitor. His first coherent thought was that his shoulder hurt like a bitch.

A woman's face moved into his field of vision. "Mr. Castillo?"

Philip tried to figure out whether he should own up to his identity, but the nurse nodded as if he had responded and said, "I'll let the doctor know you're awake. And you have a friend waiting to see you."

Her face disappeared and in a few moments another took its place—a man with reddish-blond hair and fair skin. Philip thought for a disorienting moment that he had been unconscious for so long that Owen McNally had had time to lose a tremendous amount of weight. Then he realized that this must be another of Lizzy's allies, Owen's brother. Philip cast about hazily for the brother's name.

"Philip," the man said, "I'm Andy McNally."

"Dr. McNally," Philip heard the nurse's voice from some-where behind Andy, "I'll let the police know he's awake."

"Okay," Andy said over his shoulder.

Philip could hear the light tread of steps as the nurse left the cubicle.

"Lizzy ...?" he managed to rasp out.

"She's fine." Andy glanced back toward the door, then leaned toward Philip. "I know you're not in the best condition for this, but you need a story to tell the cops. They think you were the victim of a mugging in Kennett Square. Tell them you're here visiting me. I was in Sedona a couple of years ago—you can say I came to your counseling business for a reading, or whatever it's called, and we kept in touch. You got a hankering for Mexican and went to a restaurant in Kennett Square. You got mugged and shot in the parking lot."

"Mexican?"

"Trust me on this—you wanted to go to a Mexican restaurant and you went to Kennett Square." McNally lowered his voice further. "Lizzy got you there and took your wallet to make it look like you had been shot in a mugging. That's just for you," he added, "don't tell that part to the police."

Philip nodded.

"If you can't remember parts of the story," said McNally, "just tell the police your memory is hazy about what happened—it's not uncommon in people who have undergone severe trauma."

"Severe?"

"You lost quite a bit of blood, but you'll be fine. Remember what the story is—" and he ran through it again.

Visiting Andy ... hankering for Mexican ... shot in a restau-rant parking lot. He supposed it made some sort of sense.

6

<hr>

Brady Plott dropped a Wawa bag onto his desk and himself into his chair. At the adjoining desk, Bruce Denninger banged away, two-fingered, on his keyboard.

"Got some info about the guy that got mugged behind Dos Sombreros," said Brady.

"Oh, yeah?" said Den, not looking up.

"Name's Philip Castillo. He's visiting from Arizona."

"March seems like a weird time to leave Arizona and come to PA."

"Yeah, no kidding. He's visiting a friend—Andrew McNally. McNally's actually a doc at Mercy—or at least does some moonlighting there. He was at the hospital with Castillo when I was there. He's the one who IDed him."

"Is Castillo a doc, too? You said he had some medical papers on him when he was found."

"No. He's some kind of counselor in Sedona. He was still unconscious when I went over there earlier. They're going to call me when he comes around."

"What did you find out from the people at the restaurant?"

"Just that some teenage girl ran in and said someone was in

the parking lot and had been shot. They said she looked a little banged up—there was some blood on her cheek."

"Was she involved in the mugging?"

"She didn't say anything like that to the folks at the restaurant." Brady considered. "Maybe she put her ear down to the guy's chest to see if she could hear a heartbeat and got some of his blood on her."

Den raised an eyebrow.

Brady shrugged. "Just speculating."

"Who's the girl?"

"No one knows. She didn't hang around."

"See if you can find her."

"Will do."

Den hammered on his keyboard for another minute, then said, "This guy got jumped in the parking lot and no one saw it?"

"He was in the back parking lot. But I'm wondering what he was doing back there—it was late, there must have been spaces out front."

"Ask him about that," said Den.

"Yup."

"Was his car in back?"

"No, the only cars in back belonged to the employees." Brady pulled a paper-wrapped object from the Wawa bag, unrolled it to reveal a hoagie, and took a giant bite. He wiped some tomato juice from his chin as he powered up his computer. He ate and typed for a few minutes, then said, "Got the autopsy report back on that guy in the basement of the Pocopson house. Guess what he died of."

"Blood loss from the shot to the thigh?"

"Nope."

"Smoke inhalation?"

"Nope."

"He didn't burn to death, right?"

"Right."

Denninger sighed. "Okay, I give up."

"Stroke."

"Stroke?"

"Yup."

"How old was he?"

"Forty-nine."

Denninger sat back in his chair. "Some forty-nine-year-old guy's walking around the basement of a house belonging to Gerard Bonnay, who died of a stroke during a break-in at his company three months ago, and Louise Mortensen, who has disappeared off the face of the earth—the basement of a house decorated with accelerant-impregnated curtains that were probably used to burn it to the ground ... a guy, I might add, who was carrying a Sig Sauer and has a bullet wound to his thigh, and he dies of a *stroke*?"

"Yup."

Denninger rubbed his hands down his face. "Fantastic."

7

Late in the afternoon, Andy finally talked Lizzy away from Owen's bedside and to the room at the William Penn Hotel that he had reserved for her.

When they reached the room, Andy said, "You wait in the hall for a sec, I'm just going to make sure no one else has come by to visit."

"Andy, I should go in first—unless you're carrying a gun, I'm more 'armed' than you are."

"But I'm bigger and scarier looking," he replied. "Well, not *scarier* looking—that would be Owen—but more imposing. Wait here."

Lizzy fidgeted in the hallway while Andy checked behind the drapes and in the bathroom and closet, then waved her in.

"I dropped your bags off earlier," he said. "Need anything else?"

"Not that I can think of. Thanks for everything, Andy."

"No problem. If you get hungry, just order room service. When you want to go back to the hospital, give me a call and I'll walk you back." He glanced at his watch. "Although I need to swing by my parents' house."

"How are they doing?" asked Lizzy. Owen and Andy's mother, who suffered from dementia, had been particularly unhinged at the news of her son's heart attack.

"They're all right," said Andy. "Is it okay if we wait until tomorrow to go back to see Owen?"

"Sure, that's fine."

"I'm sure you can put the time to good use by catching up on some sleep."

"You're the one who looks like you need some sleep."

"Nonsense, I'm just hitting my stride."

Andy left, with an unnecessary admonishment not to open the door to anyone except him, and she flipped the door latch into place behind him.

She undressed, wincing at the stiffness in her muscles and the pain in her back. When she tried to take off her shirt, her stomach flipped and tears sprang to her eyes—it was still stuck to her back and shoulders by the blood from the wounds she had suffered forcing herself out of the tiny concrete window well to escape from the basement of Louise's Pocopson mansion.

She ran a bath and lowered herself into it slowly, her shirt drifting up around her in the steaming water, and flinched as the heat hit her raw skin. Eventually the sting passed, and she leaned back with a sigh. The next thing she knew, the water was cool.

She opened the drain and, as the water swirled away, tried to ease the shirt off her back. Still stuck. She refilled the tub with hot water and leaned back again.

She was able to remove the shirt after the third soaking.

She carefully toweled off and pulled on a nightgown. She ran her hand over her crew cut-short, copper-red hair. Maybe she'd stop at a drugstore and pick up a new hair color. Maybe she'd go back to her natural blond.

She checked her phone and found no new messages. She

considered texting Andy, but she knew he would get in touch with her if there was any news. She was exhausted but jittery, and she decided to inventory the items she had from the visit that she and Philip had made to Pocopson.

She sat down on the bed and opened Philip's duffel bag, which she had been carrying with her since the previous night. There was the small leather packet that held a syringe and a vial containing the drug Louise had formulated to increase Mitchell's power—what Lizzy called the squeeze and Mitchell called the crush.

She also had, committed to memory, the phone number Philip had given her right before he entered Louise's house—the number that he had told her to call if she needed a new identity. He had instructed her to tell the person on the other end of the line that Philip Casal had sent her. Philip must have changed his name from Casal to Castillo when he left prison. That was why Uncle Owen hadn't found anything on Philip's crime when he had done an internet search on him.

She opened the browser on her phone and typed *castillo* into the search: Spanish for *castle*. She smiled.

She started to type in *philip casal murder arizona*, then deleted it. It was clear Philip wanted to leave that part of his life behind. That was probably one of the reasons he had changed his name, and he wouldn't have told her about what he had done if he hadn't had to explain the reason for the favor he had asked of her. It felt disloyal to get the details from anyone but him.

She turned to another souvenir she had from the trip to Pocopson. It was the list Philip had stolen from Louise's desk, and appeared to be a catalog of the jobs that Millard had performed for her—the list that contained an entry that could only refer to the murder of Lizzy's father, Patrick Ballard: *12/5 PB Philadelphia*

She scanned the other coded entries. *3/6 PC Sedona.* That

must be when they had drugged Philip, meaning that each entry didn't necessarily mean a murder.

She began another set of internet searches based on the entries. With only a date, initials, and a location, it was impossible to know for sure what they referenced, but over the next hour she uncovered several possibilities: the Willow Grove home of a state medical board investigator named John Burgess had burned down on the same date listed behind *JB* on the list. According to the dollar amount listed in the last column, that had cost Gerard Bonnay and Louise Mortensen twenty-five thousand dollars. A professor in San Diego had been paralyzed in a hit-and-run accident. Fifty thousand. A Harvard research assistant had been killed in a mugging in Boston. Seventy-five thousand. She swallowed down a lump in her throat. Had George Millard gotten the same rate for the same job on her dad?

Her next search was for information on the murder of Philip's prison mentor, Oscar. She didn't know his last name, only that he had likely been killed two or three months ago, and about three months away from the end of his twenty-year prison sentence at the Williams Correctional Facility in Arizona.

Finally, she found an obituary she thought was for the person she was searching for: Oscar Riva, seventy-two. It included a long list of children, grandchildren, and great-grandchildren who survived him. She swallowed hard as she noted the date of this death. Philip had still been in mourning for his friend when Lizzy had walked into his psychic counseling office in Sedona and had unknowingly offered up a way for him to get revenge on Oscar's killer.

She stared at the screen, then typed, somewhat reluctantly, the name of the man Philip had asked her to kill: *Tobe Hanrick*.

There was no lack of information on Mr. Hanrick.

Tobe Hanrick Associates Implicated in Shootout
    Hanrick Gang Still Active in Central and Northern Arizona
    Tobe Hanrick Sentenced to Life for Torture Killing of University of Arizona Student
    Hanrick Cellmate Found Dead - Foul Play Suspected

She clicked on the first article, which included several pictures of Hanrick. He was a good-looking man, probably in his forties, clean shaven and tan, with short, light brown hair and hazel eyes. He was not traditionally handsome—his eyes were a little too close together, his mouth a little too small, his ears a little too big. But in a picture of him grinning, obviously cropped from a larger photo based on the disembodied arm draped round his neck, the overall effect was nice enough—a friendly and approachable man.

With a thumping heart, she clicked on the article about the student and read with bile rising in her throat.

The student's name was Sarah Pearson. The picture that all the news outlets ran was one from her sister's wedding. She was dressed in a peach-colored bridesmaid's dress, white flowers woven into her long blond hair. One arm was slung around her sister's shoulders, the other extended to click the selfie. Their cheeks were pressed together, their mouths open in laughter.

According to testimony at the trial, when Sarah Pearson's father had tried to move in on Hanrick's territory, Hanrick had driven to the University of Arizona campus where Sarah was a junior. He lured her into a van with the claim that he was the uncle of a housemate who, he told her, had been in a car accident and was in the ER. Once she was in the van, he and an accomplice bound and gagged her. Three days later, Hanrick called the father and gave him directions to the isolated hunting cabin where he could find Sarah's body.

At the bottom of the article was a mug shot, and for that

Tobe Hanrick had made no pretense of friendliness or approachability. His mouth was a thin line, the muscles in his neck corded in anger, and the eyes that stared out from the photo were ones that might have dogged the thoughts of the photographer months later.

If this had been the only crime Hanrick had committed, it would be reason enough to want him dead. But it was not the only one.

She scanned through other articles about those who had had the misfortune to cross paths with Tobe Hanrick. After a few minutes, she dropped the phone on the bed feeling sick to her stomach and went to the bathroom to splash cold water on her face. She patted her face dry, then stared at herself in the mirror. Sarah had been only a few years older than Lizzy. That blond hair could have been Lizzy's before she cut and dyed hers when she was on the run from Louise Mortensen and George Millard.

Now that she knew what Hanrick had done, Philip wasn't the only one who wanted him gone. Lizzy might not have been able to protect her father or Uncle Owen or Philip from the evil that existed out there in the world, but she had the power to make sure that Tobe Hanrick didn't cause any more suffering than he already had.

8

Louise opened her eyes and took a deep breath, enjoying the feel of the crisp bed linens for a moment before she turned her head to check the time. Almost seven o'clock—she had slept through the whole day. And, she had to admit, she was starving.

She got up and pulled on the terrycloth robe. Hoping she would not have to venture from the suite in a robe and pajamas, she went to the bathroom and opened the closet door. Her dress, now clean and carefully pressed, hung on a padded hanger, and the pumps, which had suffered during her walk from the house to the outbuilding where George had hidden Owen McNally's SUV, were polished. A small supply of underclothes lay neatly folded on a shelf. Next to her own dress hung two others—one a light gray wool with black trim, the other a rich emerald. She fingered the material appreciatively.

She took a shower, put on the gray dress, then found the phone that Maja had given her and pressed zero.

Maja answered almost immediately. "Good evening, Dr. Mortensen. I trust you are feeling rested?"

"Yes, thank you. And thank you also for the extra clothes. You did a wonderful job selecting them."

"I'm glad that they are to your liking. I didn't pick them out myself, but I will pass on your appreciation. Would you like to join Herr Viklund in the dining room?"

"Yes, thank you. Should I meet you in the foyer?"

"I will come to your room," said Maja, and disconnected.

There was a knock on the door less than a minute later, and Louise opened it.

"Please follow me," said Maja, and led Louise down the corridor.

When they reached the entrance hall they turned right, down the main corridor of the complex. They approached the double doors that led to the dining room where she and Gerard had dined with Theo. Louise slowed, but Maja continued walking, leading Louise through a few more turns before opening a door and stepping aside to let Louise enter.

This room was much smaller than the dining room with which she was familiar. The entire opposite wall was hung with floor-to-ceiling drapes in a subtle geometric pattern and a color palette similar to the one in her suite. The furniture was of a spare, streamlined design. A square dining table was set with fine white china, gleaming silverware, and sparkling crystal.

"There are appetizers on the side table," said Maja, "as well as still and sparkling water. Is there some other type of drink I could bring for you? A cocktail? A glass of wine?"

"Sparkling water will be fine, thank you."

Maja poured, added a wedge of lime with a pair of silver tongs, and handed the glass to Louise. "Please make yourself at home. Herr Viklund will be with you in just a few minutes." She stepped into the corridor and closed the door behind her.

Louise strolled to the table and glanced over the appetizers—

toast points topped with small swirls of gravlax and tiny sprigs of dill. They looked delicious, but she didn't want to have her mouth full of canapé when Theo arrived, so she reluctantly turned away.

She circled the table, then walked to the drape-covered wall. She found a separation in the fabric and pulled the curtain back slightly, expecting to see the woods that surrounded the compound. Instead, there was elegantly detailed paneling. She shrugged and let the drape fall back into place.

Theo arrived a moment later.

"Louise, I hope you found the accommodations to your liking, and were able to get some rest."

"Yes, the suite is lovely. I've never been in that wing of the house before. Or this dining room."

"The main dining room always struck me as being too large for two people. You must be hungry." He picked up the plate of toasts and held it out to her.

Louise took one gratefully, and Theo followed suit.

"Excellent," she said.

Theo poured himself a glass of water. "I didn't get a chance to say earlier how sorry I was to hear of your husband's passing. Gerard Bonnay was a fine man, and his death is a loss to us all."

"Thank you."

"It's been quite some time since you and Gerard visited," said Theo.

"Yes, at least two years."

"And how long since your first visit?"

"It was not long after I graduated from medical school, so ... almost thirty years."

There was a light knock at the door, and Theo called, "Come in."

The door slid open, and Maja stepped in, followed by her tray-carrying assistant.

"Louise, please have a seat," said Theo. "You can assess the quality of the chef's other offerings."

He pulled out one of the two chairs at the table for Louise, then sat himself.

Maja placed a salad at each plate, bowed slightly to both of them, and she and the young man with the now-empty tray left the room.

"May I pour you some wine?" asked Theo.

"Yes, thank you."

Theo removed a bottle from a silver bucket at his elbow and poured for Louise, then for himself.

"Do I recall correctly that you and Gerard had quite an extensive wine cellar?" he asked.

Since Theo had never been to their home, Louise knew he could only know this if Gerard had mentioned it. She smiled sadly—he had been proud of his cellar. "Yes, but it was much more Gerard's collection than mine."

Theo swirled his wine, sipped, and nodded. "I certainly recall the two of you talking about your lovely home outside Philadelphia. It's such a shame that circumstances dictated our dramatic course of action."

"Yes, although I don't know what else we could have done."

"So, the drapes worked as anticipated?"

She thought back to the previous evening.

She had started in her study, snatching up the files for Ballard and Mitchell, files that would have silenced any doubts that her adversaries had about her role in the creation of the pair's special talents. Then she had gone to the window, flicked a flame from the lighter she had been carrying ever since things had started to come unraveled, and touched it to the bottom of the drapes. She jumped back as the flames leapt up their length. She hurried from room to room and window to window, setting the lighter to the bottom of the drapes, staying only a moment to make sure the flames had taken hold.

"Yes, just as you described they would," said Louise.

"My supplier is very reliable," said Theo. "And you were able to save your research documentation in electronic form?"

Louise sighed and set her fork aside. "Most of it, but not all. George was scanning the records and giving me the contents on flash drives, and I do have those. I had him start with the most recent records and work backwards, but I'm missing the documentation of the earliest experiments."

"Ah, yes. May I also say how sorry I was to hear of Mr. Millard's death."

"He was a great help to me and Gerard over the years. Thank you again for making the introduction."

"And were his services satisfactory?"

"Oh, yes," said Louise, but her tone was equivocal.

"Except perhaps for the last few months?" Theo probed.

"Well, yes. If he had been able to eliminate Ballard, we might not be in this position."

"Very disappointing," said Theo. "And a shame that he was not able to complete the scanning of the records. But you do have the records of the two subjects you were in touch with, correct?"

"Yes. Elizabeth Ballard and Mitchell Pieda." Her voice hardened even beyond her normal tone. "As you know, it was Ballard who killed Gerard."

Theo nodded gravely. After a moment of respectful silence, he asked, "And do you know where Ballard and Pieda are now?"

"I don't know where Mitchell went after he left Pocopson, but he has an aunt who lives in Jenkintown, outside of Philadelphia, which is where he was living before he moved in with me and Gerard. It's possible that he went there."

Theo raised an eyebrow. "It would not be too difficult for

someone with access to even the most broadly available data to track him down there."

"No, but he might not think he has reason to guard against being found. He no doubt knows that George is dead, and that I have no incentive to go to the authorities. From his point of view, the game might be over."

"For a young man with his skills," replied Theo, "the game is never over."

Louise nodded.

"I'll have someone check the aunt's house in Jenkintown," said Theo.

"I don't know what her name is, or exactly where she lives."

Theo waved his hand. "No matter. We'll find her. If he's naive enough to run to his aunt's house in these circumstances, all the easier. Tell me more about his ability."

"I don't know that there's much I can add to what I've already told you. He's able to cause cranial bleeds through the power of his mind. He called it the crush. The power is minimal under normal circumstances—he killed a work colleague, but it took many days of him spending considerable time with the target. However, I formulated a steroid-based drug that greatly magnified his power. Under the influence of that drug, he can kill almost instantaneously."

"Do you have any of this drug available to you?"

"No, but it would be easy to reformulate, with the appropriate equipment and reagents."

"Excellent," said Theo with a smile. "And Mr. Pieda's ability to cause strokes was not his only skill."

Louise had resigned herself to the fact that, considering that Theo was hiding her from the authorities, she owed it to him not to hold back any information related to her experiments. "I wish I had been able to spend more time studying that," she said. "He can read certain people's thoughts under certain circumstances.

He was able to read our housekeeper Juana's thoughts. In some cases, he was able to read Gerard's thoughts. He said I was difficult to read. And every indication was that he couldn't read George's thoughts, probably because George always had his mental defenses up around Mitchell."

"Although you found a way around that," Theo said, the admiration clear in his voice.

"Yes. A slight variant of Rohypnol lowered the subject's defenses. We tried it out on George, proving that it worked even on someone who knew he had been drugged and had reason to resist having his thoughts read, and then used it successfully on Philip Castillo to find out where Ballard and her godfather were headed after they left Sedona."

"And you would be able to formulate more of this drug?"

"Oh, yes." After a moment, Louise continued, "We need to keep in mind that the Rohypnol drug is a facilitator, but not always necessary for Mitchell to read a person's thoughts. If you send someone to find him, Mitchell might be able to ascertain information from that person that we would rather he not have."

"I think I have a solution for that. A young woman I'm grooming to take a larger role in my business affairs. In fact, it is my niece, Rey. Did you ever meet her?"

"Yes, I did have the pleasure of meeting her, perhaps five years ago. She was at Georgetown, studying law, correct?"

Theo nodded. "That's right."

"An intelligent young woman, and composed beyond her years."

"Yes, she has already been a tremendous help to me. We could send her to get Mr. Pieda without giving her more information than she needs to discharge that assignment, and fill her in on the details later."

"It seems an awkward position to put her in."

Theo smiled. "We will explain the reason for the limited background. She will understand."

Louise smiled back. "Well, she is certainly a good candidate to encourage cooperation from Mitchell," she said.

Theo laughed. "Yes, I can see that that might be the case." He took a sip of wine. "What was your relationship like with Mr. Pieda? Cordial? Competitive? Adversarial?"

"It was a business relationship with high stakes," she said. "As you can imagine, under those circumstances, it had its ups and downs."

"Would you say it ended on an up note or a down note?"

She shrugged. "A neutral note."

"Really? I would have thought that with the situation as unsettled as it was, and the stakes as high, your relationship with Mr. Pieda might have been strained."

Louise hesitated. She was not a good liar—Gerard had always handled any situation that required smooth deception. And Theo—a man who had access to the specialized tools of arsonists—was unlikely to be shocked at any collateral damage that might have occurred.

She took a sip of wine. "It's more accurate to say that before the night of the fire, I could have said our relationship was on an up note, but when Ballard and Castillo showed up in Pocopson after Owen McNally's heart attack, Mitchell was away, helping his aunt with a family matter. When Mitchell got back to Pocopson, Castillo knocked him out and left him behind one of the outbuildings. Mitchell might have assumed that George and I had seen what happened to him on the security monitors."

"And, when the fire spread from the house to the outbuilding," said Theo, "that you had abandoned him."

"I didn't know for sure that he was tied up," she said stiffly. "The security cameras don't show the area behind the outbuildings."

"No, but that was really the only logical conclusion as to why he didn't emerge from behind the outbuilding once Ballard and Pieda had gone into the house. That, or that he was still unconscious and therefore helpless."

Louise kept her eyes on Theo's and her face impassive, but under the table her knuckles whitened as her fingers closed on her linen napkin.

Theo waved a hand. "I don't blame you for doing what you did. In fact, I admire it. I have always admired your ability to keep your eye on the prize regardless of distractions along the way. But it's important for us to know that Mitchell Pieda has reason to dislike you. Perhaps even to hate you."

Louise gave a single, curt nod.

"And what is the prize for Mr. Pieda?"

"Money," she said promptly, then considered. "Not so much money itself, as what it can provide. Status. Access to the finer things in life."

There was a knock at the door and Maja and her assistant entered and served the entrées.

When they had withdrawn, Theo asked, "What do you know about Philip Castillo?"

"Castillo?" She shrugged. "He styles himself a new age counselor. Ballard saw him several times, and obviously they formed enough of a bond that she and McNally were able to convince him to come out to Pennsylvania from Arizona and break into my home."

"What do you think motivated him to throw his support behind Miss Ballard?"

"I really don't know."

"Do you think he and Miss Ballard are romantically involved?"

"George thought not, and his assessments of such things were usually reliable."

"Did you know Castillo had been in prison?"

Louise raised her eyebrows. "No."

"For second-degree murder."

Louise stared.

"He was nineteen," continued Theo. "He stabbed another young man."

She drew her eyebrows together. "I would have expected George to have discovered that."

"His name was Casal when he went to prison."

"Still."

"Casal. Castillo. Is he Mexican? Or perhaps Native American?"

"It's possible."

"Does he look Mexican or Native American?"

"I suppose so."

"Any family?"

"I haven't any idea. Why are you so interested in him?"

Theo swirled his glass of wine. "Over the last decade or so, I have been exploring some business opportunities in the Southwest that someone of Mr. Castillo's appearance—and temperament—might facilitate." He took a sip. "I can't imagine that being a new age counselor pays very well," he said contemplatively.

Louise shifted in her seat. "Would you like to hear about Elizabeth Ballard?"

Theo held up his hand. "I have plenty to consider for now."

The conversation for the remainder of the meal was about a paper Louise had presented at a conference the previous year. When Maja and the young man had cleared away the dessert plates, Theo stood, came to Louise's side of the table, and pulled out her chair for her.

"I will very much look forward to continuing our conversation tomorrow," he said.

She stood. "Theo, I know I'm putting you in an awkward position by coming here. Should we be making plans for my departure?"

"Nonsense. I couldn't be more pleased to have you as my guest, and I can assure you that you won't be bothered as long as you're here."

"But I can't stay here forever."

"We must give you a chance to tell the rest of your tale," he said. "Then we can decide how to proceed."

9

———

The next morning Philip was moved from the ICU to a room. Philip suspected that the fact that it was a private room was thanks to Andy McNally's influence. Just as the nurse finished getting him settled, a young man with cop written all over him appeared at the door.

"Mr. Castillo? I'm Detective Brady Plott of the Lenape Township Police Department. How are you feeling?"

"Not bad, all things considered."

Plott removed a small spiral notebook from his pocket. "We certainly haven't given you a very friendly welcome to Pennsylvania."

"Just in the wrong place at the wrong time, I guess."

"Can you describe what happened?"

Philip gave him the story Andy had prepped him with: visiting Andy ... hankering for Mexican ... mugged behind the restaurant.

Plott shook his head. "That's a shame. I understand that Dr. McNally lives in Villanova."

Since Philip had no idea where Andy lived, he remained silent.

"Kennett is quite a drive from there," Plott continued.

"I was in the mood to do some exploring."

"What made you choose that restaurant?"

"I heard it was good."

"Oh, yeah? I'm always looking for good Mexican myself—do you remember who gave you the recommendation?"

"Must have been McNally."

"So," said Plott, "you drove to the restaurant and parked the car."

"Yup."

"Where did you park it?"

Philip appreciated that Andy had no doubt been keeping the cover story bare bones in the hope of making it easy for him to remember, but he was wishing Andy had provided a few more details.

"Parking lot."

"Do you remember which one?"

"The restaurant parking lot," said Philip, hoping the restaurant had a parking lot.

"In back?"

"Yeah, I think so."

Plott waited for a moment, evidently hoping Philip would elaborate, then said sympathetically, "The car's not there now."

"Damn. Mugger must have gotten my keys and taken it."

"Too bad it wasn't in front. Better lit out there."

"Yeah, too bad," said Philip.

Plott nodded encouragingly. When Philip didn't say anything, he said, "Good thing that girl saw you back there."

"What girl's that?"

"White girl between sixteen and eighteen with very short red hair. She ran into the restaurant and let them know you were out back."

"That was lucky."

"Does she sound like anyone you know?"

"Nope."

"Why did you park in back anyway?"

Philip started to shrug, then thought better of it when his shoulder protested. "Can't recall."

Plott nodded. "Yeah, a bullet wound can play havoc with the old brain cells."

Philip shot him a look, then decided he was being sincere.

"Did you drive out from Arizona?" asked Plott.

"No. Flew."

"Rented the car?"

"Yeah."

"If you can give us the name of the rental agency, we can get the license plate and keep an eye out for it."

"Great," said Philip, wishing Plott were a little less the eager beaver when it came to helping out a crime victim. "It was Budget."

Plott nodded and jotted a note.

"Can you describe what happened to you?" he asked.

"I can't really recall anything after I got to the restaurant. Like you said, the brain cells."

The nurse stepped into the room. "How are you feeling, Mr. Castillo?"

"Tired." At least he didn't have to make that up.

"Brady," she said to the detective, "that's enough for now. He needs some rest."

"I can imagine," said Plott sympathetically. He slipped the notepad back into his pocket. "We'll do our best to get your belongings and your car back. If you do remember anything about the mugging, or think of anything that might be helpful, please give me a call." He put a business card down on the bedside table.

"Will do," said Philip.

"Especially that girl—I'd love to talk with her. She might have seen something that would help us track down the mugger."

"Yeah, maybe. I'll let you know if I think of anything."

"Or maybe she was involved."

"Doesn't sound like it."

Plott shrugged. "Either way, it would have been better if she hadn't run off. But don't worry—we'll find her." He gave a wave and left the room.

Philip lay back. The police finding Lizzy was exactly what he was worried about.

10

———

Lizzy got a roll of quarters from the front desk of the hotel and found a pay phone in a largely deserted conference area. If she was going to Arizona to kill a man, a fake identity seemed like a good idea, and if she was going to call a number she had been instructed to memorize and not write down, it seemed smart to make that call from a pay phone.

She picked up the handset, then returned it to the cradle. She was reaching for the handset again when she saw two maintenance guys coming down the hall toward her, talking and laughing. She glanced around, spotted a restroom a few yards away, and slipped into it. Maybe if she was calling a man to get a fake ID, she shouldn't even be seen near the phone from which the call was made. It wasn't like she had any experience with this sort of thing.

She looked at her reflection in the restroom mirror as she listened to the men's voices recede. Her face was more pale than could be explained by the week since she had last been in the Arizona sun. She reached up to run her hand across her brutally short crew cut and suddenly she missed the long blond hair she had cut off when she was on the run from Louise. When she was little, her mother had let her hair grow long because that was better than risking Lizzy getting angry with the stylist. After her mother had died, she had kept it long out of habit. When all this was over, she would grow it out again.

When she could no longer hear voices from the hallway, she returned to the pay phone. She took a deep breath and picked up the handset. There was just one promise standing between her and this all being over. She would go to Arizona to take care of Tobe Hanrick, not only because she had promised Philip that she would, but also because if she didn't, she knew Philip would try to do it himself, and she couldn't think of a way that would turn out well for Philip.

Lizzy pressed in the number Philip had given her, then fed quarters into the phone at the instruction of the automated voice.

"Hello?" The voice was quiet, almost whispery.

"Hello. I'm calling because Philip Casti— Casal gave me this number."

"Philip Casal? It's been a long time since I heard that name."

"He said to call this number if I needed a new identity."

"How do I know you know Philip Casal?"

"He's medium height, kind of wiry build. Dark hair and dark complexion. Dark eyes."

There was no response.

"He was at Williams," she said. "For killing someone."

"Who?"

"What?"

"Who did he kill?"

"A rancher's son."

"What was his name."

"Um ... I don't know." Lizzy's heart was beating hard now. Maybe she should have done that search on Philip's background after all. What if she wasn't able to convince this person that Philip had actually given her the phone number?

"Why did Casal kill the rancher's son?"

"He was doing something bad to an animal."

"What was he doing?"

"I don't know. That's all he told me." The heavy handset was slippery in her grasp.

"You haven't told me anything that anyone might not easily find out about Philip Casal."

Lizzy racked her brain. What could she say that would prove she knew Philip? "He was friends with a man named Oscar who was killed at Williams. Oscar told him the lesson of the Ruby Slippers."

Silence.

"The lesson of the Ruby Slippers is that you have the power within yourself to help yourself out of your own problems, but sometimes you need help realizing it." She was blathering now. "And snakes and ladders. The lesson of snakes and ladders is that the snakes are your vices, and they trip you up, and the ladders are your virtues, and they help you along—"

She heard a quiet laugh at the other end of the line. "Yes, I see you do know Philip Casal."

Lizzy slumped against the wall.

"I've owed Philip Casal a favor for a good many years," said the voice, "and I've never been one to like owing a favor. I'll be glad to finally pay off that debt. What do you want?"

"Pardon?"

"Driver's license?"

"Yes."

"Snap a couple of selfies. Don't smile. Then I'll give you an email address to send them to."

She took a couple of pictures and sent them off.

After a moment, the voice was back. "I'm not going to be able to match the hair. What color is your hair when it's not red?"

"Blond."

"That'll be easier. Hold on."

She heard the sound of the phone being placed on a hard surface, and then some sort of shuffling noise in the background. A minute ticked by, then two. The automated voice asked for more money and she fed in more quarters. Lizzy hoped the transaction could be completed before she ran out of coins. She felt a rivulet of sweat trickle down her spine.

Finally the voice was back. "Okay, I got a good one. It helps that all teenage girls wear their hair long and straight these days. And because you're a student of the Ruby Slippers," there was a soft laugh, "it's a premium product—it'll pass a background check, like for a gun. But you can't use it at a TSA checkpoint."

"That's fine."

"Where do you want it sent?"

"Can you send it to a hotel?"

"Sure."

"You could send it to the William Penn Hotel in Philadelphia. Let me look up the address ..." she said, tapping on her phone.

"Don't bother, I'll look it up. What name should I send it to?"

Lizzy groaned internally. "Andrew McNally." It was the name the room was reserved in.

"Okay. I'll get this in the mail to Andrew McNally today. You should have it tomorrow, the next day at the latest."

"Wow, that's fast."

"Damn straight."

"Thank you."

"You tell Philip Casal we're even now."

"I will."

And the line went dead.

11

———————

Philip was congratulating himself that the discussion with Plott that morning had gone about as well as the circumstances and his condition would allow, when more alarming thoughts began to sour his mood. Specifically, thoughts about what had been in the pockets of the jacket he had worn to Pocopson, which was likely now in the hands of the hospital—or the police.

He hit the call button at the side of his bed, and in a few moments a nurse appeared.

"Everything all right, Mr. Castillo?"

"I was wondering—do you have my belongings?"

"I can't imagine they kept your clothes. They would have been quite a mess."

"How about what was in my pockets?"

"I'm sure the police have that." She must have noticed his worried expression. "I know it's inconvenient, but I'm sure you'll be able to replace anything that the muggers took as soon as you're discharged."

As she turned to go, he said, "I need to speak with Andy— Dr. McNally. Can you call him?"

The nurse looked at him critically. "You really shouldn't be having visitors. If you ask me, Dr. McNally is taking advantage of his association with the hospital—"

"Please," interrupted Philip. "I was carrying something important and I'm afraid the mugger got it. It's going to be a load off my mind if I can talk to Dr. McNally, then I can stop worrying about it and get some rest."

She sighed. "All right. I'll see if I can track him down."

A HAGGARD-LOOKING Andy arrived an hour later. "Hey, Philip, what's up?"

"I realized there were a couple of things in my pockets that could cause us problems, depending on whose hands they fell into."

Andy shot a look toward the door, then sat down on the chair next to Philip's bed. "Oh yeah? Like what?"

"I took three papers from Louise Mortensen's office. One was a list of jobs Millard did for Mortensen. Lizzy has that. I also found medical records for Lizzy and Pieda. I couldn't take the whole file, but I took a summary sheet from both of them and put them in my jacket pocket. They have Lizzy and Pieda's names on them."

Andy ran his fingers through his hair. "Shit." He was silent for a few moments, then said, "If they really dig into that stuff— and it seems unlikely if they think you're just some poor slob who got mugged on his way to dinner—maybe we can say that Lizzy and Pieda were clients of your counseling business. I suppose it's plausible that you might have medical information about them on that basis."

"And what if they find out that they both live in the Philly area?"

"You're visiting to check up on them."

"And I haven't bothered mentioning their names before now?"

"Jesus, Castillo, I know it's thin—let me know when you come up with something better."

Philip dropped his head back on his pillow. "Sorry. I've been thinking about it and haven't come up with anything better."

Andy sighed. "Let's hope they lose interest before we need to start explaining even more oddities." He paused as a cart trundled past in the hallway, then continued. "If they find Pieda, he's going to be just as interested in avoiding a connection with the Pocopson fire as we are. I'm not as worried about Pieda telling them what really happened as I am of him telling the cops a story that doesn't match up with whatever we tell them. Of course, if they discover that Lizzy and Pieda were both Vivantem babies, that would be dicey, but it's hard to see how they'd just stumble across that information."

"There's another problem," said Philip. "I don't know what happened to my phone."

Andy groaned. "Great."

"How thoroughly did the house burn?" asked Philip.

"The house pretty much burned to the ground, except for the kitchen. Parts of the basement are relatively intact."

"If I dropped the phone in Pocopson, those are the areas it would likely be. There or outside."

Andy flopped back in the chair. "It definitely wouldn't be wise for me to go snooping around Mortensen's property." He shook his head. "I think we just continue to lay low, and try to get you out of here and back to Arizona as soon as possible. Although you clearly can't be discharged for a couple of days."

Philip smiled bleakly. "I'm a fast healer."

"Let's not push it if we don't have to. There was a lot of damage to your shoulder, and you lost a lot of blood." Andy rested his head on the back of the chair for a moment, then hauled himself forward. "Oh, here's a fun fact for you." After a glance toward the door, he continued. "Mitchell Pieda can read minds."

"Are you kidding me?"

"I kid you not. Seems like Mitch had the old one-two punch in terms of weaponry—causing strokes and reading minds."

"My initials were on the list of George Millard's jobs," said Philip slowly. "And we know that Pieda came to my office for a consult under an assumed name. Maybe that woman I met at the Cowboy Club got me drunk so that Millard could bring Pieda to my house and read my mind to find out where Owen and Lizzy were. Although," he added, "I think I would have noticed Millard and Pieda showing up at my house no matter how drunk I was."

"They might have given you something, like scopolamine or flunitrazepam."

"Jesus. How do you know about the mind reading?"

"Because while he and Lizzy were rescuing you, he read Lizzy's mind."

"Wait a minute—*Mitchell Pieda* helped rescue me?"

"Yeah, Lizzy got his help getting you to the restaurant parking lot in exchange for letting him go."

"Jesus," he said again. "Where's Pieda now?"

"Who knows. But what we have in our favor is that he has every reason to hate Louise Mortensen—as far as he's concerned, she left him to burn behind the outbuilding where you guys had tied him up."

"Yeah. I guess that's good for us."

Andy pulled out his cell phone and glanced at it. "Listen, I've got to run. Do you need anything? Other than having me make any semi-melted cell phones in Pocopson disappear?"

Philip tried to sit up, and couldn't contain a wince. "There is one other thing."

"*Another* thing?"

"I need to talk with Lizzy."

Andy opened his mouth to protest, but Philip interrupted him. "I agree she shouldn't come here—we don't want her sitting here if the Lenape cops decide to drop by again—but if you could get me a phone, or loan me yours, I could call her."

"Why?"

Philip hesitated. "I asked her to do me a favor, and now I realize I don't need her to do it."

"What was the favor?"

"I can't say."

Andy raised an eyebrow.

"It doesn't matter in any case, since she doesn't have to do it."

Andy sighed. "I'll give her the message. I think it's important to keep as many layers as we can between you and Lizzy. I've been discouraging her from coming to visit you, but if they do end up tying you to what happened in Pocopson, I've got to believe they'd check any calls you make, so a phone call from you to Lizzy isn't a good idea. And since they can tie you to me, we probably shouldn't even be making calls to Lizzy from my phone."

Philip lay his head back on the pillows. "Yeah, you're probably right."

At that moment, the nurse came into the room and pulled up at the sight of Andy. "Dr. McNally, are you still here?"

"I just got here," protested Andy.

"You may be a doctor at this hospital," she said, "but in these circumstances you're a visitor. I need you to let Mr. Castillo get some rest."

Andy sighed, then stood. "I'll give Lizzy the message," he

said to Philip, "and as soon as you're up and about—and out of PA—you can give it to her again yourself."

"Thanks, Andy."

The nurse cleared her throat loudly.

"Okay, okay, I'm leaving," said Andy. "Hang in there, Castillo. A couple more days, and you'll be basking in the Arizona sun."

12

———————

Bruce Denninger trudged into the police station, a smear of soot on his cheek and a funk of smoke on his clothes.

"Man, whoever burned the place in Pocopson really wanted it burned," he said, tossing his coat toward the back of his chair, from which it slid to the floor. "Anything on the mugging?"

Brady tapped on his keyboard. "I'm checking out Live Scan to see if I can find that girl at Dos Sombreros who allegedly found Castillo in the back parking lot. They said she had short red hair—*real* short and *real* red. Maybe she was in on the mugging but didn't expect it to go down the way it did."

"Worth checking."

Brady turned his chair toward Den, crossed his arms, and leaned back. "Don't you think it's surprising that in a place like Lenape Township, in one night, the house of two local celebrities burns down with an armed man in the basement, and a guy from out of town gets shot behind a restaurant a couple of miles away?"

"Sure, it's unusual—hell, mischief night is a veritable crime fest around here—but what have you got to tie them together?"

Den drew his eyebrows together. "You have something to tie them together?"

"I had a productive morning," said Brady with a grin. "I got the ballistics report back on the bullet they took out of Castillo. He got shot with the same caliber gun that the guy in the basement in Pocopson was carrying."

Den sat back. "Sig Sauer, right? Not exactly unusual, but it is interesting."

"That's not the only thing. *Castillo* isn't his original name."

"Oh, yeah?"

"What do you think Mr. Castillo's name used to be?"

"I give up."

"Philip Casal."

"Okay."

"And guess what life-altering experience preceded Mr. Casal's name change?

"Damn it, Brady, can you ever just tell me something without playing twenty questions?"

"Twenty questions is more fun," said Brady cheerfully, "but if you're going to be a spoilsport ... he went to prison. And guess what—"

Den wagged his finger at Brady.

Brady sighed dramatically. "Casal did four years in Williams for second-degree murder."

Den sat forward. "You don't say."

"I do say," said Brady. "Got in an argument with some guy and knifed him."

"Did you get that from him?"

"No, I did a search on the driver's license he used to reserve his rental car."

"I wonder if the people whose medical records he was carrying would know anything we should know about Mr. Casal Castillo."

"My thoughts exactly," replied Brady. He consulted the small notebook that lay open on his desk. "I got an address for one of the names on the documents. Mitchell Pieda. Want to pay Mr. Pieda a visit?"

"Can't hurt."

Brady stood, retrieved his coat from the back of his chair, and pointed to his cheek. "Soot."

Den pulled a handkerchief out of his pocket and scrubbed at his cheek, then raised his eyebrows questioningly.

Brady gave him the thumbs up.

"How about the other document Castillo had?" Den asked as he tucked the handkerchief back in his pocket. "What was the name on that one?"

"Elizabeth Ballard," said Brady. "We're still looking for her, but if she's in the system, Dottie will find her."

13

———————

Mitchell was flipping through the issues of *GQ* that his aunt had saved for him when he heard a knock at the door. Neither he nor his aunt had friends who were in the habit of dropping by unexpectedly, so a knock inevitably meant someone asking for money, or asking if they had found Jesus.

His aunt had left for the doctor's office half an hour before, having declined his admittedly unenthusiastic offer to drive her. He pushed himself out of the Naugahyde recliner, which he had chosen over the couch that his aunt had been using as her sick bed, and went to the door.

He looked through the peephole to see a black Chevy Impala parked on the street at the end of the walk and two men on the porch who didn't look like they were there to ask for money or offer salvation. They looked like cops.

He considered for a moment whether he could pretend he wasn't home, but it was likely that they had heard his footsteps. He probed their minds, but the door seemed to present a mental as well as physical barrier.

He opened the door.

The older one held up a badge. "Good morning. Are you Mitchell Pieda?" He pronounced it PIE-da.

"Pieda," said Mitchell, emphasizing the long E, "like Piedmont. Yes, I'm Mitchell Pieda."

The older man put away the badge. "I'm Detective Denninger and," he nodded toward the younger man, "this is Detective Plott of the Lenape Township Police Department."

"Hello," said Mitchell.

"We're investigating some crimes that took place in Pocopson and we'd like to ask you a few questions."

"I can't imagine how I could help you with anything that's going on in Pocopson."

"Might be a wild goose chase, but we'd still like to ask you a few questions."

Mitchell shrugged and stepped aside. "Sure."

They entered and he closed the door behind them, then turned to them, his hands in his pockets.

"Could we sit down?" asked Denninger.

"Sure." Mitchell led them to the living room and gestured them toward the couch. He perched on the edge of the recliner.

The two cops lowered themselves onto the couch, and the older one got out a small spiral notebook and pen.

"There was a fire in Pocopson a couple of days ago, and we've identified a person of interest." He paused.

Mitchell scanned his thoughts, but they were inaccessible. The younger detective, though, was easier to read.

"Yes?" said Mitchell.

Denninger took a paper out of his jacket pocket, unfolded it, scrambled off the couch, and held it out to Mitchell. "Do you recognize him?"

Mitchell wouldn't have needed to be able to see the image in Plott's mind to know the photo Denninger was handing to him was likely to be Philip Castillo. He examined it for a few moments, then shook his head. "No, I don't think so." He handed the photo back. "What makes you think I might know him?"

"He had a document that had your name on it."

Mitchell didn't have to fake being startled—he hadn't seen that coming. "Really? What kind of document?"

"Some kind of medical record."

Mitchell sat forward. He tried to get more information from Plott's thoughts, but either his own alarm or Plott's excitement was interfering. "He had a medical record with my name on it?"

"Not a full medical record, just one page. It looked like some sort of summary sheet."

"How could he have gotten that?"

"We think he got it from the house that burned. It was owned by Louise Mortensen and the late Gerard Bonnay, who ran the Vivantem fertility clinic."

Mitchell scanned Plott's thoughts to see if they knew that he was a Vivantem baby, but sensed nothing. He shrugged. "Sorry, I can't help you."

"We're just starting the investigation," said Denninger, "and this and a couple of other documents that he had with him are the only leads we have at the moment. Maybe as we find more information, we can run it by you—maybe trigger some memory of where you might have crossed paths with this guy."

A couple of other documents introduced possibilities that ratcheted up Mitchell's concern a few more notches. He scanned both their thoughts but could get nothing concrete.

"Can I see the documents?" asked Mitchell. "Maybe I could tell you more if I saw them."

"I'm afraid not. The information in them would be confidential."

"I could just look at the one that had my name on it."

"We don't have them with us at the moment, but we'll keep

your offer in mind." Denninger nodded to Plott, and they extracted themselves from the couch. "Thank you for your time, Mr. Pieda," said Denninger, back to the PIE-da pronunciation. "If you think of anything that might be helpful to the investigation—even if it doesn't seem important to you—please give us a call." He handed Mitchell a card.

"Sure," said Mitchell. "I'll do that."

He followed them to the front door and watched as they drove away.

What documents had Philip Castillo taken from the Pocopson house?

14

———

"Now, tell me about Elizabeth Ballard," said Theo. They were again in the small dining room, finishing their entrée of brook trout.

"She's a naive young woman who has no control over her ability," said Louise without hesitation.

"An ability that's considerably greater than Mr. Pieda's, correct?"

"Not when Mitchell's on the steroid drug."

Theo swirled his wine. "Yes, if one were to compare Pieda's steroid-enhanced ability to Ballard's natural ability, Pieda might win more points. But what if Ballard's ability was also enhanced? What then?"

After a moment, Louise said, somewhat reluctantly, "I suspect it would be even greater."

"And mind reading? Any sign of that in Miss Ballard?"

"Not that I'm aware of."

"Any sense as to whether she would have been more or less susceptible to Mr. Pieda's mind-reading ability?"

Louise considered, then said, "I don't know. There's nothing to suggest that the ability to cause strokes would have an effect one way or the other on susceptibility to mind reading, but it was an unintended consequence of an experiment that was aimed at achieving telepathy, so there may be a connection."

Theo took a sip of wine. "And it took her parents some time to realize what their daughter could do?"

"Yes. By the time her parents—and Elizabeth, for that matter—realized that she was causing her mother's strokes, her mother's condition was quite advanced. They took Elizabeth to a family cabin in the Poconos to keep her away from people, and once her mother died—"

"Of a stroke?" asked Theo.

"Yes, of a stroke," said Louise. "Once her mother died," she continued, "her father brought Elizabeth back to the Philadelphia area, to a house as far away from the city as he could get and still commute to his job at William Penn University."

"How old was Miss Ballard when she killed her mother?"

"Seven."

"That must have left quite a psychic scar."

"No doubt," said Louise blandly.

"And what then?"

"Ballard's father and Owen McNally spent a decade keeping her isolated, but then she killed a woman who harassed her and her father."

"Ballard killed the woman on purpose?"

"I doubt it—hence my assessment that she has no control over her ability. She would have no practical reason for killing a stranger."

Theo nodded. "Please, go on."

"Her father needed to keep her away from the police. You can imagine the result if a group of law enforcement officers tried to take into custody a girl who causes strokes when she's angry or frightened. Gerard stepped in and told him we could protect her."

"And then Mr. Millard killed her father."

"Yes. Gerard and I believed it was the only way we could keep control of Elizabeth. I must say we underestimated the tenacity and resourcefulness of her godfather."

"And you tried to kill Owen McNally with a dose of potassium chloride."

"Yes. In that case, I underestimated his weight," she said irritably.

Theo swirled his wine. "You said she causes strokes when she's angry or frightened. I can imagine she would have been angry with the woman who harassed her, and no doubt as a small child she would have periodically been angry with her mother, as all small children are. But how do you know she can cause strokes when she's frightened?"

"We tested her."

"How did you do that?"

"We locked her in a room with ..." Louise's voice trailed off, and she looked uncomfortable for the first time.

"With someone who frightened her?" prompted Theo.

"He was a small-time crook named Anton Rossi. Gerard told him that Elizabeth was," she paused again, "a prostitute. That she had been told to pretend to resist Rossi's advances."

"And so Mr. Rossi persisted even when Miss Ballard objected."

"Yes."

"Interesting," said Theo, sounding unconcerned. He took a sip of wine, then set down the glass. "And what is the prize for Elizabeth Ballard?"

"Her whole life has been built around creating an environment where her ability doesn't pose a danger to others. That was orchestrated by her parents and her godfather, but she has bought into that goal. Or at least she had," she said, her voice turning grim, "until she decided to kill Gerard."

"Which she did because she learned—or at least suspected—that Gerard was responsible for her father's death. And, indirectly, for the death of her mother, as well as her other unintended victims."

"Yes."

"And then she came after you because she learned or suspected that you tried to kill her godfather."

"Yes."

"And so her motivation now is ...?" He looked at her expectantly.

After a moment, Louise said, "I think it's safe to assume that she might come after me."

Theo nodded gravely. "All the more reason for you not to hurry away from the safety of my compound." He sat back in his chair. "And where do you suppose she is now?"

"I assume she's somewhere in the Philadelphia area, waiting for McNally and Castillo to be discharged from the hospital. As far as she knows, with Gerard and George both dead, and with Mitchell having betrayed me, I've exhausted my resources, so she may not consider me a threat, at least for now."

"But at the moment, neither McNally nor Castillo are in a position to help her."

Louise sighed. "There's also McNally's brother, Andrew. He helped Owen McNally get Ballard away from us when we had her at the Pocopson house."

"Is she close to Andrew McNally?"

"I'm not sure what her relationship is with him."

"She has a growing band of allies."

"Yes," said Louise. She was silent for a moment, then continued, frustrated. "I'm afraid I haven't executed this operation as smoothly as I would have liked to."

Theo shrugged. "It's not really your usual occupation."

She scowled. "No."

Maja and a young woman whom Theo introduced as Elsa arrived to serve dessert—almond tart and Earl Grey tea—then retired.

Theo added milk and a sugar cube to his tea. "I imagine you will be anxious to get back to your research."

"Yes, but I'm not sure when I'll be able to do that. Or where. I obviously can't go back to the Vivantem headquarters. In fact, I imagine I'll need to leave the country and go into hiding, although that also," she added, "is not my usual occupation. I'm not sure how I would do it. I must admit that I've been hoping you might be able to help me with that."

"That would be no problem," he said comfortably. "You know how much I admire your work, Louise, and I believe I can provide the facilities you would need to continue it right here on the property."

"But for how long?"

"As long as is needed."

"The police and the government have long memories," she said. "It might be quite a long time."

He waved a hand. "That is of no concern to me. It could be a permanent arrangement."

She hesitated, her tea cup halfway to her lips. "Permanent?"

"Certainly. No lack of room. And no lack of resources for you to pursue your research. You need only tell me what you desire and it will be provided."

Louise gave a strained laugh. "I'm fifty-nine years old, Theo. I could live another thirty years. I doubt you want me creeping around your compound when I'm ninety years old."

Theo gave an urbane laugh. "Not unless you were still enjoying your time here."

"Well." She put her cup down. "It's ... a very generous offer, Theo."

"Give me an opportunity to demonstrate what such a life could offer," replied Theo with a smile. "Then you can make up your mind."

15

———

Brady slammed down his desk phone. "Den, they found Casal's rental car in a lot a couple of blocks from Dos Sombreros. And guess what was in the back seat?"

Den glared at Brady.

"Oh, come on, humor me."

"Take out menus from Dos Sombreros."

"Nope."

"Jimmy Hoffa?"

"Nope."

"The gun that matches the bullet in George Millard's leg?"

"Nope."

Den sighed. "I give up."

"The crime scene techs found a stain they think is blood."

Den smiled wolfishly. "Did they swab it?"

"They're doing that now."

"Even if it's not Castillo's, it sounds like the events of that evening didn't go down exactly like he told us."

"Let's go talk to him again," said Brady.

Den tapped a pen on the blotter on his desk. "There's nothing illegal about having been in jail, and Castillo's not going anywhere. I think we should talk to the guy in Jenkintown again. I feel like he knows more about Castillo than he's letting on."

"Sounds good," said Brady.

They stood up and retrieved their jackets from the backs of their chairs.

"What about the other medical record—what was the name on it?" asked Den.

"Elizabeth Ballard."

"Any luck finding Ballard?"

"Not yet. There's an Elizabeth Ballard who lives in Parkesburg whose dad was killed in a mugging back in December."

"Another mugging?"

"Yeah. She was sixteen at the time—would be seventeen now. Preston checked out the Parkesburg house and no one was home. They're going to swing by again. Mom's dead—*not* a mugging," he said, in response to Den's raised eyebrow. "Guess what the cause of death was."

"Brady, goddammit ..."

"Died of a stroke ten years ago."

"Like Gerard Bonnay and George Millard."

"Exactly. There are a surprising number of people dropping dead of strokes."

"We should do a search for other people in the area who've had unexpected strokes."

"Will do."

"And ask Dottie to check on who Ballard's guardian is."

"She's on it."

"Ask her to get a move-on—we want to have all the information we can when we talk to Castillo."

16

———

Philip woke to a buzzing sound—some new monitor? He would have thought at this point they would be removing monitors, not adding them.

He looked around for the source of the sound and spotted a cell phone sitting on his bedside table. The phone buzzed again, and the screen lit with an incoming text. Philip picked it up.

It's Andy. Police realize you were involved in fire, they're coming to arrest you. If you can get to the entrance I'll pick you up.

Philip groaned and replied with a text: *No clothes*

I stopped by earlier you were asleep but I put some clothes in the closet

The fact that Andy McNally had stopped by his room and Philip hadn't even been aware of it gave him an unpleasant turn at his lack of diligence, but he supposed he had to cut himself some slack—he was still on the mend.

He swung his legs off the bed, trying to ignore the stab of pain from his shoulder. He removed the tape securing the IV line and pulled out the needle, then grabbed a few tissues from a box next to the bed to stanch a surprising amount of blood. He bent his arm to hold his makeshift bandage in place and pushed himself to his feet. He swayed for a moment, then walked gingerly to the closet.

Inside hung a pair of jeans, a T-shirt, a flannel shirt, socks, and a pair of leather boots. They matched Philip's usual apparel, although at a higher price point: Pendleton shirt, Ariat boots. At least the jeans weren't designer. The addition was a baseball hat. He was not normally a baseball hat kind of guy, but having the ability to hide his face seemed wise.

He shrugged out of his hospital gown and, keeping his ear tuned for footsteps in the hallway, put on the new clothes. He flushed the bloody tissues down the toilet and hoped that the plaid of the shirt would disguise any stain that might leak through the fabric. He had to stop periodically to steady himself with a hand on the wall when a spell of dizziness hit him. He had told Andy that he could get to the entrance, but he wasn't going to be able to make it much further than that.

He stepped to the door and glanced into the hallway. It was oddly quiet, not a doctor or nurse or orderly in sight. He stepped out of the room and started down the hall. He knew which direction the elevator was from the couple of nurse-escorted walks he had taken.

The wait at the elevator seemed interminable. He expected any moment for someone to tap him on the shoulder and ask him what he thought he was doing out of bed, but there was no way he could handle the stairs. Finally, the doors opened and he stepped in. Based on the looks the other passengers threw his way—fortunately, all visitors, not hospital staff—he was not looking his best.

When the doors slid open, he hung back, leaning against the wall while the other occupants stepped out. One of them, a young woman, turned back.

"Are you all right?" she asked.

"Yes, thanks. Just got some bad news."

"I'm sorry to hear that. Is there ..." She trailed off.

"Thanks, I'm fine. Just need a minute."

She nodded. "Sure. Well ... good luck."

She started down the hall, glancing back once.

She was wearing a coat and carrying a handbag, like she was on her way out. Philip hoped that if he followed her, he'd end up at the entrance where Andy was waiting.

He got as far as the lobby, then had to lower himself onto one of the couches. He could feel the tug of the sutures against his skin and was pretty sure his wound had opened up.

He pulled out the phone and laboriously pressed out a text.

Got to lobby not sure how much further I can get

Can you get to the entrance? came the response.

He sent back a thumbs up, pushed himself up from the couch, stifled a groan as his shoulder protested, and started his unsteady way to the entrance.

He was almost there when he heard a voice call from the vicinity of the information desk, "Sir, are you all right?"

Philip turned as much as he dared without losing his balance and waved his good arm. "Yup, thanks for asking."

He turned back to the door, but not before he saw the security guard—a middle-aged man with a buzz cut and sharp eyes —leave the desk and walk toward him. "Are you a patient, sir? Have you been discharged?"

Philip saw the sequence of events like a movie playing in his mind's eye: if they hadn't already connected him with the burned house and dead body in Pocopson, as Andy's text suggested was the case, then certainly his attempt at an unauthorized departure from the hospital would cause them to look further into why Philip Castillo of Sedona, Arizona, had come to Pennsylvania. They wouldn't have to look far to find enough to put him back in prison.

And he hadn't been exaggerating when he had told Lizzy that he would rather die than go back there.

The guard had almost reached him, but Philip had no energy to run. He wondered illogically if he could possibly delete the texts from Andy so as not to implicate him in whatever was about to happen, when another man appeared at his side—young, blond-haired, blue-eyed.

"Mr. Castillo," he said with a Scandinavian accent, taking Philip's arm, "I'm so sorry I was detained. The car is right outside."

The guard slowed, then stopped a few yards from Philip and the new arrival. "Do you gentlemen need any assistance?" he asked.

"No, thank you," said the young man. He steered Philip toward the door. "Dr. McNally sent me," he whispered.

Philip stepped outside, to where a sleek black limo idled. The young man led him to the car, a steadying arm on his elbow, and opened the back door.

Somehow this didn't seem like Andy McNally's style. Philip glanced back to the entrance where the security guard was standing, a walkie talkie at his mouth.

Sometimes the devil you didn't know was preferable to the devil you did.

He lowered himself into the limo and the young man pressed the door shut behind him.

The phone in Philip's hand buzzed with a text: *Safely away, I believe?*

That was definitely not the Andy McNally he knew.

Who is this? he replied.

An ally. Texting is so awkward. We can communicate more easily if you turn on the monitor.

There was a video monitor next to the seat. Philip reached out with his good arm and turned it on as the car glided away from the curb. A face appeared—a more mature, and more aristocratic, version of the driver.

"How do you do, Mr. Castillo," said the man. "I'm Theo Viklund. I'm pleased to make your acquaintance." He even shared the driver's accent, although his was less pronounced. "I apologize for the ruse of pretending to be Andrew McNally, but it was in fact the case that the police had tied you to the arson at Dr. Mortensen's home and the murder of Mr. Millard. I felt that convincing you that I was Dr. McNally was the most expeditious way of enlisting your cooperation."

"Who are you?"

"As I said—an ally."

"You provided the phone? And put the clothes in my room?"

"Yes."

"How did you do it?"

"We merely had to wait for you to be asleep."

"Do you work for Louise Mortensen?"

Viklund smiled, but there was a coldness to the expression that suggested irritation rather than amusement. "No. But I do have access to her resources."

"And what resources would those be?"

"That is better explained in person."

"Where are you taking me?"

"To a place you will be able to recover in peace, without concern about interference by the authorities."

"And where would that be?"

"My home. You will arrive here within a few hours. If at any time during the trip you wish to take a break, just ask the driver."

"And what if I ask him to take me somewhere other than your home?"

"To what end? I would just have to call the police with an anonymous tip about a sighting of a person of interest in the

Pocopson arson and murder, and you'd be right back where you were, except in handcuffs."

Philip grimaced.

"If you need any pain medication," said Viklund, "there's a pill and some water in the center console."

Philip glanced over. Sure enough.

"I will give you some privacy for the drive," continued Viklund. "I look forward to meeting you in person." The monitor went black.

Philip leaned back in the seat, trying to find a comfortable position. He would have been tempted to unbutton his shirt and check the size of the blood stain on the bandage, but he wasn't about to assume that Viklund wasn't still watching him.

He turned his attention out the window, trying to memorize the route they took—generally west—and the turns they made, but the quiet hum of the tires on the road was soothing, and he felt a little light-headed from the additional loss of blood.

In a few minutes his eyes drifted shut and he slept.

17

———

Mitchell hurried to the door, hoping to get to it before a second knock increased the chances that the sound would break through his aunt's NyQuil-induced slumber. The two cops from Lenape Township stood on the porch.

Mitchell opened the door.

"Good morning, Mr. Pieda," said the older one, back to the incorrect pronunciation. "Detective Denninger and Detective Plott."

"I remember."

"Can we come in for a minute?"

"My aunt's sick. She's in bed, taking a nap."

Denninger dropped his voice. "We'll be quiet."

Mitchell scanned Denninger's thoughts and found them just as opaque as during his first visit. He turned his attention to Plott, but sensed nothing other than a general excitement that masked any more detail. He sighed and stepped aside. "Let's go in the kitchen."

He led them to the kitchen and remained standing.

"Mr. Pieda," said Denninger, "we've uncovered some information that makes us even more convinced that the man whose picture we showed you yesterday was involved in the fire and murder in Pocopson. We'd like to ask if you'd be willing to come to the hospital where he's recovering from a gunshot wound to see if you recognize him."

"I already told you, I don't know who he is."

"I know you didn't recognize him based on the photo we showed you, but sometimes seeing people in the flesh is different." A mobile phone buzz emanated from Denninger's coat pocket. He reached for the phone as he continued talking. "We could arrange it so that he wouldn't be able to see you—" He glanced down at the phone, then did a double-take. Mitchell could see the text of the message as if he were holding the phone himself: *Head over to Mercy. Someone drove Castillo away from the hospital.*

"Damn!" exclaimed Denninger.

Plott raised his eyebrows in surprise.

"What is it?" asked Mitchell innocently.

"Unanticipated complication," muttered Denninger. He passed the phone to Plott, who read the message.

"Sorry to hear that," said Mitchell. "So, should we go to the hospital?"

"Not right now."

"Oh no? I thought you were anxious for me to see him," said Mitchell, enjoying himself.

"He's not at the hospital anymore." The scowling Denninger took the phone back from Plott.

"He was discharged?" asked Mitchell.

"Not discharged."

"He's on the run? How concerned should I be if a person who's suspected of arson and murder, and who had a paper with my name on it, is now on the run?" Mitchell tried to inject some concern into his voice.

"We're going to head over to the hospital now and check things out. If there's any information you should be aware of, we'll be in touch."

Mitchell followed the pair to the door.

"If you see the man whose photo I showed you," said Denninger, "or can think where he might have gotten the document with your name on it, please give us a call."

"Will do."

Mitchell eased the door shut behind them. The two cops had a brief exchange at the car—the sound of slightly raised voices came to him through the door—then they climbed into the Impala and departed with a squeal of tires.

Had Elizabeth Ballard and her allies spirited Castillo away from the hospital? Owen McNally surely couldn't be in any condition to be driving, but maybe his brother was responsible for Castillo's unplanned departure.

He was still standing at the window a few minutes later, his hands in his pockets, his mind fumbling through a string of uncomfortable speculation and unappealing options, when another car pulled into the space vacated by the Impala. A red Tesla. The door opened and a woman stepped out—slender, blond-haired, and fair-skinned, wearing a blue suit and white blouse. Much to his surprise, she strode up the walk to his front door and knocked smartly on it. After a moment of indecision, he stepped to the door and opened it.

"Mitchell Pieda," she said, pronouncing it correctly, "my name is Rey Viklund." She put out her hand. "I'm a friend here to help." She had a slight Scandinavian accent.

He scanned her thoughts. He couldn't get any details, just a general impression of a woman on a mission. A very pretty woman.

He took her outstretched hand. "Pleased to meet you."

"May I come in?"

He glanced up and down the street, quiet in the late morning of a weekday. "My aunt's asleep—she's in bed with a cold. Let's talk outside." He stepped onto the stoop and closed the door behind him.

"The police were asking you about Philip Castillo, yes?" she asked.

He hesitated, then said, "Yes."

"They believe he was involved in the Pocopson fire and the death of George Millard."

Philip scanned her thoughts but didn't sense anything beyond what she had said, as if she had been given a script but not the story behind it.

"That's what they said."

"And because he was carrying a document with your name on it, they suspect you have some connection to the fire."

"They didn't say that."

"Perhaps not, but I can assure you that is the case."

"How do you know?"

"I do not know myself, but my uncle knows."

"Who's your uncle?"

"A powerful man who wants to help you. Like he helped Philip Castillo."

"Your uncle is the person who got Castillo out of the hospital?"

"Yes."

Mitchell ran his fingers through his hair. "Why would your uncle help Philip Castillo and me? We're not exactly playing on the same team."

"Because he has become powerful by forming alliances with other powerful men."

"Castillo?" asked Pieda, disbelievingly.

"My uncle believes he has potential that has not yet been tapped."

After a moment, Mitchell asked, "And your uncle wants to form an alliance with me?"

"My uncle says that your powers have already been tapped, but in no way tapped out." She hesitated. "Does that make sense to you?"

"Yes, I suppose so." He regarded her. "He didn't share what my powers are with you?"

"No. He said he had reason not to."

He sensed some slight irritation at the fact that information was being withheld from her, but no deception on her part.

"And how did your uncle visualize this alliance working?" he asked.

"It is best if he explains it to you himself, and to do so he invites you to his home."

"Where is that?"

"Just a few hours away."

Mitchell thrust his hands in his pockets and looked abstractedly out at the Tesla.

"When the police can't find Castillo," she said, "they'll come back for you. And eventually they will find out something about you that you wouldn't want them to find out. You can stay here," her gesture took in the modest house, the unkempt lawn, the tacky lawn ornaments, "or you can come to somewhere that I believe will be much more to your liking."

Mitchell considered Rey's offer. It was obviously not without risk, but if the police continued to dig into the Pocopson arson and murder, it was all too easy to imagine the progression of events from there: the police questioning him, linking him to the fire, investigating his ties to Louise Mortensen and Vivantem, identifying him as the person who had been at the scene when

Attorney General Russell Brashear collapsed and then died of a massive stroke. In the best case scenario, he would land in prison, and he had seen enough of Philip Castillo's memories of his incarceration that he didn't want that to happen to him. In the worst case scenario, he would land in some secret government research facility, the subject of God only knew what experiments.

He nodded once. "Okay."

"Does your aunt know about the police's visits?"

"No."

"That's good. You can tell her that you're taking an impromptu road trip with some friends."

"How long until I can come home?"

"I don't know, but you should plan to be away for some time."

"I'll need to pack some things."

"No need. It's better if we leave before your aunt wakes up. We can provide you with whatever you need."

"All right. I'll leave her a note."

He stepped back into the house and didn't try to stop Rey when she stepped in after him. He went to the kitchen, jotted the message that Rey had suggested on a notepad decorated with a chorus line of hippos, and put it under the salt shaker. Then he shrugged on his coat and started for the door.

"Just one minute," he said, and turned down the short hall leading to his aunt's bedroom. When he got to the closed door, he could hear her rattling snore. He sensed Rey at the other end of the hallway, sensed her displeasure at this deviation from her script.

He cracked the door open and looked in. His aunt lay on her back, mouth open, a litter of wadded-up tissues scattered over the bedspread, a spine-sprung copy of Danielle Steel open beside her. He looked in at her for a moment, then eased the door shut.

He was humiliated to feel his throat tighten with impending tears. What had Louise Mortensen and Elizabeth Ballard gotten him into?

18

Andy headed into Mercy Hospital for another check on Castillo. He himself was feeling better than he had in a couple of days. In the aftermath of Owen's heart attack, and of Lizzy and Castillo's escapades in Pocopson, he had been doing a near-continuous circuit: Owen's hospital room to Castillo's hospital room to Lizzy's hotel room. When he had a free hour, he ran over to his parents' house to check on his parents, who had not taken the news of Owen's heart attack well.

Andy had gone almost two days without any sleep after the shit hit the fan. It had been an unpleasant flashback to his first rotation in the ER as a medical student, but the previous night he had gotten four uninterrupted hours and he was feeling pretty chipper.

"Hey, Pete," he called as he passed an orderly in the corridor. "How's the new baby?"

Pete grinned. "Almost as pretty as her mother," he called back.

Andy was actually humming when he stepped into Castillo's room and sensed that his day was about to take a turn for the worse.

Two men, looking like cops out of central casting, turned from the nurse to the new arrival.

"Dr. McNally," the nurse blurted out, "your friend disappeared."

AFTER AN HOUR in the Lenape Township police station interview room, the cops were running out of new ways to ask him the same questions.

The older cop was taking the lead, while the younger one sat in a chair behind Andy. Maybe he was supposed to be a threatening presence, but it would have been more effective if he hadn't looked like a grown-up Fred Savage.

"So, the man who Mr. Castillo left the hospital with," said Denninger. "You have no idea who he was?"

"Nope."

"Or who sent him?"

"Nope. I didn't realize he ran with a limo-driving crowd."

"And you say you met Mr. Castillo in Sedona."

"That's right."

"What were you doing in Sedona?"

"Vacationing."

"And in what circumstances did you make the acquaintance of Mr. Castillo?"

"I went to his business for a reading."

"And now he's visiting you in Pennsylvania?" asked Denninger, with a raised eyebrow.

"Yup."

"Could you describe your relationship with Mr. Castillo?"

"Nope."

"No, you couldn't describe it?"

"As I have already said—more than once—I don't see any

reason I should share the details of a long-ago vacation with you."

Denninger sat back, annoyed. "Dr. McNally, we have reason to believe that Mr. Castillo may have been involved in an arson in Pocopson."

"Doesn't seem like his style, but who knows what he got up to when I was at work."

"And a murder."

Andy frowned. "That certainly doesn't seem like his style. What in the world makes you think that?"

"I'm afraid I can't share the details of an active investigation."

"Then I'm afraid I can't speculate on what felonies my friend may or may not have been committing when I wasn't keeping an eye on him."

"Maybe he was working with someone."

"Maybe."

Denninger pulled up the top sheet of the notepad in front of him, glanced at the second page, then let the first page fall back into place.

"Do you know someone named Mitchell Pieda?" He pronounced it PIE-da.

"PIE-da?" asked Andy. "Nope."

"Elizabeth Ballard?"

"This is getting tiresome, gentlemen."

"Dr. McNally—"

There was a knock on the door and a uniformed officer stuck his head in. "Detective Plott, message for you."

The younger detective sighed, stood up, and headed for the door. "I'll be right back, Den."

Denninger massaged the back of his neck with a large hand. "I'm going to grab some coffee. Any for you, Dr. McNally?"

"Sure. Thanks."

"Milk or sugar?"

"Black."

Denninger stepped out of the room, closing the door behind him.

Andy pulled his phone out of his pocket. The cops might be monitoring what happened in the room, but without a warrant of some kind, he guessed they couldn't find out who he had called. And with a warrant, he had enough calls to Owen from his phone that one more couldn't make a difference.

"Hey, what's up?" answered Owen.

"I'm having a little chat with the men in blue of the Lenape Township Police Department."

"What?" exclaimed Owen. "Why?"

"Because they are interested in my relationship with a bunch of different people. Philip Castillo. Mitchell PIE-da. Elizabeth Ballard."

"Holy crap! What are you telling them?"

"I'm telling them I don't know anything."

"Do you need a lawyer?"

"I'm thinking it might not be a bad idea."

"Should I call one for you?"

"Yup."

"Are they listening to you?"

"I don't know. The guy who was questioning me just got called out of the room."

"Where are you?"

Andy gave Owen the location of the police station.

"Okay, I'm going to find a lawyer and send him over there."

"Thanks."

Andy ended the call and tried to keep from fidgeting.

Ten minutes passed, then the cops returned, Plott in the lead and looking alarmingly enthused. Denninger followed, his hands coffee-free.

Plott sat down in the seat Denninger had vacated. "So, Dr. McNally," he began with a grin.

Andy raised his eyebrows.

"You've never heard of Elizabeth Ballard?"

"I didn't say I had never heard of her. I said the conversation was getting tiresome."

"Ah, that's an important distinction, because if you *had* said you had never heard of her, it would be a little hard to believe."

"Oh? And why's that?"

"Because it appears she's your brother's ward."

Andy hoped his expression hadn't changed.

"Owen McNally is your brother, correct?"

Andy sat back in his chair. "Gentlemen, this has been fascinating, but I'm done with this conversation."

Plott flipped open a notepad. "According to the county records, Elizabeth Ballard was the daughter of Charlotte Ballard, who died when Elizabeth was seven, and Patrick Ballard, who died in December during a mugging in Philadelphia. Owen McNally was designated as Miss Ballard's guardian, although there's no record of Mr. McNally having filed the appropriate paperwork after Mr. Ballard's death." He glanced up at Andy. "Seems unlikely that there would be two unrelated McNallys whose names have been connected with crimes in Kennett Square."

Andy stood. "We're done here—"

Denninger and Plott also stood, and Andy was wondering how long it would take Owen to get a lawyer to the police station when there was a knock on the door. This time the person who stepped into the interview room wasn't the uniformed cop, but a middle-aged man wearing a loosened tie. Andy could see the uniform standing in the hall behind him.

"Detectives, can I speak with you for a moment?" asked the new arrival.

Denninger and Plott exchanged looks.

"Sure, Lieutenant," said Denninger. He turned to Andy. "Just have a seat for one minute, Dr. McNally."

Before Andy could respond, the three men stepped out of the room. Through a small glass window, Andy could see the uniform positioned directly outside the door. He sighed and sat down.

Five minutes passed, then Andy could see Denninger talking to the uniform. A moment later, Denninger stepped into the room, his face red and his mouth tight.

"I apologize for the inconvenience of bringing you down to the station, Dr. McNally," he said stiffly. "You're free to go."

Andy stood. "Not that I'm complaining, but what changed?"

"Nothing you need to worry about. Officer Preston will drive you back to the hospital."

"Okay."

Denninger stood aside to let Andy step into the hall. Somewhere in the back of the station, Andy could hear voices raised. One sounded like Plott, one sounded like the lieutenant.

"Sounds like young Plott isn't too happy about the change of plan," said Andy.

Denninger smiled humorlessly. "Kids."

"They grow up so fast—one day you'll look back fondly on this."

"Officer," said Denninger, "please drive Dr. McNally back to Mercy."

The cop headed for the entrance, and Andy followed him out. They climbed into a police cruiser and a short time later pulled up at the hospital entrance, the cop never having uttered a word.

Andy looked over at him. "Well, it's certainly been jolly."

The cop glared at him.

Andy climbed out of the car, which pulled away almost

before he had swung the door shut. He ran his fingers through his hair, then started toward his car in the parking lot, pulling his phone out of his pocket as he walked.

WHEN THE NURSE arrived in Owen's room, she found him typing feverishly on his phone.

"Dr. McNally," she said, "you can't get yourself all worked up—it's going to slow your recovery. Do you need me to take your phone away?"

"No, I'll be more worked up if I don't have it," he said, not looking up.

She reached out a hand and he snatched the phone back. She rolled her eyes. "I'm not going to take your phone—not *yet*, anyway. I just want to take your blood pressure."

He surrendered his arm to the blood pressure cuff, typing awkwardly with the thumb of his other hand.

She tutted at the reading. "Dr. McNally, you really need to—"

Owen's phone rang.

"I need to take this." He reclaimed his arm and stabbed *Accept.*

She put her fists on her hips. "Dr. McNally, I really must insist—"

"Just this once," he said to her, then spoke into the phone. "I'm trying to figure out what kind of lawyer to call—"

"Looks like I don't need a lawyer," said Andy as the nurse glowered, then stalked out of the room. "They let me go."

"What? What's happening?"

"Evidently, shortly before I got to Mercy, Castillo walked to the hospital entrance, got in a limo, and was driven away. How he got that far under his own steam is a mystery to me. When I got to his room, unaware that he had decided to check himself out, the police were there, and they took me to the station and were asking a bunch of questions about Philip and how I knew him and where the limo had come from. They obviously had the medical summaries for Lizzy and Pieda that Castillo got from Mortensen's house. Then they got called away and when they came back they started asking me really specific stuff about Lizzy. They knew her mom and dad were dead, and they knew her guardian was named Owen McNally. But they must not have had a chance to do much research beyond that, because they called you *Mr.*, not *Dr.* Then their lieutenant called them out, and a couple of minutes later they're apologizing for the inconvenience and driving me back to Mercy."

"Why did they let you go?"

"I haven't any idea." Andy had reached his car. He chirped it open and dropped into the driver's seat. "Do you think Mortensen has that kind of pull, to get a police investigation called off? She wouldn't want the police questioning me anymore than we want it."

"I wouldn't have thought so, but who knows," said Owen. "I can't imagine that Philip would have just walked out of the hospital and climbed into a car sent by Louise Mortensen."

"But if he got in the car of his own accord, don't you think he would have gotten in touch with one of us?"

"Yes, I would think so."

They were both silent for a few moments, then Owen said, "Maybe it's not that they're dropping the investigation. Maybe they had some other reason for letting you go. Maybe," he said, his voice rising, "they want you to lead them to Lizzy."

"Yeah, it's a possibility. But whether the cops are hoping I'll lead them to Lizzy, or whether Louise Mortensen is spiriting people away in limos, we need to circle the wagons." After a moment, he said, "Or send the wagons off in different directions."

"What do you mean?"

Andy sighed. "I'm not sure. We need to have a strategy powwow. And Lizzy should move out of the hotel. If it was Mortensen who picked up Castillo, she would know you're at Penn U Hospital, and it would have been easy for her to follow me and Lizzy from there to the hotel. I'd recommend Lizzy go to Ruby's house. As far as we know, Ruby's the only one who no one suspects is playing for Team Lizzy."

"Yes, that makes sense."

"Can Ruby pick Lizzy up somewhere near the hotel? Ideally without someone seeing Lizzy get into Ruby's car?"

"I'll call her and find out."

"By the time Lizzy and Ruby get to Ruby's place, I'll be at the hospital and we can call them."

"What if the police follow you?"

"I'll do my best to make sure that doesn't happen. No need to lead them right to *Mr.* Owen McNally."

"And then we'll scatter the wagons?"

"We might want to send Lizzy away, and maybe even Ruby, but I'm staying here. You're stuck with me, bro."

19

The sound of the car door opening roused Philip and he opened his eyes to see the man from the videoconference standing outside.

"Welcome, Mr. Castillo."

Philip tried to push himself out of the seat, but a bolt of pain shot from his shoulder straight to his brain.

"This may help," said Viklund. He gestured to a portly man dressed in a suit and tie, a black leather bag on the ground at his side. The man stepped forward, holding a sling. "If you'll allow the doctor to put on the sling, I believe you'll be more comfortable."

Philip hesitated, then nodded. "Okay."

The doctor leaned into the car and fastened the sling carefully around Philip's arm. Just having a moment to orient himself made him feel better.

Once the sling was in place, Viklund gestured to the chauffeur, who had been hovering in the background. He stepped forward with an elegant wooden cane.

"You have been sitting for some time and might be light-headed. This will help you maintain your balance." He took the cane from the chauffeur and held it out to Philip.

Philip swung his legs out of the car and levered himself up, the doctor lending a discreet assist with a hand on his good elbow.

They were standing in a circular drive in front of a low building of metal and glass sunk into the landscape.

"Thank you, doctor," said Viklund. The portly man stepped back and Viklund took his place at Philip's elbow. "Your guest room is not too far," he said to Philip.

Leaning as little as possible on the cane, Philip made his way across the flagstone terrace that led to the front door. He noticed a wheelchair parked unobtrusively off to one side and felt a grudging pang of gratitude to Theo Viklund that he had given him the chance to make it to the guest room under his own power.

They passed through the door into a large entrance hall, and then continued straight back down a long corridor, their footsteps muffled by the carpet that ran its length. They passed a number of closed doors, and Philip was wondering how far back the building went, and if he would in fact be able to make it to the guest room, when Viklund stopped at one of the doors, pushed it open, and stepped aside to let Philip enter.

Philip nodded toward the door. "After you."

Viklund smiled. "Certainly." He stepped into the room and Philip followed. The chauffeur and doctor stayed in the corridor.

The colors were the reds and tans of the desert southwest, the rug a Wide Ruins pattern, the bed's headboard fashioned from unfinished wood. A Navajo wedding basket hung on the wall, the undyed pathway from the basket's center to its rim correctly oriented, as far as Philip could tell, toward the east. In the absence of any windows, rustic iron lamps cast a warm glow.

"I regret that our more fully appointed guest quarters are not available at the moment," said Viklund. "They are either presently occupied or being prepared for other occupants."

Philip crossed the room and eased himself down on the bed. He would have preferred to remain standing, but he sensed he would be pushing his luck. "And who might that be?"

"I will fill you in once you're rested."

"I'm going to need to let some people know that I'm okay," said Philip. "They're going to wonder what the hell's going on if I just disappear from the hospital and they don't hear from me."

"You can call them on the mobile phone I used to text you."

"I'm not calling them with a phone you gave me."

Viklund smiled again. "So suspicious. But of course I can hardly blame you." He appeared to consider. "We know that Andrew McNally has been visiting you in the hospital, and we know how to find him if we need to, so you'd not be giving anything away if you were to call him."

Philip tried to find a flaw in this reasoning and couldn't. "That would work great if I knew what his number was."

"You'll find it programmed into the phone," said Viklund. "I'll step out so you can make the call. When you're done, just press zero and the doctor will come in to see if there is anything we can do to make you more comfortable. Then you can get some rest."

Philip nodded.

Viklund stepped out of the room and closed the door.

Philip got the phone out of his pocket, opened the Contacts, and pressed the entry for *Andrew McNally*. He was relieved when it rang to voicemail.

"Andy, it's Philip. As you probably know by now, someone sprung me from the hospital. Sounds like the police were getting close to connecting me with what happened in Pocopson. I'm fine—it looks like I'll have a chance to rest up where I am now. I'm calling from a phone that this person gave me and I have every expectation that the calls are being monitored, so don't call me back on this number. I'll be in touch again as soon as I can." He hesitated. "Please make sure you've conveyed the message I gave you, and do everything you can to make sure the recipient takes it seriously. And it's a good idea for me not to know where that person is." He ended the call and put the phone on the bedside table.

He expected the trio in the hallway, no doubt listening in to his conversation, to come in as soon as his call was done, but when a minute ticked by with no arrivals, he remembered Viklund's instructions and hit zero on the phone.

The doctor entered almost immediately. He rebandaged Philip's shoulder, took his pulse and blood pressure, and offered him a pain pill, which Philip declined. When the door closed after him, Philip heard a click. He pushed himself to his feet and crossed to the door. It was, not surprisingly, locked.

He returned to the bed and lay back on the mound of pillows. If he was going to be locked in, he might as well make good use of the time.

He closed his eyes and slept.

20

Lizzy slipped out of the hotel via a service entrance leading to the hotel's loading dock. She texted her location to Ruby and pretty soon a white van turned into the back street and pulled up to where she stood.

Lizzy slid open the van's side door and hoisted her suitcase into the back. "Hey, Ruby. Thanks for coming."

"I thought it would look more appropriate pulling up to the back of a hotel in a van than in my car," said Ruby DiMano in her usual brisk tone, "and it will be easier for you to hide in back."

Lizzy clambered into the back of the van and slid the door closed, then tried to get comfortable on the hard metal floor. "Where are we going?"

"To my apartment."

"What's happening?" she asked. Ruby had told her nothing during their brief phone call, other than the fact that Owen and Andy thought it was best that she leave the hotel.

"Hold on, I want to make sure no one's following us."

When Ruby DiMano had first met Lizzy, she was an informer for Louise Mortensen's husband, Gerard Bonnay. But when Bonnay had had Lizzy's father killed—a hit made to look like a mugging—Ruby had switched sides and helped Owen and Andy spirit Lizzy away from the Pocopson house where Gerard and Louise were holding her.

It should have been a quick drive from the hotel to Ruby's apartment in Overbrook, but Ruby wended her way around the streets of West Philly for fifteen nerve-jangling minutes before declaring them free of any tails.

"So, what's happening?" repeated Lizzy from the back of the van.

"Mr. Castillo left the hospital."

"He did? I thought he wasn't going to be able to leave for at least a couple of days."

"That's what we all thought. A limo showed up and picked him up at the entrance."

"A limo?" asked Lizzy, shocked. "Was it Louise?"

"She's the first person who occurred to me," said Ruby, "but no one knows. Maybe the McNallys will have more information when we talk to them."

They had just reached Overbrook and were sitting in the tiny apartment when Ruby's phone rang.

She activated the speaker. "Hello. We're both here."

"Hi, it's Andy and Owen," they heard Owen say. "Were you guys able to get away from the hotel without being seen?"

"I think so," said Ruby.

"Ruby should join the Secret Service," said Lizzy.

"Heaven forbid," said Ruby.

"You know about Philip?" Owen asked.

"We know he left the hospital," said Ruby.

"I got a message from him," said Andy.

"Really? That's great!" said Lizzy. "Where is he?"

"He wouldn't say, just that he was somewhere where he would be able to rest up."

"Did he tell you who picked him up?"

"No. He said that someone was probably monitoring the phone he used to leave me the message, so I wasn't supposed to call him back."

"That doesn't sound good," said Lizzy, casting a worried glance at Ruby.

"I know, but he didn't sound panicked or upset, just tired, which would be totally understandable," said Andy. "I'm not thrilled about the situation, but for the time being I think we need to assume he's okay. He did say, though, that it was best that he not know where you are, Lizzy."

"That makes it sound like he's afraid of Mitchell reading his mind again," Lizzy replied.

"Possibly. Or Louise may have other mind-reading Vivantem offspring working for her. Or it may be for an entirely different reason—there are other ways than mind reading to get information out of a person."

"Andy," Owen admonished.

"Sorry." Andy cleared his throat. "In any case," he continued, "I think we should take a tip from Philip and start a policy from here on out that we not share any information among ourselves that would be useful to Louise if one of us were to fall into her hands. Lizzy, I hate to say it, but I think you're going to have to disappear, at least for a little while, until things blow over. Ruby, how about a return trip to the Keys with Liz?"

"I'm afraid I can't, Dr. McNally. I need to be here to help out with my brother-in-law."

"How about you, Andy?" asked Owen. "Maybe you can take Lizzy somewhere."

"Uncle Owen," said Lizzy, "Andy has to be here to keep an eye on your parents."

"Right, right," he replied. After a pause, he said, "Maybe I—"

"Absolutely not," interrupted Andy. "The doctors said you

need plenty of rest, otherwise you risk causing even more damage to your heart."

"I can go off somewhere by myself," said Lizzy. "Lots of seventeen-year-olds go on trips by themselves."

"Like who?" said Andy.

"I don't know any personally, Andy," she retorted. "I don't know any other seventeen-year-olds."

Andy was silent for a moment, then said, "Maybe it's not a bad idea. Lizzy could go somewhere by train or bus."

"The disadvantage of any mode of transportation that runs on a schedule," said Owen, "is its predictability. If they found out Lizzy was on a particular train, all they'd need to do would be to wait for her at the destination. It's limiting and doesn't provide much flexibility."

"I could borrow your SUV," said Lizzy.

"You don't know how to drive," said Owen.

"I do so," she said. "Dad used to let me drive around Parkesburg. Sometimes I would drive him to the train station in the mornings and drive Ruby back to the house. Or the other way around in the evenings."

"But," said Owen, "that's illegal."

There was silence on the line for a moment, then Lizzy heard the first honest laughter she had heard from Andy since she had returned to Pennsylvania. After a moment, Owen joined in, sounding a bit sheepish. She and Ruby exchanged smiles. Finally, Andy said, "Well, Dudley Do-Right, you can make a citizen's arrest when all this other stuff blows over."

"Okay," said Owen, "I agree that comparatively speaking it barely registers on our current scale of illegality—and, in fact, is probably a big help." He paused. "But if you can drive, why didn't you drive Philip away from Pocopson yourself, rather than getting Mitchell Pieda to help you?"

"I've never driven in the dark," said Lizzy, "and it didn't seem like the best time to try it for the first time. Plus, I had to let Mitchell go anyway so he wouldn't spill his guts to the police about us."

"Very sensible," agreed Owen. "However, if we're trying to limit any connections between me and Andy and you, my SUV is probably not the right choice for a getaway vehicle."

"You could use the van," said Ruby.

"I can't take your van. How will you drive your brother-in-law around?"

Ruby hesitated, then said, "He's declining. I don't think he's going to need the van anymore."

"Oh, Ruby, I'm so sorry," she said, taking Ruby's bony hand in hers.

They were all silent for a moment, then Andy said, "I hate that the circumstances make it an option, but it would solve the problem. Even if the cops know that Ruby has been visiting Owen in the hospital, there's no reason for them to connect her with Lizzy or Lizzy's disappearance. Plus," he added, "Owen must have had two dozen visitors, and the cops can't check them all out."

"It's very generous of you to offer the use of your van, Ruby," said Owen, "and, Lizzy, it's convenient that you've driven around Parkesburg before, but your driving experience is pretty limited."

"I can practice on back roads," said Lizzy.

"I could go with Lizzy for the first day," added Ruby, "just to get her used to the van."

"That would be great," replied Andy.

"There are other logistical challenges," said Owen. "What about money? Using a credit card to pay for a hotel room might alert someone to your location."

"I can stay in the van—it's big enough," said Lizzy.

"What about buying gas?" said Owen, beginning to sound desperate.

"We can give her cash," said Andy.

"And you don't have a driver's license," said Owen. "If you're going to be driving anywhere other than to and from the Parkesburg train station, you should have a driver's license, and it would be tricky to get you one, especially on short notice."

"I don't have one now, but I should have one soon—tomorrow or the day after."

Lizzy described her conversation with Philip's friend, trying her best to make it sound like a straightforward business transaction. When she was finished, she glanced over at Ruby. Ruby actually had a somewhat pleased expression on her face. "So, I'm set with the license," Lizzy concluded in the face of Uncle Owen and Andy's silence.

Then there was some noise in the background on the other end of the call, and Owen said, "Hello, Doctor—would you mind giving us a few more minutes?"

"Actually, I think we're almost done," said Andy. "Owen, why don't we let the doctor poke and prod you for a few minutes, and I'll just step into the hallway and wrap up any last details with the ladies."

They heard some faint protest from Owen, but Andy had evidently taken the phone off speaker. In a moment, he continued, a background hum of other voices and the muffled squawk of a PA system suggesting that he had moved from the room to the hallway. "I guess we just need to wait until the license shows up, load you up with some cash, and get you on the road."

"Sounds good," said Lizzy.

"I just have one quick message for you, Liz."

Ruby stood up. "I'll let the two of you speak privately, while I put on some tea." She stepped through the door that led to the bathroom that separated the living room from the kitchen in the tiny apartment.

"What's up?" Lizzy asked. Her stomach was knotted—what else could Andy need to tell her privately other than some ominous update on Uncle Owen's condition?

"Philip gave me a message for you," he said.

"Oh? What is it?"

"He says you don't need to do the favor he asked you to do after all."

After a moment, Lizzy said, "Really?"

"That's what he said." He waited a beat, then continued. "I'm going to ask even though I know it's none of my business. What favor did he ask you to do?"

"I can't say. It's a secret."

Andy sighed. "I know you don't want to hear this, Lizzy, but we really don't know much about Philip. He seems like a nice guy, and I know that you and Owen both benefited from his ... counseling services, but to be blunt, his willingness to go to Pocopson with you and break into Mortensen's home is part of the reason we're in this situation. We have to be super careful about anyone who knows what's going on."

"I know that," she said shortly.

"I know you do. Anyway, I didn't want Owen to know about this favor Philip had asked for because it's the kind of thing he would stress about, and stress is the last thing he needs at the moment." She heard him sigh. "Well, in any case, whatever the favor was, you don't have to do it anymore, so I guess it's a moot point."

21

—————

Rey drove the Tesla to the Schuylkill Expressway toward King of Prussia, picked up the Turnpike west to Harrisburg, then turned south. Soon she left the highway and continued on two-lane roads. Mitchell couldn't believe that the only route to their destination was such a circuitous one—he guessed Rey must be taking an indirect route on purpose. The thought that she wanted to disguise the location of their destination wasn't comforting, but he consoled himself with the thought that if she or her mysterious uncle had some nefarious plan in mind for him, they probably wouldn't care whether or not he knew where he was going.

Mitchell periodically scanned Rey's thoughts but couldn't get anything useful beyond the fact that her uncle had sent her for Mitchell, and that she herself was curious to learn the reason behind her assignment.

Eventually they turned off the road onto a paved drive and drove through a metal gate, which trundled closed behind them. In about half a mile, they pulled up in front of a low metal-and-glass building that was almost indistinguishable from its surroundings. They climbed out of the car.

"Where are we?" asked Mitchell.

"This is my uncle's home," said Rey.

She led Mitchell across a flagstone terrace to the front door, then into a large entrance hall. She turned to the left and led him to an unobtrusive corridor.

The corridor curved to the left, the right side lined with windows. After a few yards it began a gentle rise so that when they stopped at the door at the end of the corridor, they were twenty feet above the ground. She pushed open the door and led him through.

The room was a near replica, in ambiance if not in detail, of the library in Pocopson. Thick Persian rugs covered the floors, club chairs faced a gas fireplace. Unlike the Pocopson library, however, the walls opposite the door and to his right were floor-to-ceiling windows, giving an impression of the world's most elegant tree house. A glass door led to a balcony.

Rey gestured to doors leading off the main room. "Bedroom. Bath. Kitchen."

"This is very nice," said Mitchell. He walked to the windows and looked out at the wooded grounds, then turned back to Rey. "When will I get to meet your uncle?"

"Very soon. He regrets that he can't meet you in person, but I'll set up a videoconference for you." Rey went to an antique table standing against one wall and touched a button. The hunting scene above the desk that Mitchell had taken to be an oil painting disappeared, replaced by a view of a room that was so similarly decorated to the one in which Mitchell stood that it appeared to be an extension of it. "He'll be with you in just a few minutes. You don't have to wait by the desk—you'll hear a chime when he arrives." She pulled a mobile phone out of her pocket. "We don't get cell reception here, but if you need anything, you can press zero on this phone and someone will come immediately. I also need to ask you not to leave the room. My uncle would prefer that we not risk having you run into his other guests."

He nodded. "All right."

"Please make yourself at home." She smiled encouragingly at him, then stepped out of the room and closed the door behind her.

He took a tour of the suite, taking a bottle of sparkling water from the well-stocked refrigerator and popping his head into the elegantly appointed bedroom.

In a few minutes, he heard the chime and went to the desk. The monitor displayed a man standing next to the chair at the doppelgänger of Mitchell's desk.

"Mr. Pieda, I'm pleased to meet you. I'm Theo Viklund. I hope your trip here was comfortable, and that my emissary was congenial."

"Very congenial," said Mitchell. "Also very mysterious. I don't really know why you've brought me here."

"Yes, I certainly owe you an explanation. Please, have a seat," said Viklund, gesturing from the monitor to Mitchell's chair, then sitting himself.

Mitchell sat. "I understand I'm not the only person you've helped out," he said.

Theo nodded. "I assume you are referring to Philip Castillo. Yes, he is here at my compound."

"I thought he was in the hospital."

"He was, but he can rest more comfortably here. And he's not the only person who is enjoying refuge here."

Mitchell raised his eyebrows. "Oh?"

"Yes. Dr. Mortensen is my guest as well."

Mitchell tried to hide his alarm. "What is she doing here?"

"The same as you—avoiding the unwanted attentions of the authorities."

"How do you know Louise?"

"She and I have been friends and colleagues for many years. The recent events—the attorney general's investigation, Mr. Millard's death, and of course her husband's death—have obviously been traumatic for her, and I felt that she needed my support to get the situation under control. And, if I may speak frankly, to get herself under control."

"What do you mean by that?"

"The Louise Mortensen I knew a year ago would never have left a colleague behind as she herself escaped."

"You know what happened in Pocopson?"

"Yes."

Mitchell realized he was perched on the edge of the chair and sat back, trying to match the cool demeanor of his host. "You can imagine I'm not too thrilled about the idea of encountering Louise after what happened."

"I can certainly understand that, and that is why Rey asked you to stay in your suite unless you are escorted by one of my employees—just temporarily." He smiled. "And I hope that your quarters are pleasant enough that staying there for a time will not be an inconvenience."

"How long do you think I'll have to stay here?"

Theo waved his hand. "I have already arranged to have the interest of the Lenape Township police directed elsewhere."

"Really?" Mitchell hesitated. "How did you manage that?"

"Called in a favor from a friend of a friend. Of course," he continued, "there is still the matter of the attorney general's investigation."

"What do you know about that?"

"I know you were responsible for the attorney general's death."

Mitchell was silent.

"It will be best if you stay here until I can divert the AG's attention as well. And perhaps," he added, "by that time I will have been able to convince you to stay for other reasons."

"Rey mentioned your interest in forming alliances."

"In the case of you and Mr. Castillo, absolutely. In the case of Louise, it is more a matter of a favor to an old acquaintance."

"What could Philip Castillo possibly offer to someone like you?" Mitchell asked, then added, a little awkwardly, "For that matter, what can I offer?"

"Mr. Castillo's involvement will come later, but I am counting on you to clear the way for that involvement."

"Clear the way?"

"There are forces who would stand in the way of progress—some private concerns, some in government. I have a colleague who would be grateful for assistance in clearing those barriers, and I'm anxious to provide that assistance. And when I throw my support behind a cause, I always share the benefits with those others who have supported it. I believe that you, Mr. Pieda, are the man to do that."

22

———————

It was late afternoon and Louise and Theo were walking the paths of the grounds, enjoying an unusually balmy March day.

"Did you ever find Mitchell's aunt's house?" asked Louise.

"Indeed we did. And we found Mitchell as well."

Louise cast a sideways glance at Theo. "And what is he up to?"

He glanced at his watch. "I imagine he's resting up in his suite."

Louise stopped and Theo turned back to her, eyes amused.

"He's here?" she asked, her voice stony.

"Yes. And he's not the only guest who arrived today."

Louise's eyes narrowed. "Ballard?"

Theo shook his head. "No, Miss Ballard is staying at a hotel not far from her godfather's hospital room."

"Then who?"

"Philip Castillo."

"He's out of the hospital?"

"He is now. He also is resting in his quarters."

"And what are you planning to do with them?"

"My plans for Pieda are no doubt quite similar to the plans you had for him—to eliminate individuals who are standing in my way. My plans for Castillo ... I haven't quite decided yet how those plans might play out."

"I'll be interested to find out what you decide," she said somewhat peevishly, "if you care to share that information with me."

"We're partners, Louise. I would certainly share information on any developments that would impact you."

They resumed walking and after a few moments Louise said, "You're collecting quite a band of accomplices at your compound."

"I don't imagine they will be here long—I will likely relocate them to one of my other homes. I believe the seclusion could be appealing to you, but perhaps less so to Mr. Pieda and Mr. Castillo."

"Gerard used to call it 'the wilds of Western Maryland,'" said Louise. "But I imagine it provides the benefits of privacy while also being relatively close to scientific and medical institutions in Washington and Baltimore."

"But there are so many places I could be that would be much more convenient to those cities."

"Yes, I suppose so," she said. "So why here?"

"Are you familiar with the attractions of the area?"

"Not specifically."

"The Catoctin Mountains? Their reputation as a rejuvenating retreat?"

There was a long pause, then Louise said, "Camp David?"

Theo nodded.

"You set up your base here so you would be near the President?" Louise sounded as surprised as it was possible for her to sound.

Theo waved his hand dismissively. "Not the president. With

a few rare exceptions, they are figureheads with no real power. It is the men and women with whom they surround themselves who are the true power brokers, and only the closest and most trusted advisors are invited to accompany the President to Camp David. If I focus on the people who are there, I know I'm not wasting my time on someone who will be of no use to me."

"And to what use are you putting them?"

"Why, all sorts of uses. Some in support of my own goals, some in support of the goals of others who may in time prove to be able to support my own goals."

They continued walking in silence for a minute, then Theo asked, "Do you know anything about jousting?"

Louise raised an eyebrow. "I'm afraid not."

"It's a fascinating study—the techniques, the strategy."

"Strategy?"

"Absolutely. It wasn't just a matter of two knights happening upon each other in a forest glade and hurtling toward each other pell mell. They relied on others to support their goal—squires, attendants. Each had a very specific role to play. And in the actual joust, there were so many considerations to be factored in—for example, the length of the lance. If your lance was longer than your opponent's, then obviously you would strike him before he could strike you, but a longer lance is heavier and harder to control. You might assess your opponent as unskilled and decide that he would be likely to miss you with a point-on attack, opening the opportunity for you to use a less elegant but very effective strategy of sweeping him off his horse with a lance held perpendicular to the direction of the charge."

"Interesting," said Louise.

"They had quite clever ways of training young men for jousting," continued Theo, undeterred by Louise's lukewarm response. "They used a construction called a quintain. It was painted to look like a man—a Saracen, in fact, since this was the era of the Crusades—holding a wooden sword out to the side. The student would aim at the quintain, and if the lance hit off-center—the result, for example, of the student not heeding his instructor's direction—the quintain would spin around and hit the unfortunate student with the wooden sword."

"Operant conditioning," said Louise.

Theo smiled. "Exactly. The goal of all this practice was to enable the young knight to perfect his technique to the extent of being able to use his lance to spear an iron ring suspended by a thread."

"Don't you mean a brass ring?"

Theo waved his hand. "The brass ring was an invention of carousel-makers in nineteenth- and twentieth-century America. The rings in the medieval jousting fields were iron."

Louise narrowed her eyes. "Theo, I know you better than to think you are telling me this as idle conversation."

"Quite right," he replied. "There's something I'd like to show you."

He turned onto another of the paved paths, and soon Louise could see among the trees a building just as discreetly disguised in its surroundings as the main house. Its facade was windowless. Theo walked to the door and pressed a code into a keypad, then opened the door and stepped aside to allow Louise to enter.

They stepped into a lab, all antiseptic white and stainless steel, concrete floors polished to a high sheen bouncing back light from fluorescent fixtures. A man—Louise guessed him to be in his late sixties—sat on a stool at a microscope at a lab table, his hand resting on the fine focus knob. She noticed that he was missing the thumb on his left hand.

Ignoring him, Theo began to circle the room, gesturing to the equipment that lined the walls.

"Spectrophotometer ... ultracentrifuge ... ion torrent

sequencer ... high performance liquid chromatography equipment ... mass spectrometer." He neared the end of the circuit. "And remind me what this one is?" He raised his voice slightly, obviously directing the question toward the man at the lab table, although his gaze remained fixed on the piece of equipment.

"Flow cytometry cell sorter," came the monotone reply.

"Flow cytometry cell sorter," repeated Theo with a nod. He waved his hand toward a large Mac on a worktable. "And access to the records of every governmental and private research organization in the world, with no possibility of being traced. You are limited only by your ability to read the language in which the documentation is written—and even that is becoming less of an issue with AI translation." Theo stepped to the man's side. "Dr. Mortensen, I'd like to introduce you to Ed Rinnert, who will be serving as your research assistant. Dr. Rinnert was responsible for obtaining all the equipment you see here."

The man climbed stiffly off the stool. Louise extended her hand and the man shook it, not meeting her gaze.

She glanced between the man and Theo. "Not Edmund Rinnert of New Hampshire State?"

"The very same," said Theo cheerfully.

The man nodded, his eyes focused somewhere near her shoulder.

"Why, I recall reading your paper on LC-MS/MS-based proteomics of primate germ cells—it must have been ten years ago."

"Twelve," said Rinnert, his voice barely audible.

"Very impressive," said Louise. "Really groundbreaking in many ways. But I thought ..." She sorted through her mental files, then located the fact that had been eluding her. "You were reported missing several years ago."

"Three years," said Rinnert.

Louise glanced again between the man and Theo. "You've been here for three years?"

Rinnert nodded.

"Edmund got in a little trouble with some falsified test results," said Theo, "and didn't have any family to turn to. Terrible to find yourself an isolated individual in that type of situation. I was pleased to be able to offer him refuge." He picked up a paper from the table next to Rinnert's microscope, glanced at it, then let it fall back onto the table. "Edmund has been working on ..." He turned to Rinnert. "I know I'll butcher it. Please describe your area of research to Dr. Mortensen."

"Modulating embryonic developmental pathways using engineered G-protein coupled receptors," said Rinnert.

"Yes, quite so," said Theo. "There were some significant findings in the first year, but lately it's been slow going. I think we'll turn our attention elsewhere for the moment. Do you concur, Edmund?"

Rinnert nodded.

Theo turned to Louise. "I'm sure Dr. Rinnert will relish having the opportunity to work with you, Dr. Mortensen—to enjoy that collegial interaction that, admittedly, has been missing in the last few years."

"Relish" was not a word Louise would have chosen to apply to the man who stood before her. She had attended a talk given by Edmund Rinnert a year or two before he disappeared, and she recalled him as a jovial, enthusiastic presenter, given to dramatic hand gestures. She didn't recall noticing his missing thumb at the talk.

"It will be a pleasure to work with you," she said to him.

"Likewise."

"I'd like you to work with Rinnert to create more of the Rohypnol drug you gave to Mr. Pieda's targets," said Theo, "and the steroid drug you used to enhance Mr. Pieda's ability to cause strokes."

Louise shot a look at Rinnert.

"Don't worry," said Theo. "Edmund is the soul of discretion. There's nothing that we're working on here that I wouldn't feel completely comfortable discussing in front of him."

Rinnert said nothing.

"What will you need to formulate those?" Theo asked Louise.

Louise listed the requirements.

Theo looked to Rinnert. "Anything we're missing?"

Rinnert shook his head.

"It appears we're in luck," said Theo, rubbing his hands together. "I'd say no time like the present. Louise, would you mind terribly starting on that right away? I believe I may have an opportunity to put one of those drugs to use in short order."

After a moment, Louise replied. "Yes, all right."

"Should you need anything, you know how to get in touch with Maja." He turned toward the door, then turned back to her. "And Louise, for understandable reasons, we can't have you wandering the grounds with the other guests who are at the house. Please let Maja know when you're ready to go back to your suite and she'll accompany you. Just a precaution against any unplanned encounters."

Louise nodded.

"Excellent. I'll leave you to it." Without a glance toward Rinnert, he let himself out the door, and they heard a snatch of hummed tune floating through the air before the door closed on it.

23

—————

Brady Plott opened the door to his daughter's bedroom. A Cinderella nightlight cast a soft glow, illuminating a room decorated entirely in Disney princess. His wife, Carly, wouldn't be getting Kaitlyn out of bed for another hour, but the last time Brady had left the house without giving Katie a goodbye kiss, she had pitched such a fit that Brady had had to promise he would kiss her goodbye regardless of how early he left.

He bent over the bed, pushed a tumble of brown curls off her forehead, and kissed her.

"Hey, Lady Katie," he whispered. "I'm heading out."

She rolled over and rubbed her eyes. "So early?"

He stifled a laugh—she sounded just like her mother.

"Yup. Uncle Den has some early morning work for us to do."

"Okay," she said, almost back to sleep.

Brady kissed her again, closed the door behind him, and ran lightly down the stairs. Carly was pouring coffee into an insulated mug, looking almost as sleepy as Kaitlyn.

"Thanks, hon," he said as she handed him the mug. "You know, you don't have to get up when I have to leave early."

She yawned. "I know. I might go back to bed." She blew him a kiss. "Morning breath. Best to keep your distance."

He saluted as an alternative, and headed for the car.

Once around the corner, he pulled to the side of the road, got out his phone, and tapped out a text.

Need to take day off—Kaitlyn's sick and Carly's away

In a moment a response came back from the lieutenant. *Okay don't forget to call the com room*

"No shit," muttered Brady as he tapped the speed dial for the station's communications center.

That call out of the way, he plugged Andrew McNally's home address into his GPS and pulled away from the curb.

THE SUN WAS JUST COMING up when he arrived at the expensive-looking condo complex in Villanova. He circled the building and confirmed his Google Street View reconnaissance of the previous night: the parking garage had three exits, and he would be able to watch only two at once. He found a spot on the street where he could watch the two closest to the main road.

He had spent the previous afternoon complaining to Den about the cancellation of the investigation, and to the lieutenant about the cold case he had put them on. When the lieutenant got tired of his complaining and told him to take the rest of the afternoon off—big deal, it was already four o'clock—he had gone home and complained to Carly. There was no reason, no explanation--just an infuriating *I'm the boss and that's how it is.*

Brady was pretty sure if McNally led him to Philip Castillo, the lieutenant would rethink his position.

He waited only about twenty minutes before he caught a glimpse of the car he had been hoping to see—a sweet cherry red Lexus sport coupe registered to Andrew McNally. Unfortunately, it had left the parking garage from the one exit that Brady couldn't see from his position and was already almost at the intersection at Lancaster Avenue.

"Figures," he muttered as he started up the car.

The Lexus turned left, which made sense—McNally worked at Bryn Mawr Hospital. By the time Brady had reached the intersection, the Lexus was lost to view, and he had to wait for the traffic to clear to make the turn.

Traffic was heavy even at this early hour, and Brady split his attention between trying to pick the fastest lane and glancing down side streets in case Bryn Mawr wasn't McNally's destination and he had turned off Lancaster Avenue.

He swore as he passed the entrance to the Blue Route. McNally could be headed toward Plymouth Meeting or Chester, and even if Brady guessed right, he would probably never catch up with the Lexus. He continued on to Bryn Mawr and drove through the hospital's parking lots without much hope of seeing McNally.

With a sigh, he resigned himself to going back to the condo to wait for McNally to return. He figured he had some time to kill and decided to make a stop at a Wawa for a breakfast hoagie.

He negotiated the scrum of early morning traffic and went inside. He entered his order at the self-serve kiosk, paid at the register, and then joined the other customers waiting for their orders.

"Kaitlyn," he heard, and the sound of his daughter's name made him turn toward the speaker, who stood next to him. He was a tall, heavyset man with fair hair and skin. "I told you not to do that," said the man into his phone, speaking with an accent of some sort—maybe Swedish or Norwegian.

Brady faced forward again.

"Because I'm the boss, that's why," continued the man.

Brady smiled ruefully at the echo of his conversations with the lieutenant the previous day.

"Because when the boss says not to do something and you do it anyway, bad things happen."

Brady's smile faded.

"And not just to you," continued the man, "but to other people, too. There's no telling what bad things might happen."

Brady looked back at the man. He was gazing placidly at the crew behind the counter. Brady glanced around at the other customers waiting for their orders. None of them was paying any attention to the man on the phone. He wasn't speaking loudly, and considering the bustle in the store, Brady doubted that his one-sided conversation was anything more than part of the ambient noise to anyone else.

"What kind of bad things, you ask?" said the man. "Hard to say. Could be anything."

Brady turned to face the man directly. He didn't look startled, as Brady would expect someone to look if a stranger interjected themselves into a private conversation.

"Who are you talking to?" asked Brady quietly.

The man pulled the phone away from his ear, and Brady could see that its screen was black.

The man glanced at the phone. "Would you look at that. She hung up."

Brady took a step toward him, his face a foot from the man's. "Who's Kaitlyn."

The man smiled and nodded toward his phone. "That was who I was talking to. Some people just don't know how to take no for an answer." He shook his head and dropped the phone into his pocket. "Hope she heeds my warning. Because bad things could happen to Kaitlyn if my warnings aren't heeded."

"One-sixty-five!" called one of the employees behind the counter.

"Your number's up," said the man.

"Someone else can get it," said Brady.

"As you like. I must be going. Have to go see my girl. She's so spoiled—like a fine lady of the manor, always thinking she knows best." He turned away from Brady, but Brady caught what he said next over the buzz of the store. "Lady Katie."

The man walked toward the exit. Brady followed him and as they stepped out the door he grabbed the man's arm.

"What did you say?" asked Brady, his voice rough.

The man raised an eyebrow. "I said that I have to go see my girl. I said she's spoiled. That she thinks she knows best."

"After that."

"I didn't say anything after that."

"Who are you?"

The man looked down at Brady's hand where it still gripped his arm, then back at Brady. "Who are *you*?"

Brady dropped his hand.

The man shook out his coat sleeve. "I'm guessing you eavesdropped on my phone call and that you must know someone named Kaitlyn. She must be very special to you, to follow a complete stranger, to accost him in public."

Brady glanced around them. They had attracted some curious stares from fellow customers.

"Maybe you thought I was talking to your Kaitlyn," continued the man calmly. "Maybe you have reason to be worried about your Kaitlyn. On that basis, I'll overlook what happened. I don't want to call the police and report that you harassed me. I don't want to get you in trouble with them, or with your Kaitlyn." He interlaced his fingers, inverted his huge hands, and cracked his knuckles. "They break our hearts, these ladies of the manor. We must be careful not to break theirs, yes?"

The man turned and crossed the parking lot to a black sedan with tinted windows. It was parked in the space furthest from the building and closest to the road, its front facing the store so that Brady couldn't see the license plate. Brady started walking toward the sedan, but jumped back at the honk of a car horn. By the time he had dodged several other cars, their drivers no doubt desperate for their morning dose of caffeine, the black sedan was already turning onto the road. Although the car itself was pristinely clean, the license plate was too dirty to read the number, although it looked like the Maryland design. Odd, since Maryland required a front as well as rear plate.

He stood looking after the sedan as it disappeared down the road, then returned to his own car and dropped into the driver's seat. After a minute, he got out his phone and called Carly.

"Hey, what's up?" she answered, sounding considerably more alert than she had been when he had left the house.

"Just checking in. What are you guys up to?"

"I'm unloading the dishwasher and Katie is coloring. The excitement level is pretty high."

"Listen, turns out Den doesn't need me today after all, and I think I'll take the rest of the day off. Want to go over to Camden, to the aquarium? Tell Kaitlyn it's where Ariel lives."

"Hey, Katie," said Carly, "guess what Daddy wants to do today?"

"Drive the police car?" Brady heard faintly over the line.

"No."

"Turn on the siren?" She pronounced it *sigh-a-ron*.

"No."

"I give up."

"He wants to take us to see where Ariel lives. You interested?"

Brady heard an affirmative shriek from the phone.

"I think that would be a yes," said Carly.

"Great, I'll see you in a bit."

He ended the call and looked in the direction in which the sedan with the tinted windows had disappeared. He played the scene through in his mind. Had he let his imagination get the better of him? Had he really heard the man say *Lady Katie*. He had certainly said *Kaitlyn* any number of times, but it wasn't an uncommon name—there was another Kaitlyn in Katie's class, and another at Sunday school.

If he had misunderstood the situation, then he was lucky that the man hadn't made a bigger deal of Brady's behavior.

And if he hadn't misunderstood the situation ...

All he could think of was the man's huge hands, and his daughter's unmarred skin, her slender wrists, her delicate neck.

Today he'd have a day with his girls.

And tomorrow he'd go to work on that cold case.

24

Lizzy spent the night at Ruby's Overbrook apartment. The next morning, Ruby drove into West Philly to meet Andy McNally, leaving Lizzy in the apartment to pace obsessively from the sitting room through the bathroom to the kitchen and back, until someone in the store over which the apartment was located thumped on the ceiling. Ruby returned an hour later carrying a knapsack and a FedEx envelope.

"Is this what you were waiting for?" she asked, handing Lizzy the envelope. "It showed up at the hotel this morning, addressed to the younger Dr. McNally."

As Lizzy opened the envelope, Ruby continued, "If it's your new identity, don't tell any of us what the name on it is. If we're not supposed to know where you are, we probably shouldn't know what name you're traveling under either."

Lizzy nodded. "Okay."

She was startled by how much the photo looked like her—or at least her when she had long blond hair. Tracy Coates from Beloit, Wisconsin. She almost said it out loud, just to try it out, but stopped herself.

Ruby handed her the knapsack. "This is from the Dr. McNallys."

Lizzy unzipped the knapsack, which contained five envelopes. She took one out and opened it up. It was filled with bills.

"Holy cow, how much is in there?"

"Five thousand dollars. That should hold you for a while."

"Jeez." Lizzy looked uncomfortable. "I wonder if they have enough money to keep giving me loads of cash."

"I know a good place we can hide it in the van," said Ruby.

They went out to the van and Ruby showed Lizzy where she could hide the envelopes in the wells into which the back seats could be retracted. Then they loaded their luggage—Lizzy's suitcase from her trip back to Pennsylvania from Arizona and a small overnight bag for Ruby—and Ruby climbed into the driver's seat. "I'll drive us out of the city. Any idea which direction you want to head?"

"West."

Ruby shot her a suspicious look.

"Since I'm not exactly an expert driver yet," Lizzy said, "I want to stay out of busy areas. West seems like a good direction to head."

"Northern Pennsylvania would have lots of back roads you could use, and a lot of small towns you could stay in."

"I don't want to go toward the Poconos."

The Poconos was where Lizzy's mother, Charlotte, had died.

Ruby nodded. "West it is." She started up the van and pulled away.

They took the Schuylkill Expressway to the Turnpike. Ruby pointed out signs and their meanings, narrated the rules of the road, and commented on the vagaries of other drivers. When Ruby wasn't lecturing, Lizzy read the Pennsylvania driver's manual on her phone.

Ruby got off the Turnpike at Morgantown and turned the vehicle over to Lizzy.

They got on a two-lane road headed west. The biggest challenge was that Lizzy's father's car had been much smaller than Ruby's van, and whenever they approached an object near the road—a parked car or the occasional Amish buggy—Lizzy would pull far to the left, unless there was a car coming in the opposite direction, in which case she would stop to wait for traffic to clear, eliciting honks from the cars behind her. After ten minutes, Lizzy's look of determination was beginning to veer toward grim and a sheen of sweat covered her forehead.

"Pull off here," said Ruby as they approached a largely deserted parking lot in front of an under-construction warehouse. "We can practice a little more without all these antsy people distracting you."

One side of the parking lot was being paved, and was separated from the rest of the lot by barrels between which yellow nylon rope was strung.

"Let me out over there," said Ruby, gesturing toward the roped-off area, "and then you drive by the barrels and I'll hold my hands apart to show how far away from them you are."

After a few passes for which the van's distance from the barrels was too great for Ruby to indicate, Lizzy started getting a better sense of the width of the van. After a dozen passes, she was able to consistently bring the van to within about two feet of the barrels.

Ruby waved her down and climbed back into the van. "Very good," she said briskly.

They spent an hour in the parking lot, aisles standing in for roads and light poles serving as a sedate slalom course. Ruby ran Lizzy through a parallel parking exercise that prompted Lizzy to refer to her as Sergeant DiMano. When they had exhausted the possibilities in that lot, Ruby drove them to a sparsely populated mall parking lot for more practice.

When they finally ventured back onto the road, Lizzy was feeling much more confident about her driving skills, and the lack of honks indicated that the other drivers were happier as well.

After an uneventful half hour, Ruby said, "You're doing very well. Want to try the highway?"

"Sure," said Lizzy.

"Okay. Let me drive again so we can do a reconnaissance run to make sure it's not too busy."

Ruby drove to the nearest westward-heading highway. Traffic proved to be light, so she pulled off at the next exit and swapped seats with Lizzy.

"For the first merge, you just keep your eyes on the road, and I'll watch for traffic. I'll tell you what car to pull in behind. Be sure to keep your speed up so that the traffic on the highway doesn't have to slow down for you."

Lizzy started down the entrance ramp at a somewhat sedate speed.

"It will be better if you can go a little faster," said Ruby.

Lizzy increased their speed slightly as they reached the end of the ramp.

"The truck—" said Ruby.

Lizzy pulled to the left and the blast of an air horn drowned out Ruby's "Not yet!"

Lizzy jerked the wheel to the right as the truck blasted by, and the van lumbered onto the shoulder of the road. Ruby reached over and grabbed the wheel to steer the van away from the guard rail, but in the last few feet before they came to a stop, they heard the teeth-grinding screech of metal on metal.

Ruby puffed out the breath she had been holding.

"I'm sorry," cried Lizzy, "I thought you meant to pull in behind the truck!"

"I wasn't very clear about that," replied Ruby. "Let's swap places—I want to get us away from the entrance ramp, then we can check things out."

There was no indication of any effect on the van's operation, so Ruby continued on to a turnoff about a mile further on and they climbed out. A dirty silver streak ran the length of the van's side.

"Oh, Ruby, I'm so sorry!" Lizzy looked ready to cry. "I ruined your van!"

"Nonsense. It's not ruined—it's just a little cosmetic damage. We'll get it fixed up when things are back to normal." She patted Lizzy's arm. "But maybe you should stick to the back roads for a little while."

25

P hilip had slept for most of the day and a half since he had arrived at Theo Viklund's home. An attractive young woman named Elsa—as blond-haired and blue-eyed as the young man who had picked him up at the hospital—arrived periodically with meals that were all of a theme Philip thought of as Gourmet Mexican. Under the assumption that Mortensen's lackeys had slipped him a drug in Sedona, Philip at first thought he should avoid eating or drinking anything, but that wasn't a sustainable plan. If Viklund really wanted to give him a drug, Philip suspected there wasn't much he could do to stop it. And although he wasn't a huge fan of Mexican, gourmet or not, it was better than hospital food—and certainly better than prison food.

Despite the stress of not knowing what was going on, Philip found Viklund's home more restful than the hospital. It was quiet, the room was comfortable, and he wasn't continuously disturbed by people taking his temperature or checking his pulse.

In the evening, Elsa appeared with an invitation for Philip to dine with Theo Viklund.

She led him through the twists and turns of the corridors to a dining room that was a somewhat larger and more elegant version of Philip's bedroom—or of his office waiting room back in Sedona, for that matter: Navajo rugs in a variety of patterns hung on paneled walls and covered the floor, a pair of elaborate, and likely antique, kachina dolls stood on a sideboard of rough wood, and a rustic table with an Equipale chair on either side anchored the room.

"Please help yourself to a beverage," said Elsa, gesturing toward the sideboard. "Herr Viklund will be with you shortly." She stepped into the hall and closed the doors behind her. Philip heard the familiar click of a lock.

He went to the sideboard and was both amused and irritated to see, among bottles of wine and liquor, a bottle of Knob Creek bourbon. Viklund had certainly done his homework. If Andy McNally's guess was right about what had happened to Philip in Sedona, the beautiful woman who had lured him out of the Cowboy Club had likely drugged the shot of Knob Creek she had poured for him. He stuffed his hands in his pockets and made a circuit of the room, examining the decor.

He turned toward the doors when he heard the click of the lock being disengaged, and Theo Viklund stepped through and crossed to him, hand extended.

"Mr. Castillo, I hope the rest has speeded your recovery? No cane, I see."

After a brief hesitation, Philip shook Viklund's hand. "Much better, thanks." He gestured to the decor. "You've got quite a collection here."

Viklund strolled to the sideboard, dropped an ice cube from a bucket into a crystal tumbler, and poured himself a shot of bourbon. "I'm fascinated by Southwestern American culture, and specifically by Native American culture." He raised the bottle toward Philip with raised eyebrows.

"No, thanks."

"Is there something else I could get you?"

Philip picked up a bottle of water from the sideboard and twisted off the cap.

Viklund returned the bottle of bourbon to the table and raised his glass.

"Skål."

Philip raised his bottle and they drank, then Viklund gestured him to one of the chairs at the table.

"So," Viklund asked when they were seated, "are you Native American?"

"Why does it matter?"

"You could perhaps answer some questions about the Navajo rugs for me."

"You should ask an expert. I wouldn't want to give you a bum steer."

"Quite right," said Viklund.

"It's interesting that this room is decorated in a way you might assume would be appealing to me. Same with the room I'm staying in, and the food you're serving me. And you don't strike me as a guy who would normally be serving Mexican food or decorating with kachina dolls."

Viklund smiled. "Why else would I do those things if not because I enjoyed them?"

"To make me feel comfortable."

"But that is the goal of every good host, is it not?"

"Not to the extent of redecorating rooms."

Viklund shrugged. "I have the resources. It is a bit of a hobby for me."

"Why would you go to all this trouble? For that matter, why would you spring me from the hospital, at the risk of attracting the attention of the police?"

Viklund waved his hand. "Any such attention can easily be dealt with."

"How?"

"As you asked before, why does it matter?"

"Because when someone does me such a big favor, I like to know why. And what they might expect in return."

"I admire your caution, Mr. Castillo. Perhaps it was only to obtain your views on Native American material culture."

Philip raised an eyebrow.

There was a knock on the door and Viklund called, "Come in."

Elsa opened the door and an older, stouter, but similarly Scandinavian-looking woman stepped in, carrying a tray filled with plates and bowls. Philip could smell chili powder. She stepped up to the table and Elsa lifted two bowls from the tray, but Viklund held up his hand.

"I think perhaps Mr. Castillo has had enough of that cuisine for now." He turned to Philip. "Is there some other type of food that you would enjoy?"

"Pretty much anything else."

Viklund laughed. "Of course." He turned toward the women. "Agnes, please bring us pretty much anything else."

She nodded expressionlessly and carried the tray out of the room, followed by Elsa, who closed the door behind them.

Viklund took a sip of bourbon. "Your time in the hospital must have been quite stressful."

"I don't imagine anyone enjoys being in the hospital."

"Especially if you were concerned that your next stop might be prison."

Philip was silent.

"Your conviction and imprisonment as a teenager seemed quite unfair. It must have left you with a distrust of the legal system."

"I don't imagine anyone totally trusts the legal system."

"And the name change from Casal to Castillo suggests that you're intent on leaving that part of your life behind."

"You don't expect me to make this any easier for you than it evidently already is by answering your questions, do you?"

Viklund shook his head. "No, of course not. I must remember my goal of being a good host. Let's speak no more of that for now."

Viklund regaled Philip with some background of the Southwestern decor. He may have gotten it to appeal to Philip, but he seemed knowledgeable about the significance of the dolls and the manufacturing process of the rugs—far more so than Philip himself.

Eventually Agnes and Elsa returned with the replacement dinner—bowls of yellow pea soup, crusty bread and salads—and an accompanying bottle of wine. Viklund uncorked the wine as Agnes served the meal. He poured for himself and Philip and raised his glass.

"To finding common ground," said Viklund.

Philip watched as he drank, then raised his own glass and took a sip.

Agnes and Elsa retired, Viklund resumed his seat, and the conversation continued, this time focused on Arizona itself—the mountains and desert, the flora and fauna. Viklund claimed never to have been there but was as well informed about it as he had been about the rugs and kachina dolls. Viklund paused periodically, providing openings for Philip to engage in the conversation more actively, but when Philip remained silent, he continued the monologue, seemingly unperturbed.

Eventually Agnes and Elsa returned again—Agnes to clear the table, and Elsa to serve dessert: rhubarb cake and espresso.

Philip drained the small cup as they withdrew.

"Maybe we should talk less about where I'm from, and more about where you're from," he said.

"I've been here so long, I feel like a native."

"Based on the people you surround yourself with, you've built a Little ... Stockholm? Oslo? right here in ... wherever we are. Pennsylvania or Maryland, I assume. Or ..." He tried to picture the state just to the south of Maryland, but his mental map was hazy. "West Virginia," he said after a moment. That didn't seem quite right.

"Come in," called Theo, although Philip hadn't heard a knock.

The door opened and a man stepped in. An alarmingly large man.

"Lucas," said Viklund, "I believe Mr. Castillo may need some help returning to his room. He's looking a bit sleepy."

He did feel sleepy. Not so much sleepy as ... he cast about for the right description. Woozy?

Drugged?

Goddamn.

26

Louise was immersed in an unauthorized perusal of the files of the NIH when a light laugh behind her forced her attention back to the lab. She turned to see Theo standing at the door.

"Fascinating, isn't it?" he asked.

"Yes, it is." She glanced around the lab. "Where is Edmund?"

Theo strolled over to the desk where she was working and glanced at the monitor. "He left half an hour ago."

"Oh. Well." She stood so she didn't have to crane her neck to speak with Theo. "Where did he go?"

"He has his own quarters," said Theo. He glanced at his watch. "It's quite late. You missed dinner. I'll ask Maja to bring something to your suite."

"Thank you."

"I brought some news."

"Yes?"

"The attorney general's office has discontinued its investigation of Vivantem."

Louise raised an eyebrow. "I'm not surprised that they've had to put it on the back burner, with the founder dead and the new CEO missing."

"It's not on the back burner," said Theo. "It's closed."

Louise examined him for a moment, then said, "That is certainly good news. I gather I have you to thank for that."

Theo waved his hand. "It was a matter of a few phone calls. The Lenape Township Police Department—one detective in particular—was actually more of a challenge to call off than the AG's office."

Louise hesitated. "The police are definitely off the arson case?"

"And murder."

"And murder."

"Yes," said Theo. "Assuming, of course, that their prime suspect—you—doesn't reappear in public. And in other news," he continued, "we got a chance to put the Rohypnol drug to use this evening."

"On Castillo?"

"Yes. Mr. Pieda was able to obtain some useful information from him."

"What did he find out?"

Theo waved his hand. "Nothing you need worry yourself about."

Louise opened her mouth, then clamped her lips together. After a moment, she asked, "What are you going to do with Castillo and Pieda?"

"I will enlist them to my cause."

"What about Ballard? Will you be bringing her here as well?"

"If she would ever emerge from the hotel," he said with mock irritation, then smiled. "No, in reality, I am happy to leave Miss Ballard where she is—at least for now."

"And how do I factor into this plan?" asked Louise.

"Your medical and scientific expertise is vital to my plans."

"Like reformulating the drugs."

Theo began wandering around the lab. "Yes, that has certainly been most helpful, but I know what you're capable of, and in comparison to some of the work you've done, those were mere parlor tricks. You created children with extraordinary talents—I'm most interested in that. And in exchange for your support, I can continue to protect you from the unwanted attention of the authorities."

"You've known me for many years, Theo. Why are you enlisting my help with your plans now?"

"You were immersed in your work at Vivantem."

"True."

"I look for people to enlist to my cause who can focus their attentions exclusively on our joint undertakings. I believe the focus that our current arrangement offers will enable you to do work you wouldn't have been able to conceive of even a short time ago." He returned to where she stood and gestured toward the lab stool. She sat, and he pulled up a stool and sat as well. "I believe you could find a life of relative isolation attractive, as long as research facilities are available. But even for you, my offer would not have been appealing had I approached you before the attorney general's investigation, before Gerard's death, before the debacle with Elizabeth Ballard and Mitchell Pieda, before the situation progressed to a point that burning down your home was the only way out of it."

She was silent.

"Now, however, I believe what I'm offering could be quite attractive to you."

After a moment, Louise said, "I'm hardly in a position to negotiate."

"Am I misunderstanding your character so much?" he asked with a smile.

"No. The scenario does hold some appeal. It's not what you're offering, it's what you're taking away. It's been many years since I've had to take orders from someone else."

"I would hardly consider it taking orders—we're partners."

"It's hardly an equal partnership when one person holds all the cards."

"I believe I would play the cards in a way that would benefit us both."

Louise looked down at her hands and realized that she was fidgeting with her wedding ring. She laced her fingers together in her lap. "Just so I'm sure I'm clear, the proposal is ...?"

"I will protect you from the authorities and will continue to provide you with state-of-the-art facilities and all the data you could possibly need for your research. That is the prize—the iron ring—that I'm offering you. In exchange, I would ask you to agree to stay here in the compound except if and when I arranged for you to travel, obviously under a false identity. And you would provide me with the results of your research, for me to do with as I see fit."

After a long pause, Louise spoke. "Very well."

Theo stood and held out his hand. "I'm so pleased, Louise, and so excited—for both of us."

She stood and shook his hand.

"May I accompany you back to the house?" he asked.

As they walked back to the main building, the only illumination the lights that lined the walk, Louise thought she heard the sound of steps behind them. She turned but could see no one.

"Probably Lucas," said Theo easily. "My bodyguard. I asked him to stay by the lab in case you needed anything."

"You asked him to stay outside the lab, unannounced?"

"I didn't want him to be a distraction."

When they reached the main building, Maja met them at the door and took Louise's coat.

"Maja," said Theo, "Dr. Mortensen will be dining in her suite. I regret I will not be able to join her, but please have Agnes make something special. It's a night to celebrate."

"Certainly, Herr Viklund," replied Maja.

"Good night, Louise."

Louise nodded to him.

Maja led Louise to her suite. When they got there, Louise said, "I'd like to keep my coat with me. That way I can step outside without you having to take the time to bring it to me."

"It's no problem, Dr. Mortensen, I'm happy to do it. Just press zero on your phone should you need anything."

Maja stepped into the corridor and closed the door noiselessly behind her, Louise's coat draped over her arm.

Louise walked to the window and looked out, the wooded landscape visible only for the dozen feet illuminated by the lights from the room.

She didn't like the turn her relationship with Theo was taking. When she had appealed to him for help when the situation with Ballard and the Attorney General began to deteriorate, she had known that she would need to repay him in some way. However, she had pictured it as a reckoning up between equals, made from some foreign country with no extradition agreement with the United States, and under a new identity.

Could she even trust Theo's description of activities beyond his compound? Had the AG's investigation actually been closed? She got out the phone he had provided and looked for the browser app, but she couldn't find it. In fact, the phone was missing most of the standard apps.

With an ever-growing sense of misgiving, she went to the bathroom closet to get her handbag, which she hadn't needed since she had arrived at Theo's compound. She reached into the pocket where she kept her mobile phone.

Empty.

Her heart beat accelerating, she checked the main compartment of the handbag, and eventually removed all the items onto the vanity.

Her phone was gone.

Twenty minutes later, Maja arrived with caviar atop a bed of ice and a plate of blini. She opened and poured from a split of Champagne.

"Do you have any special requests for dinner?" she asked Louise.

"No, thank you, that will be enough for this evening."

Maja looked uncertain. "Perhaps some soup?"

"No. But thank you."

"Very well. Let me know when you'd like me to come back for the dishes."

After Maja left, Louise went to the table, scooped some caviar onto a blini with a small mother-of-pearl spoon, and ate it. She didn't doubt it was top quality, but it tasted no better to her than sardines dug out of a tin can. She took the glass of Champagne back to the window.

When she had finished the Champagne—as well as the caviar-free blinis, which she ate when she began to realize the foolishness of drinking on an empty stomach—she reached for the mobile phone to call Maja, then hesitated. She crossed to the door and turned the knob.

She had expected it to be locked, but the door swung open. The corridor was empty. She stepped out and listened for the sound of footsteps. All was silent.

She went back to the dining table and picked up the plates and glass, then returned to the corridor and walked slowly in the direction of the entrance hall, her heart thumping.

As the curve of the corridor brought the entrance hall into view, she saw a large man standing motionless and silent at the end of the corridor. His feet were slightly apart, his hands clasped loosely in front of him. He turned in her direction.

"Good evening, Dr. Mortensen," he said in the Swedish accent Louise was beginning to loathe. "I'm Lucas. Is there anything I can help you with?"

"I didn't want to bother Maja. I thought I'd bring my plates out."

"It will be better for you to stay in your suite—you never know who you might encounter if you are wandering around Herr Viklund's home unescorted. I will ask Maja to collect the plates."

"All right. Thank you for your help."

"Certainly, Dr. Mortensen."

She felt his eyes on her as she retreated down the corridor and let herself back into the suite. In a few minutes, Maja appeared with a tray onto which she loaded the plates and glass.

"Is there anything else I can get for you, Dr. Mortensen?"

"No, thank you, Maja," said Louise.

"I wouldn't suggest leaving your suite without me," said Maja. "Herr Viklund's home is quite large and the corridors can be confusing. I'm happy to take you anywhere you'd like to go. Within the complex," she added.

"Yes, I'll certainly do that from now on."

27

———————

izzy and Ruby stayed in a motel the first night and then, after breakfast the next morning, drove to a car rental where Ruby got a Mitsubishi Mirage for the drive back to Overbrook.

Ruby walked Lizzy back to the van.

"Don't drive after dark," she said.

"I won't."

"And stay on the backroads."

"I will."

"Want me to show you that trick to get the driver's door to unlock again?"

"No, I think I've got it."

"Just jiggle the key."

"Ruby," said Lizzy, exasperated, "I know. You showed me twice."

Ruby sighed. "I hate leaving you here by yourself."

"Yeah, but it's for the best."

"It didn't work out so well when we left you in Smoketown," Ruby said pointedly.

"That was a while ago."

"It was just a few months ago."

"Yeah, but a lot has happened since then."

"That's true." After a moment Ruby added, "I could stay with you for another day or two."

"No, you need to get home to your sister and brother-in-law."

"Yes, I suppose I do." Ruby scowled at the van. "Are you sure you don't want to go shopping for supplies before I head back?"

"No, I'll stop at a Walmart tonight and pick up what I need. They probably like it better if you're staying in their parking lot if you've bought something from them, right?"

"Yes, I imagine so. Call us and let us know how you're doing. It should be all right for you to let us know you're okay without any details about where you are, right?"

Lizzy hesitated. "I think it would make me homesick to talk to you or Uncle Owen or Andy."

"How are you going to get updates on the senior Dr. McNally's condition?"

"Maybe you can text me any important information like that. And I'll text you to let you know I'm okay."

Ruby examined Lizzy closely for a moment, then said, "At least once a day."

"Yup, at least once a day."

Ruby appeared about to say something else, then changed her mind and gave Lizzy a quick hug. She stepped back. "At least you probably don't need to go too far. It will be helpful for us to be able to get together again quickly depending on how things develop."

"Sure."

"You take care of yourself, Lizzy."

"You too, Ruby."

Ruby crossed the parking lot to the Mirage, started it up, then turned onto the road, heading east.

Lizzy jiggled the van's balky lock open and climbed in. She

got out her phone and tapped in her destination: *Williams AZ.* Thirty hours. She clicked Options and selected *Avoid highways.* Thirty-eight hours.

She sighed, put the van into drive, and pulled away.

She couldn't tell Ruby that the real reason for not wanting to talk with her or Uncle Owen or Andy was her fear that it would break her tenuous resolve to kill Tobe Hanrick.

28

—————

Philip woke up the next morning feeling considerably less terrible than he had after the prostitute George Millard had hired had slipped something into one of his drinks in Sedona. So it hadn't just been the drug that had inflicted the suffering after all—the eight shots of bourbon had played a part as well.

He was wearing the same clothes he had had on the night before, minus the boots, and was lying on top of the bedclothes, covered by a cotton blanket of a Southwestern-themed design. No detail too small, he thought sourly.

In the bathroom adjoining the bedroom, Philip undressed and cleaned up as best he could with the bandage still on his shoulder, then worked his way into fresh clothes.

He tried the door, which, not surprisingly, was locked. He pressed zero on the Viklund-provided mobile phone.

In a moment, there was a knock on the door.

"Come in."

Elsa entered.

"How are you feeling, Mr. Castillo?"

"Great. Just wanted to let Viklund know I'm up and about."

"Very good, I'll take you to see him."

She led him down the corridor, continuing on past the room where he had dined with Viklund. The doors were open and Philip glanced inside. The Southwestern decor was gone—there were no rugs on the walls or tchotchkes on the sideboard. It looked like a partially dressed stage—which, he thought, was pretty much exactly what it was.

She led him to a conservatory, windows overlooking the wooded landscape, where Viklund sat at a cafe table flanked by two metal chairs. He stood when Philip entered.

"Good morning, Mr. Castillo. I hope you're feeling well?"

"I'd feel better if I didn't keep getting drugged."

"I apologize for taking the liberty. But I'm sure you know that this was not your first such experience."

Philip was silent.

"I do owe you an explanation," said Viklund. "Please," he continued, gesturing to the other chair, "have a seat."

They both sat.

"Coffee?" asked Viklund, lifting a silver coffee pot.

Philip raised an eyebrow.

Viklund smiled. "You are no doubt suspicious that it was the espresso that contained the drug, and you would be right. Allow me to serve myself first."

Viklund poured coffee into his own cup, placed the coffee pot within Philip's reach, and drained his own cup.

"You asked me before if I worked for Louise Mortensen. It is more accurate to say that Dr. Mortensen works for me. In fact, she is here at the compound."

"You don't say."

"I do," said Viklund. "I have supported Dr. Mortensen and her research for many years, and I was happy to come to her aid when she had exhausted her options."

"That was big of you."

"It will likely not surprise you to learn that my friendship with Dr. Mortensen was not the only motivation for the assistance I provided to her. She will be an invaluable resource for me—she has a truly innovative mind, and I believe her innovations will open opportunities for me and my allies."

"And how long do you expect her to be innovating for you and your buddies?"

Viklund smiled, and Philip almost felt bad for Louise Mortensen. "Oh, I have every reason to expect that Dr. Mortensen will be supporting my work for many years to come."

Philip nodded.

"And, as you may already suspect," continued Viklund, "Mitchell Pieda is here as well. The presence of Dr. Mortensen and Mr. Pieda at the compound is why I—regrettably—must lock the door to your room. It wouldn't do to have you run into either of them wandering the corridors of my home."

Philip smiled thinly. "Yeah, that would be awkward."

"You are a master of understatement, Mr. Castillo." Viklund refilled his own cup, then held the coffee pot over Philip's cup. At Philip's nod, he filled his cup as well. "I believe you are aware of Mr. Pieda's special skills. There's not only his ability to create strokes, but his ability to read minds. Some people have a natural resistance to this ability, but as with so many things, science gives us a recourse. The drug you were given—here and in Sedona—is a derivative of flunitrazepam and makes the subject more susceptible to Mr. Pieda's mind-reading ability."

"And what did ol' Mitch ask me this time?" asked Philip, more casually than he felt.

"He asked what the prize is that you seek."

Philip tried to keep his face neutral. "And what did he find out?"

"He perceived your relief that you weren't aware of Miss

Ballard's location and therefore could not provide it to us. That made me curious, because we believed Miss Ballard to be in a hotel near the hospital where her godfather is recovering from his heart attack. I had two employees watching the hotel, and they confirmed that although Dr. McNally's younger brother had indeed come and gone yesterday morning, he had only gone to the front desk, not to the room. That seemed odd, so this morning they checked the room while the housekeeper was cleaning. It seems that Andrew McNally had ended his reservation the previous day." He took another sip of coffee. "I was none too pleased to hear that, and those two employees have now been ... reassigned, shall we say."

"How do they like their new assignment?" asked Philip, deadpan.

Viklund smiled thinly. "It is a permanent assignment, so I can only hope that they are satisfied with where they ended up."

Philip looked back at him, expressionless.

Theo continued. "Mr. Pieda also confirmed the fact that you were intent on staying out of jail based on the unpleasant experiences of your first incarceration."

"You wouldn't need a mind reader to figure that out."

"And he found out that you want a man in prison in Arizona named Tobe Hanrick dead."

"Interesting."

"Perhaps to you. I must say I have no interest in personal vendettas—except my own, of course. However, there was another motivation that did interest me."

"Which was?"

"Your desire to kill him yourself, rather than having Miss Ballard do it for you. That is of interest to me, because I believe that were Miss Ballard to try to take on the task you set before her, it would not only be emotionally damaging to her, but would also put her in danger. And I have no interest in having

Miss Ballard be more traumatized—either emotionally or physically—than she has been already. So, in that sense, I do have an interest in helping you to kill Mr. Hanrick, so that Miss Ballard doesn't have to."

"Why do you care what happens to Ballard?"

"She is an extraordinary result of Dr. Mortensen's experiments. It would be a shame if she were to die in an attempt to fulfill a promise made to a friend."

"And a shame if she fell into the hands of someone other than yourself. I don't see why you wouldn't want to add Ballard to the list of extraordinary people you have working for you."

"I won't deny it would be quite a coup to enlist Miss Ballard to my cause, but from what Dr. Mortensen has told me, for my purposes she is not quite ... how shall I say it ..."

"Bloodthirsty enough?" suggested Philip.

Viklund smiled. "Exactly. So, while I have no designs on her myself—at least for now—I nevertheless would not like to see her come to any harm, with a view to a possible future alliance." He laughed. "I can see you are unconvinced as to my motives, Mr. Castillo."

"Sorry to be a skeptic."

Viklund waved his hand. "No matter. I won't ask you to try to find out where she is—from one of the McNally brothers, for example."

"I figure that since Ballard would have told them about Pieda's ability to read minds, they have probably made it a point not to know where she is either."

"I have no doubt that you are correct. We shall speak no more of Miss Ballard for the time being, except to ensure that we prevent her from trying to discharge her obligation to you. We need to get you to Arizona," said Viklund. "If Miss Ballard is headed there, I suspect she will need to go by car or bus or train, since a TSA check at an airport would alert any authorities who might be looking for her to her presence. Any realistic option will take her several days. You can recuperate here for a day or two, then we will fly you out to Arizona."

"If flying is a problem for Lizzy, it will certainly be a problem for me," said Philip.

"Not the flying I have in mind," said Theo. "It has been quite a few years since I or any of my associates have had to resort to a commercial airline flight."

"And once I make sure Ballard can't get herself into even more trouble by killing Hanrick, what then? You're going to recruit me into your army?"

"Or perhaps into my own Knights of the Round Table."

Philip snorted.

Viklund shook his finger at Philip. "There is a bit of the knight errant about you, Mr. Castillo. You take great risks for those who have earned your loyalty. Miss Ballard, your damsel in distress. The old man you befriended in prison."

"He wasn't an 'old man.'"

Viklund held up a placating hand. "A poor choice of words. But what I wish to convey is that I admire your commitment to a cause, and I admire your willingness to break the narrow-sighted strictures of the law in service of a higher moral code. You have been a loyal friend—to Miss Ballard and Mr. Riva and no doubt to many others—but perhaps it is time for you to have an opportunity to champion your own cause." He paused, but Philip was silent. Theo continued. "I believe that when this Hanrick business is taken care of, you and I might explore other mutually beneficial opportunities. As someone who is, or at least looks, Native American, you could be useful to me. As you may have noticed, all my staff are Swedish, and they would appear out of place in certain settings and circumstances. Since I became aware of your involvement in matters related to Dr.

Mortensen, I have been thinking about opportunities that would be facilitated by having a colleague who could operate in the Native American community."

"What kind of opportunities?"

"No need to get into that detail yet. I would first like to assist you with your goal."

Philip was silent for a moment, then said, "Why are you telling me all this? If I were running the kind of operation it sounds like you're running, and told someone what you've told me about it, I'd want them out of the way as soon as I got what I wanted from them."

"I assume you are using 'out of the way' as a euphemism for dead, but I would hardly have to resort to such extreme measures. As you might surmise from the fact that I'm sheltering Dr. Mortensen—a well-known person who is suspected of involvement in arson and murder, not to mention unethical medical experimentation—I have quite a bit of control over the authorities' interest in my business. And I similarly have quite a bit of control over the authorities' interest in others' business. If you were to do anything that would be against my best interests, it would be quite simple to get you into the hands of those authorities. And it's quite likely that once you were in their hands, they would not believe a word you told them about the mysterious man you met in Maryland. Mr. Pieda was able to confirm for me your deep aversion to the idea of going back to prison. It would be all too easy for me to make that happen. Do you believe me?"

Philip nodded once.

"So we should pursue the initial goal of keeping Miss Ballard from coming to harm in her pursuit of Mr. Hanrick?"

Philip was silent for a long moment, then said, "Yes."

Viklund nodded and sat back in his chair. "One thing that was not entirely clear to Mr. Pieda was the desired circumstances of Mr. Hanrick's death. Do you merely want him dead? Or do you want to kill him yourself?"

Philip stared at the calm face asking him if he wanted to commit murder. Finally, he spoke.

"I want to kill him. And I want to be looking in his eyes when he dies."

29

Owen was finishing up the dinner of chicken breast and salad that Ruby had prepared for him. The chicken seemed a little dry and the salad dressing a little sparse, and he was contemplating the meal of fettuccini alfredo that he would prepare when he regained control of his kitchen.

He had been discharged that morning with strict orders not to exert himself in any way. Andy had called Ruby as she drove back from Western Pennsylvania and hired her to stay with Owen to make sure no exertion took place.

Ruby had declined Owen's invitation to join him for meals.

"Dr. McNally, we would just spend the whole meal trying to think of things to talk about."

"I never have trouble thinking of things to talk about," said Owen plaintively.

"I'll bring you your meals in the dining room, and I'll eat in the kitchen," she said, and that was that.

He levered himself out of his chair, paused to catch his breath, and began gathering up the plate and utensils.

Ruby appeared at the door. "I'll take those, Dr. McNally," she said, taking them from Owen.

"It's not like I had a heart transplant," said Owen. "I can clear my dishes myself."

"Don't be silly," said Ruby briskly. "You need to rest."

Owen trundled after her down the hall to the kitchen, Ruby's base of operations. "I've been doing nothing but resting. I'm tired of resting."

"You have to think of getting better as the job you need to do." She rinsed the plate and utensils and put them in the dishwasher.

"It's a pretty deadly boring job," he said grumpily.

"Would you like dessert?" she asked.

Owen perked up. "Dessert?"

"I got something called oat-based fruit crumble."

After a brief pause, he said, "That was very thoughtful of you."

"I'll bring it to you. Do you want to have dessert in the living room?"

"Yes, that sounds nice. Can you bring me some tea as well?"

"Yes," she said, putting on the kettle.

Owen went to the living room and picked up an old copy of *Progress in Neurobiology*. He lowered himself into his favorite chair and flipped through a few articles until he came to "Uncertainty and stress: Why it causes diseases and how it is mastered by the brain."

"Very helpful," he muttered, and tossed the magazine onto the table.

A few minutes later, Ruby came into the living room with a tray and transferred a plate of crumble and a steaming mug onto the table.

Owen leaned forward, sniffing suspiciously. "What's that?"

"Peppermint tea."

"Isn't there any real tea?"

"That is real tea."

Owen drew his brows together. "You do know I'm a medical doctor and am familiar with the effects of various foods on the human body, don't you?"

"Yes. Is there anything else I can get for you?"

He sighed. "No, thank you. Except for the fake tea, dinner was very nice."

"I'm glad you liked it. I'm going to turn in. You can leave those there when you're done, I'll get them in the morning."

He glanced at his watch. "It's quite early."

"I need to go over to my sister's house early tomorrow, but I should be back here in time to make breakfast."

"Ruby, please take your time. I know your brother-in-law is doing poorly, and you should spend as much time as you need with him and your sister. I'm more than capable of fixing my own breakfast. And my own lunch, for that matter."

She narrowed her eyes at him.

He looked resolute.

"It shouldn't be necessary," she said, "but I appreciate the offer." She glanced around the room, evidently looking for something that should be wiped down or straightened up.

"Good night, Ruby. And thank you again for everything."

"Good night, Dr. McNally." She left the room, and he heard her go to the front and back doors, heard the rattle of hardware as she checked the locks, the beep as she set the alarm, then her measured tread on the stairs. For a few minutes there were the sounds of her moving around on the second floor—steps, running water, more steps, then silence. They were soothing sounds. He had to admit that he appreciated having someone else in the house, especially with things so discombobulated.

He ate the crumble, which was actually quite good, then made a half-hearted attempt to get interested in the "Uncertainty and stress" article. He got to the end of the first page and realized he hadn't any idea what he had just read.

He tossed the magazine aside for the second time and went upstairs, stepping over the fourth stair, which squeaked. He went to his office and powered up the monitor, then pulled up his bank account information.

He had reviewed his account balances and was scanning his stock portfolio when he heard the beep of the alarm announcing a door opening, Andy's voice—"Wendy, I'm home," à la Jack Torrance—and another beep as Andy deactivated the alarm.

Owen pushed himself out of his chair and hurried down the stairs. "Shh—Ruby's in bed," he whispered between fast breaths.

Andy raised his eyebrows and glanced at his watch.

"She has to get up early to go to her sister's."

"Oops. Sorry about that," Andy whispered back, looking genuinely contrite. He held up three bottles of beer. "Look what I brought."

"You brought a three-pack?"

"The rest are in my car. I'll bring you another one tomorrow."

They went to the kitchen and Andy popped the caps off two of the bottles and put the third one in the refrigerator. "That's for Ruby. No cheating."

They clinked bottles and sat down at the kitchen table, Owen still a bit out of breath.

Andy looked at him critically. "How are you feeling?"

"Okay."

"No, seriously. How are you feeling?"

"Tired."

Andy waited for more, but Owen was silent. Finally, he said, "Not sure if this is going to make you feel better or worse, but the attorney general's office called off the Vivantem investigation."

Owen put down his beer. "Really? When?"

"I saw it in the news today. I almost missed it—it was buried on the electronic version of a back page on phillychron.com."

"Why did they call it off?"

"They didn't say anything specific," said Andy. "Just general stuff about higher priorities and limited manpower."

"Do you believe that? Or do you think Mortensen pulled some strings?"

Andy sighed. "I don't know what to think. I figured she burned her house down to destroy evidence, but if she could get the investigation called off, why bother?" He drank. "Maybe she thought the fire would destroy the body in the basement."

"It seems like a complicated way to get rid of a body. Plus, she would know that no fire was likely to burn so hot and so completely as to destroy a body, especially one in the basement."

"Yeah." Andy shrugged. "It doesn't make a lot of sense, but I can't think of anyone else who would be interested in ending the investigation. Except maybe the Pennsylvania tax payers. There were a lot of complaints when Brashear first announced it."

"Yes. That's probably all it is. But we should err on the side of caution and assume that Louise Mortensen is still a factor."

"Seems wise."

Owen picked up his beer and took another sip. "I think we did the right thing to send Lizzy away. I think Sedona might have worked if we had done a better job of laying low. And if it had been further away. I realize that Louise Mortensen could probably eventually track us down anywhere, but at some point, if we make it hard enough for her, *and* if we demonstrate that we aren't running to the authorities or the media, it won't be worth her while to continue to chase us."

Andy shrugged. "I'm not sure it's a plan that's sustainable in the long haul, but getting far away and keeping your head down couldn't hurt."

"If Lizzy can just stay off the grid until I'm better, I can take her somewhere where we can really stay hidden, and I can keep an eye on her until she's ready to strike out on her own. We could go somewhere nice. Maybe the person who got Lizzy the driver's license could get her a passport and we could go to Europe. Or Asia. I always wanted to go to Japan."

"You think you look big to people here, wait until you get to Tokyo."

"Very funny." Owen took another sip of beer.

"How long do you think you'd have to hide out? When do you think Lizzy will be ready to strike out on her own?"

Owen smiled wanly. "She probably thinks she's ready now, but realistically? A year? Two years?"

"You're just going to drop off the grid for two years? What about the class you're supposed to teach in the fall?"

"I'll just tell Steck I can't do it."

Andy raised his eyebrows. "That won't go over well."

"I know. But irritating Steck really isn't my top concern at the moment."

"True." Andy considered. "So you have enough money socked away to spend a couple of years on a world tour? Hey, if I'm mentioned in your will, maybe I'll knock you off myself."

"The coffers would be pretty depleted by the time the tour was done," said Owen. "But, hey, I made it once, I can make it again."

"Not if you have a reputation for dropping classes and disappearing for years at a time."

Owen waved his hand impatiently. "It would work out." He hesitated. "I'm more concerned about Mom and Dad. And about leaving you to deal with that again."

"If Mom and Dad ended up being the only thing I needed to worry about, it would be like a vacation."

Owen looked down at his bottle of beer.

Andy ran his fingers through his hair. "Jesus, Owen, I'm sorry, I didn't mean it to come out that way. I really just meant that you shouldn't worry about that." He hesitated. "Although, to be perfectly honest, if you disappear for two years, I don't know that Mom will still be around when you come back."

Owen sighed. "I know."

They finished their beers in silence. Then Andy said, "Split Ruby's?"

"I won't tell if you won't."

30

———

Lizzy stuck to the backroads, her fingers clenched on the steering wheel, her back muscles seizing with stress. She pulled over periodically to let the faster drivers pass.

Late in the afternoon, when she had other drivers honk at her three times in less than ten minutes with no idea what transgression she had committed, she decided to call it a day. In any case, the sun was setting, and she was anxious to finish the day's drive before darkness settled in.

She pulled to the side of the road and called up directions to the nearest Walmart.

When she got there, she pulled into a space in the section of parking lot furthest from the entrance and removed some money from its hiding place under the back seats. She dragged herself into the store, got a cart, and began pushing it blearily up and down the aisles.

She loaded a couple of gallon jugs of water into the cart—once she used up the water, she could refill them at a rest area—then picked up an assortment of fruit and some prepared food that she could eat cold. In the sporting goods section, she found not only a sleeping bag but also a camp toilet that was small enough that it could be used in the back of the van. In housewares, she picked up some garbage bags to use as liners for the toilet, a pillow, and a bucket, washcloth, and towel, figuring that might be her only way to bathe for however long she was on the road.

She couldn't think of what else she might need, but that was hardly a problem—the store was open twenty-four hours a day, and she would be a couple of hundred feet from the front door.

She checked out, wheeled the cart out to the van, unloaded her purchases, took the cart to a cart corral, then returned to the van.

It was a Dodge Grand Caravan, and the two rows of seats in back folded flat, creating quite a large area for Lizzy's temporary living quarters. Lizzy pulled her purchases out of their bags, arranged them on the floor, and assessed her supplies.

She realized two misses right away. If she was going to get any sleep, she would need some sort of mattress. And if she was going to have any privacy, she would need some covering for the windows.

She climbed out of the van, retrieved the cart from the corral, and returned to the store, practically staggering with exhaustion. She found a display of air mattresses, but did "air mattress" mean she would actually have to blow it up like a balloon? She guessed that a mattress that had a built-in pump would need electricity to run. She avoided having to spend the energy to read the instructions on the boxes by splurging on a foam mattress that folded up into a tiny couch.

She wasn't sure what she could do for curtains. She finally picked up a windshield sunshade, an inexpensive bedsheet set, and duct tape.

To save herself a trip to and from the cart corral, she left the cart in the store and lugged her new purchases out to the van.

She slid the sunshade over the windshield, then climbed into the back. She pulled the sheets from their plastic wrapping, but the creativity—and the energy—to fashion curtains out of them was beyond her. At least the sheets had come with a pillowcase she would put to good use very soon.

She folded out the mattress and unrolled the sleeping bag. She draped the corners of the fitted sheet over the headrests of the driver and passenger seats, creating a tent-like area behind the seats. She stuffed the pillow into the pillowcase and climbed into the sleeping bag. Wafting her flimsy tent over her, she was dimly relieved that she would be pretty much completely hidden from passersby.

She had a vague thought that she should open one of the water jugs and brush her teeth, but the effort seemed laughably excessive, and she was asleep a minute later.

31

Lizzy came groggily awake, woken by the chime of an incoming text. As she fumbled for the text app, she noticed the time. She had slept for almost twelve hours.

Good morning ... interesting news, Ruby texted.

Lizzy opened the link to a short article on phillychron.com announcing the cancellation of the attorney general's Vivantem investigation.

Wow! She scanned the article again. *I guess that's good news right?*

I hope so

Not surprised, she texted back to Ruby, *everyone thought it was crazy to begin with*

If AG isn't interested in LM anymore, came the response, *maybe LM won't be interested in us anymore*

I hope so

Still best for you to stay away for now I think

I agree

They exchanged updates on Uncle Owen's condition—he had fixed himself coffee, scrambled eggs, bacon, and toast in

Ruby's absence that morning, and his mood seemed much improved as a result—then signed off.

She felt relieved at the news about the cancellation of the investigation—not only because it might mean they were in less danger, but also because it eliminated a distraction from discharging her promise to Philip.

She pushed aside the sheet and sat up. She was not as stiff as she had expected to be, thanks to the mattress. She was also not as cold as she had been afraid she might be. Not only was the weather comparatively warm—it had gotten down only to the high forties the night before—but she was also still completely dressed. She had not even taken her boots off before she fell asleep.

She had taken the camp toilet out of its box and was reading the instructions for setting it up when she realized she couldn't very well use it before she had some curtains rigged up. She did notice, however, that the instructions referenced special bags that could be used with the toilet—and would no doubt work better than the garbage bags she had bought. She'd see if the store carried the special bags and return the garbage bags if they did. She put the box of garbage bags in her knapsack and clambered out of the van.

The morning was bright, and cars wended their way up and down the aisles while customers trundled carts from the store to their cars.

The security guard at the entrance—gray-haired, pot-bellied, and shifting as if his feet hurt—gave her a look as she walked past him on her way to the restroom, and she realized that her haircut, which had seemed fun and fashionable in Sedona, likely gave a whole different impression here in this rural community. If she was going to elude Louise Mortensen and whatever allies she had been able to rally, her goal should be to leave no impression at all. She needed to figure out what to do with her hair.

After she had used the bathroom and brushed her teeth, she went to the hat section. A winter hat would look odd in March, as would the straw hats that were already on offer. She perused the selection and spotted an alternative. The tag identified it as a cadet cap. It was light beige, with a pretty vine pattern embroidered onto it. She tried it on and checked herself out in the mirror. It covered most of her hair. Plus, she liked the look of it. Jaunty, her mother would have called it.

She went to the sporting goods section and found the liners for the camp toilet. She started toward the customer service desk, pulling out the box of garbage bags, but then realized that she hadn't brought the receipt in with her, and she didn't feel like making yet another trip to and from the van for the amount of money she'd get back for the bags. They'd probably come in handy anyway.

She put them back in her knapsack and turned toward the check-out lines.

She paid for the cap and toilet liners and declined the plastic shopping bag. On her way to the exit, she snapped the price tag off the cap and was putting it on when she heard a rough voice behind her.

"Miss?"

She sighed as she turned around to face the security guard. She should have waited until she was outside before putting the cap on.

"I paid for it," she said, holding out the receipt.

"Yeah, I saw," he said. "Can I take a look in your knapsack?"

"Why?" she asked, taken aback.

"Do you have a problem with showing me what's in your knapsack?"

His name tag read *Wilson*. She wondered whether it was his first name or his last name. "Well, yeah," she said. She tried to keep her voice steady, but it shook a bit with nerves, and with anger. "I don't think you can just walk up to me and tell me to show you what's in my knapsack without giving me a reason why." She wasn't sure this was true, but it seemed like a reasonable position to take.

"I'm not telling you to show me what's in your knapsack. I'm asking you if I can take a look in it."

It's pretty much the same thing was on the tip of Lizzy's tongue, but she bit it back. The last thing Uncle Owen needed was to get a call from some podunk town telling him that his goddaughter was being held on suspicion of shoplifting. And that must be why the security guard wanted to look in her knapsack, right?

She sighed, unzipped her knapsack, and held it out for his inspection.

He peered in without touching it.

"Where did you get the garbage bags?"

"From here."

He raised an eyebrow at her.

"I bought them yesterday," she said.

"Why are you carrying them around in your knapsack?"

"I was going to return them."

"Why didn't you?"

"I don't have the receipt with me."

Wilson looked smug. "You don't, eh?"

"It's in the van."

"Why don't we go take a look."

She was again tempted to protest, but she gritted her teeth, turned, and stomped out of the store, followed by Wilson. As they crossed the parking lot, Wilson continued his questioning, puffing slightly.

"You say you bought the bags yesterday?"

"Yes."

"And then came back this morning to buy a hat?"

"Yes."

"You live nearby?"

"No."

"Stay overnight in the parking lot?"

"I thought Walmart let people do that."

"It's a store-by-store policy."

"There were a bunch of other people here overnight!"

They reached the van, and Wilson looked around the parking lot with theatrical surprise. "Really? And where are they now?"

"They *left*," said Lizzy. "They were on their way to somewhere else, and they left."

"Maybe you should be thinking about leaving, too."

"I'd love to," she shot back, "but I thought you wanted to see the sales receipt from the garbage bags."

He crossed his arms. "Fine. Get it."

Lizzy circled to the far side of the van, to the driver's door, and pushed the key into the lock. She tried turning it, but it wouldn't turn. She jiggled it, to no avail.

Wilson stepped up behind her. "Having a problem there?" he asked.

"I'll get it in a minute."

"I can wait here all day."

"I'll bet you can," muttered Lizzy.

He took another step toward her, almost but not quite touching her, hemming her in against the door. She turned to face him.

"Listen, girly, don't give me any lip," he said.

Girly? Lizzy had never actually heard anyone use the term *girly*. An image popped into her head of a bad guy in a hard-boiled detective movie. A hard-boiled dick. Her lips twitched.

The security guard scowled. "What?"

Lizzy shook her head. "Nothing."

"You think this is funny?"

She managed a strangled "No." She began to turn back to the door, as much to disguise the giggles that threatened to bubble up as to return to the task of getting the door open.

But then she felt his hand on her shoulder. She flinched and sidestepped, her laughter dying in her throat, suddenly afraid of the turn this encounter was taking.

Wilson sidestepped after her and tripped. He grabbed her wrist, whether to keep her from running or to regain his balance wasn't clear. If it was to regain his balance, it didn't work—he fell to the ground, and dragged Lizzy down with him. She landed on her knees with a painful thud.

"Let go of me," she cried, trying to free her wrist from his grasp, her gaze shooting around the area.

They were on the far side of the van from the store's entrance —and from the rest of the parking lot. Next to the van was a thin strip of scraggly woods, on the other side of which Lizzy could hear cars passing on the road fifty yards away. No one could see her and Wilson—and, unless she yelled, no one would be likely to hear them.

Wilson let go of her wrist and she began to scuttle away on her hands and knees, but before she could get out of his reach, he grabbed her ankle. She was about to kick out, to free her ankle from his grasp, when his grip loosened. She scrambled to her feet and turned back to him.

He was trying to push himself up, but his right side wasn't working—his leg lay unmoving on the ground, his arm buckled as he put his weight on it. He collapsed, face-first, onto the pavement.

Her heart thumping and her stomach clenched, she approached him, cautious at first. He was lying still, except for his left hand, which was clawing ineffectually at the ground. He was saying something, but she couldn't understand what it was.

She squatted next to him and put her hand on his shoulder. "Mr. Wilson?" she asked, in a tremulous voice.

"J-j-j—" His mouth was pressed onto the pavement and the sound was muffled.

"Hold on," she said, "I'm going to turn you over."

She pushed and tugged until she had succeeded in rolling him onto his back.

His face was scraped where it had hit the pavement, and the right side of his mouth was pulled down.

"Mr. Wilson, can you hear me?"

"J-j-j—" The sound was less muffled, but no more clear.

"Hold on, I'm going to get help."

His left hand shot out and grabbed her arm, and she suppressed another cry.

"Joanie," he groaned, his eyes staring wide and panicked over Lizzy's shoulder. "Joanie ..."

AN HOUR LATER, Lizzy climbed shakily back into the van. A sympathetic EMT had helped her get the door open. He had evidently chalked up her near-hysterical crying to the trauma of seeing the security guard suffer what was likely a stroke. He advised her not to try driving until she felt better.

Lizzy had thought about driving away after she had run to the store and alerted the greeter that there was an emergency in the parking lot. Then she realized that the store probably had security cameras covering the lot, maybe even ones that could pick out the van's license plate. Besides, she would have had to drag Wilson away from the tires to make sure she didn't run over him, and she didn't think she could do it. Her legs were barely steady enough to keep herself upright.

Now an equally sympathetic police officer had her—or rather, Tracy Coates's—name, date of birth, address, and phone number, and a video of her was now logged in some official database, courtesy of the officer's body camera. Other than a gentle joke about her hair color and length, the license hadn't raised any issues.

She sat in the van until the last of the emergency vehicles had left and the last of the gawkers had dispersed, then started it up and began to make her careful way across the parking lot. She could see people bustling in and out of the store, and could hear a clamor of children's voices, cut short by a curt exclamation from an adult.

She had told Ruby that she didn't want to talk with her or Uncle Owen or Andy because it would make her homesick, but now she had another reason. She had no wish to let them know that she had injured, and possibly killed, another person with the squeeze.

32

———

The same young man who had driven Philip away from the hospital drove him to an airport—Hagerstown Regional, Philip saw on the sign by the entrance—and onto the ramp to the steps of a jet. He hopped out of the limo to open Philip's door, but Philip was already out of the car. The driver turned to the trunk and removed a duffel bag.

Philip reached for it.

"I can take it on the plane for you, sir," said the driver.

"Thanks, but I can get it."

After a brief hesitation, the driver handed over the duffel. Philip draped the strap over his good shoulder.

"Herr Viklund will videoconference with you on the plane," said the driver.

Philip nodded, then climbed the steps.

A woman wearing a dark pantsuit and white blouse met him at the top of the stairs. Philip guessed her to be in her late twenties, and she had the blond hair and blue eyes of all of Theo Viklund's employees.

"Welcome aboard, Mr. Castillo," she said with the hint of the Swedish accent that was also the common denominator among

Viklund's staff. "Please help yourself to drinks or snacks, then have a seat. We'll be taking off in just a few minutes."

Philip had been on a plane only once before his flight out to Philadelphia at Owen McNally's request—a decade before, to visit a girl he had met when she and her sister were visiting Sedona from Seattle. He hadn't particularly enjoyed the experience, which had been noisy and uncomfortable.

He was clearly not going to have to worry about crying babies or nonexistent legroom on this trip. The plane was more like a living room than an aircraft, with burnished wood fittings and large, heavily cushioned leather seats.

He got a bottle of water from a buffet near the front of the cabin, then settled in. Within ten minutes, they were airborne.

He was watching the towns and cultivated fields below him give way to serrated mountains as they flew west when a video monitor next to his seat flicked on.

"Good morning, Mr. Castillo," said Viklund from the monitor. "I trust you're enjoying the ride?"

"Very nice. You've ruined me for the airlines."

Viklund's smile broadened. "Quite right. I myself am appalled by the conditions that the airlines expect their passengers to endure. And perhaps you've already met my niece, Rey, who will be accompanying you in Arizona. You should be aware of the compliment I pay you by giving up Rey's assistance here in Maryland."

Philip looked toward the woman sitting at the front of the plane. She smiled blandly back at him. "Your niece, eh?"

"Yes. Rey is my favorite niece, and I would be most displeased should anything happen to her. I trust you will keep an eye on her."

"She doesn't look like she needs anyone to keep an eye on her."

The woman's smile widened fractionally.

"You're quite right. Rey will ensure that our plans in Arizona run smoothly."

"We have plans?"

"We will shortly. It's good that we have had a few days for me to put all the arrangements in place. I've established a new identity for you. There's an envelope on the buffet."

Since Rey could obviously hear the conversation, Philip waited a moment to see if she was going to bring him the envelope. She raised an eyebrow at him. It was clear that Rey Viklund was more metaphorical pilot in command than flight attendant on this trip. He smiled at her, retrieved the envelope, returned to his seat, and opened it. It contained a driver's license identifying him as Philip Begay of Ash Fork, Arizona.

"I will arrange for you to be taken on as a temporary custodian at Williams," said Viklund, "and will further arrange for you to be assigned to an area where Mr. Hanrick will be."

Philip raised an eyebrow. "How do you plan to do that?"

Viklund waved a hand. "You needn't worry about that. Although I have to admit it has posed an interesting challenge, prison operations not being an area that I have previously had a need to delve into. A learning experience."

"So the janitor kills the prisoner, and then gets put in prison himself?"

"I'm well aware of your aversion to that outcome—and it would be suboptimal for me as well. I'm ironing out some of the details, but I feel confident I can arrange the encounter in such a way that you will be able to get away. Unless," he added hopefully, "you are willing to let someone else kill Hanrick. That would be quite easily arranged."

"I'll take my chances on your plan."

"Very well. You and Rey will go to Flagstaff and await further instructions. As soon as I have finalized the arrangements, I will let you know."

A little over five hours after leaving Maryland, they landed in Flagstaff and taxied to a satellite terminal. Rey followed Philip down the steps of the plane and pointed to a car parked next to a nearby hangar.

"That's for us."

She followed a few steps behind him, she in turn followed by the pilot, who carried her bag.

The day was cool but the sun beat down on the asphalt, which radiated the heat. As the pilot stowed their bags in the trunk, Philip shrugged out of his coat.

"You must be hot in that jacket," he said to Rey.

Rey pulled the jacket back far enough for Philip to see the gun in its shoulder holster.

He tossed his coat into the trunk and sighed. "Yeah, I figured."

33

———————

A few hours after leaving the Walmart, Lizzy pulled into the parking lot of a shopping center anchored by a Dollar General and climbed into the back of the van for a late lunch. She checked her progress on the map app and groaned. Not only did the GPS expect her to be covering ground a lot faster than she was, but she was finding driving to be exhausting, and she didn't think she'd be able to put in more than a half dozen hours behind the wheel each day.

She ate a meal of packaged cheese and crackers, an apple, and a banana, then opened the browser app and typed in various searches to see if she could find any news or police reports about a Walmart security guard who had suffered a stroke. She could find nothing.

She set the phone aside and stared out the van's window, toward where a plastic shopping bag tumbled across the parking lot before snagging on a shopping cart abandoned in the far corner. She couldn't forget the sound of that stuttered *J-j-joanie* that Wilson had uttered as his brain began to betray him and fear filled his eyes.

Maybe once she had done what she needed to do in Arizona, she would go back to Pennsylvania and ask Uncle Owen to hide her away, the way her mom and dad had tried to do. That's evidently what it would take to protect innocent bystanders like Wilson—who might have been a jerk, but not evil like Anton Rossi and Gerard Bonnay and Tobe Hanrick—from her power, and her lack of self-control.

At the same time that she wanted to be able to withdraw into some safe isolation, she also realized that traveling alone made it more likely that incidents like the one with Wilson would occur. If Ruby had been with her, it never would have happened. A female traveling on her own, especially a seventeen-year-old female, would look like easy prey to jerks—and worse. And she felt no satisfaction in the fact that, unless they were armed, they were sure to come out of an encounter worse than their supposed prey.

She considered her options. Despite Uncle Owen's concern about the dangers of the predictability of public transportation, she could leave the van here and take a bus or train to Williams, but how would she get around once she was there? Based on the time she and Uncle Owen had spent in Arizona, she got the feeling there weren't many transportation alternatives if you didn't have a vehicle of your own.

Hitchhiking wasn't out of the question, but she wanted to save it as a last resort. She had seen a dozen hitchhikers since they had left Overbrook—male and female, young and old, clean and dirty. One had been holding a sign that said *ANYWHERE WEST.*

Maybe she was thinking about the hitchhiking option backwards. And maybe a rethought approach would solve more than one problem.

She washed her meal down with a drink from one of the gallon water bottles, and got back on the road.

It took only about half an hour to spot a hitchhiker, but he was of the male, old, and dirty variety, and his scowl didn't add to his charm. Shortly after that she passed a guy and a girl about her own age. They were not noticeably dirty or scowling, but she didn't feel like taking on more than one fellow traveler.

She was thinking she might have to pull over and take a nap —or at least give her fingers a chance to release the death grip they had on the wheel—when she spotted another hitchhiker. Lizzy guessed she was in her early- or mid-twenties, medium height and probably slender under her bulky blue coat, with straight blond hair tucked behind her ears. She stood next to a large backpack to which a bed roll was attached.

Lizzy put on her turn signal and eased the van to the side of the road.

The girl hefted her pack onto her back and jogged surprisingly quickly to the passenger door.

"Hey, thanks for stopping," she said.

"Sure," said Lizzy. "I'm only going about twenty miles, is that okay?" Twenty miles seemed like a good distance to decide if the girl seemed like a promising traveling companion. If she wasn't, Lizzy would just let her off in whatever town came up in twenty miles.

"Gets me twenty miles further on," said the girl. She opened the back door and heaved her pack in, then clambered into the passenger seat. "I'm Daisy."

"Hi. I'm Tracy."

"Nice to meet you, Tracy."

Lizzy pulled carefully back onto the road.

"So, what's up?" Lizzy asked, trying to balance the need to find out enough about her passenger in the next twenty miles to know whether she wanted to extend the trip, while still keeping her attention on the road.

"It's a been a tough day to catch a ride," said Daisy.

"Although I'm glad I'm not a guy—nobody likes to pick up guys."

"Although I guess some of the people who are willing to pick up girls," Lizzy said hesitantly, "aren't necessarily the kind of person you want to get a ride with."

"That's for sure. That's why I was excited when I saw you check me out and slow down."

"I didn't 'check you out,'" said Lizzy, somewhat embarrassed.

"Sure you did. Or if you didn't, you should have. Want to be careful who you let in your car with you." She looked around. "Or van. Nice ride."

"Thanks. A friend loaned it to me. Do you hitchhike a lot?"

"I do what I have to to get where I'm going."

"Where are you going?"

"LA."

The traffic light they were approaching turned yellow. Although they were quite close to the intersection, Lizzy braked, eliciting a honk from the driver behind her.

"People sure are antsy," said Daisy sympathetically.

"Yeah. I thought you were supposed to stop for yellow."

The light turned green, and the driver behind them gunned the engine and shot around the van.

"Asshole," said Daisy.

Lizzy grinned.

They traveled in silence for a few minutes, then Lizzy asked, "Do you drive?"

"Sure. I don't have a car, but I have my license."

"What kind of cars have you driven?"

"I learned in my parents' Honda Pilot. I had a Hyundai Accent for a while. My ex-boyfriend had a Toyota Tacoma that I drove sometimes."

"Have you ever driven a van?"

"Like this one? No."

"Would you be able to?"

Daisy looked over at Lizzy. "Yeah, I'm sure I could."

"Would you mind driving for a little while? I'm getting kind of tired."

"Sure," said Daisy. "I'll give it a try."

Lizzy pulled over and she and Daisy swapped places. Daisy fiddled with the seat adjustments and the rear-view mirror positioning, then put the van in gear and gave it gas. The van jumped forward. "Oops," she said. "It's just going to take me a little bit to get used to it."

For the first few minutes, the ride was a little rough—the starts a bit jackrabbit and the stops a bit abrupt—but Daisy got the hang of it quickly.

Lizzy was gazing out the window, feeling drowsy and enjoying being a passenger, when Daisy asked, "Are you really only going twenty miles? Because I'm guessing we're coming up on twenty miles now."

"No," said Lizzy sheepishly. "I just said that in case you turned out to be a weirdo."

Daisy smiled. "I figured. I'd do it, too. So, how far are you going?"

"I'm not sure yet," said Lizzy, still wanting to have an out just in case. "But pretty far."

They drove in silence for a few minutes, then Lizzy said, "If you're going to LA, wouldn't you get there faster if you were on the main highways?"

"Sure, but you're more likely to get arrested hitchhiking on the highways." She glanced over at Lizzy. "Wouldn't *you* get wherever you're going faster if you were on the main highways?"

"Did you see the big scrape on the side of the van? I'm not very good at entrance ramps."

Daisy laughed. "Yeah, I did. Well, that shouldn't be a problem for me. Want to get where you're going faster?"

"Absolutely," said Lizzy.

"Okay," said Daisy. "Just direct me to the nearest interstate."

34

Lizzy woke, her head resting on the unsatisfactory pillow of the passenger side window. She gazed around, a bit disoriented, as she tried to rub the crick out of her neck. It was dark and the van was parked at a rest area, cars and trucks whizzing by on the interstate a hundred yards away. She thought for a semi-panicked moment that Daisy had abandoned her, and that she was trapped at the rest area by the impossibility of a successful merge into that traffic, but then she saw Daisy's backpack and bedroll in the back of the van.

As she was deciding what to do, she saw Daisy emerge from the service plaza with a white paper bag and a beverage holder with two cups. Lizzy jumped out to open the door for her.

"Dinner!" called Daisy as she neared the van.

Lizzy rubbed her eyes. "What time is it?"

"Around seven."

"Jeez, I was asleep for a long time."

"Yeah, you must have really been worn out. Where do you want to eat?"

"We can sit in back—there's a little couch back there."

They climbed into the back of the van, and Daisy laid out

the meal—cheeseburgers, fries, and a small Coke for each of them.

Lizzy realized how hungry she was, and wolfed down the burger, then leaned back against the wall of the van. "What are you going to LA for?" she asked, popping a fry in her mouth.

"Don't laugh—I'm going to be an actress. *But,*" Daisy added hurriedly, "I'm not counting on making it big right away. I have a friend who does a lot of small roles—you know, the person in the background in a restaurant scene, the cashier at a grocery store the main character goes to, things like that—and she makes pretty good money. I figure I can do that while I get the lay of the land, then start working toward bigger roles over time."

"That sounds like a good plan. Are you going to stay with your friend when you get there?"

Daisy poked her straw into her drink. "Probably not. She's not that good a friend."

"I'll have to watch for you in movies," said Lizzy. "Are you going to use your real name?"

"No way."

"Daisy's a nice name."

"It's a hillbilly name. Plus, you'll never guess what my last name is."

"What?"

"Don't laugh. Flowers."

"Your name is Daisy Flowers?" said Lizzy, delighted.

Daisy rolled her eyes. "My mom thought it was so cute. My sister's name is Rose."

Lizzy laughed. "That's great!"

Daisy held up an admonishing finger. "You said you wouldn't laugh," she said with a rueful smile.

Lizzy shook her head, still laughing. "You asked, but I never promised."

"In LA, Daisy Flowers is going to sound like a hillbilly porn star. What's your last name?"

"Ballard," said Lizzy without thinking.

"Tracy Ballard. That's a good name."

They discussed Daisy's plans—and possible stage names—until Lizzy's phone chimed with a text.

Dr McN doing well, wants a pizza

Lizzy sent back a smiley face, then typed *Everything fine here.* She added *Getting a lot of hiking done,* then deleted it and typed *Miss you guys, but I'm keeping busy.*

She muted the phone and slipped it back into her pocket.

"Who was that?" asked Daisy.

"Someone from home. I promised them I'd check in with them every day to let them know I'm okay."

When they had finished their meal, Daisy said, "I don't think we can stay here overnight. The cops keep an eye out for people trying to sleep at the rest areas. We can go to the next exit and see what the options are."

They got back in the front seats and Daisy started up the engine. She glanced at the dashboard gauges. "We need gas."

"Okay. We might as well fill up here."

Daisy drove over to the gas pumps, a pool of light in the increasing darkness. "I don't have much money," she said. "And I am doing all the driving."

"I can pay for the gas," said Lizzy. She grabbed her knapsack, got out her wallet, and opened it. There was only a twenty-dollar bill in it—barely enough to move the needle on the van's fuel gauge.

She had plenty of cash, but it was stowed in the hiding place. She should have replenished the supply in her wallet before she picked up Daisy.

"You know, I wouldn't mind having another order of fries," said Lizzy.

Daisy raised her eyebrows. "Yeah?"

"Yeah. Would you mind picking up more fries while I pump the gas?" Lizzy handed her the twenty.

"Sure," said Daisy, taking the money. She jumped out of the van and crossed the parking lot to the service plaza building.

By the time Daisy returned, the tank was full, there was another hundred dollars in Lizzy's wallet, and the remaining money was safely back in its hiding place.

35

I t was the day after Philip and Rey had arrived in Flagstaff, and Viklund was still putting a few final arrangements in place for the installation of Philip Begay as a janitor at the Williams Correctional Facility.

When they had left the Flagstaff airport, Rey drove north toward Flagstaff proper, Humphreys Peak looming over the town to the north, then turned east across the high plateau. Juniper, spruce, and pine quickly gave way to stunted trees near Winona, and finally to a panorama of scrub and sagebrush stretching from the highway to a horizon broken here and there by distant peaks.

Philip shifted uncomfortably. Anywhere north of Oak Creek reminded him of Williams, and of his four years behind bars, and the plateau's tabletop flatness and oppressively huge sky brought on an unpleasant claustrophobia that he had never felt in the canyons and arroyos of Sedona.

The resort to which Rey drove them looked like an incongruous mirage in the emptiness of the surrounding plain. He was relieved when Rey got keys to two rooms, to the mild amusement of the front desk staff. If Viklund had assumed that all he had to do to win Philip over was to throw beautiful women in his path—first Elsa and now Rey—Philip would have been disappointed in him. If that was in fact all it took, Philip would have been disappointed in himself—especially having fallen for that trick once back in Sedona.

The adjoining rooms Rey had booked for them at the resort had a communicating door, and Philip was surprised that Rey didn't insist that it be kept open so she could keep an eye on him. However, the reason became clear when Rey attached a device to the sliding glass door that led onto a balcony off Philip's room.

"If you open the door, or mess with the device, it will trigger an alarm on my phone," she said.

"Clever."

She attached a similar device to the door to the hallway.

"Hope you don't draw down on the housekeeper," he said.

"I requested no housekeeping, so you'll need to make your own bed. Don't lock the communicating door on your side."

"Okay."

She unplugged the phone from his bedside table.

"What if I want to call for room service?"

She rolled her eyes and retreated to her room with the hotel phone. She closed the communicating door, and he heard the click of the lock on her side.

That evening, he experimentally opened the glass slider, and sure enough, Rey came through the communicating door within a few seconds, her gun drawn.

Philip raised his hands. "I surrender."

She gestured him away from the door with the gun, slammed the slider shut, reset the alarm, and stalked back to her room.

Philip suspected that Viklund had chosen the resort not only because of concern for his guests' comfort, but also because there were few places where Philip could try to overpower Rey without there being a dozen, or a hundred, witnesses. He supposed he could have run—all those witnesses would have been a deterrent to Rey shooting him in the back—but once he was off the resort grounds, he wouldn't have any good options for where to go next. The desolate desert scrub was as effective a deterrent as a chain link fence.

The resort did provide plenty of diversions while they waited for Viklund's plan to go into effect. Philip wasn't a gambler, but at least it passed the time to walk through the casino, always accompanied by Rey. It was peopled mostly with men and women whose looks of strained hopefulness suggested that they could ill afford to lose the money they fed into the slot machines or bet at the tables.

At one point, out of curiosity, he told Rey he wanted to go swimming. A short time later, they were headed to the indoor pool, he dressed in swimming trunks, a T-shirt emblazoned with the casino's logo, and flip-flops that had been delivered to Rey's room, she in a light gray version of the pantsuit she had had on the previous day. After watching her sit by the side of the pool for half an hour, obviously too warm but unable to take her jacket off due to the gun holstered under her arm, he felt sorry for her, and they headed back to their rooms. He briefly thought of asking to go to the resort's gym but didn't want to force Rey to sit by in her suit while he exercised.

In the end, they spent most of the time sitting in the resort's lobby, Rey bouncing her foot and looking out the window at the surrounding desert, Philip paging through a paperback western from the gift shop.

But his mind wasn't focused on the book.

36

Mitchell sat at the bar in a restaurant a few blocks from the Capitol, the other barstools occupied by well-preserved older men chatting and laughing with well-turned-out younger women. The noise level was lively, and the ambiance screamed inside power circle.

The man on the barstool next to Mitchell's was not old enough to be considered well-preserved, but he was well-turned-out, and was attracting looks from the women, young and old. Erik, like Mitchell, was dressed in a conservative suit and tie. Unlike Mitchell, he had the same Scandinavian coloring as all of Theo Viklund's employees. His blue eyes periodically flicked over Mitchell's shoulder toward the restaurant's entrance.

Theo had introduced Mitchell to several of his employees, including Erik, and asked him to read their minds. Two had been easy to read—each had reported with a crestfallen demeanor that Mitchell's report regarding their thoughts was accurate—but Erik's mind was impenetrable. Mitchell had feared that he had fallen short in a test set him by Theo. Then Theo had sent Erik to accompany Mitchell on his assignment in DC, and Mitchell realized that the test had been for Erik, not for himself. The fact that Theo wanted Mitchell to be accompanied by someone whose thoughts were inaccessible to him did nothing to quiet his nerves.

Mitchell took a sip of the beer that Erik had ordered for him. It tasted heavy and bitter. He should have ordered a glass of wine or a cocktail. He should, in fact, have ordered something to eat—he had been too jittery to eat lunch, and it was now nearly dinnertime. He had finished barely half of his beer and he already felt a little unsteady.

Mitchell could tell the target had entered the restaurant by the stiffening in Erik's posture.

"He's here," said Erik in his light Swedish accent. "Don't turn around. We'll be able to watch him in the mirror."

Mitchell glanced up at the mirror behind the bar. The target was a lean man in his early fifties, whose March suntan no doubt reflected a trip to visit constituents in his southwestern state. He was talking animatedly with his dining partner, an older, heavier man whose back was to Mitchell. A server arrived at their table and said something to the target. Mitchell heard his laugh over the noisy buzz of the room. The target consulted with his table mate, then said something to the server, who smiled and hurried away.

Mitchell took another gulp of beer. "Why him?"

Erik shrugged. "He's been an annoyance to a friend of Herr Viklund's."

"What kind of annoyance?"

"Putting his nose in where it shouldn't be."

"Poking," said Mitchell.

"Pardon?"

"It's 'poking his nose in.'"

Erik gave him a look. "Sure. Poking." Erik glanced at his watch. "He doesn't stay long, forty-five minutes at the most."

Mitchell nodded.

"We need to get you within ten or fifteen feet of him, right?" Erik asked.

"Yes."

"And you'll need less than a minute?"

"I think so."

Erik surveyed the room in the mirror, then said, "There's a table of two women right next to him. I could pretend that I think I recognize one of them."

Mitchell looked up at the mirror again. Two women in their mid-fifties were seated at the table next to the target, several shopping bags on the booth seats next to them.

"How long can you talk with them?" asked Mitchell.

Erik laughed. "I can figure out something to say to them for at least a minute."

Mitchell didn't doubt it. The women would no doubt be thrilled that someone who looked like Erik was picking them out for attention—even if misplaced—and Erik seemed like the kind of guy who could make the faux case of mistaken identity seem charming rather than awkward. Mitchell looked down at his beer, then took a hefty swallow. He misjudged how much was in the glass, and a bit of beer escaped and dribbled down his chin onto the lapel of his jacket.

Erik grabbed a cocktail napkin from a nearby stack and handed it to Mitchell. "You okay?" he asked.

"Yeah, I'll be fine."

Erik finished his beer and set two twenties down on the bar, anchoring them with his empty glass. "Why don't you make your stop in the men's room, then come back here. We'll act like we're heading out, and then go over to their table and I'll chat with the women while you take care of the congressman."

Mitchell slid off the barstool and wended his way to the restrooms in the back of the restaurant, taking a circuitous route that would keep him as far from the target as possible.

He was relieved that no one else was in the men's room. He stepped into a stall, then shrugged out of his jacket. He loosened his tie and pulled it over his head—he didn't want to have to try to tie a decent knot after taking the drug. He took off his shirt and rolled up the sleeve of his T-shirt. Then, his heart hammering, he retrieved from his jacket pocket a packet that held a syringe and a glass vial. He filled the syringe and raised it to his arm.

He thought back to the trip into Philadelphia the day of Russell Brashear's press conference—the press conference where the Attorney General announced the investigation into the Vivantem fertility clinic and Louise Mortensen. Louise had injected Mitchell with the steroid drug in the hotel room where they had waited for the press conference to begin, and on the walk from the hotel to the courthouse, he had never felt better —that sense of invincibility that the drug provided had not yet been superseded by the painful toll that it exacted. Louise's wrist was looped under his arm, and although he suspected that the reason was to better monitor his condition in case he had an unexpected reaction to the drug, he convinced himself that there might be another reason—after all, they were partners. He could tell by the looks a few pedestrians threw them that they made a handsome couple. Looking back, he had to admit that, with the age difference, the looks might also have been triggered by speculation about the nature of their relationship. He was sure that Louise would have been less perturbed by the assumption that Mitchell was her son than he would have been.

He winced as he depressed the plunger. It hurt more than he expected it to—certainly more than when Louise did it. A dot of blood appeared, and he wished he had a Band-Aid to keep from staining his shirt.

He returned the vial and syringe to the packet and slipped it back into the jacket pocket, then redressed. He pulled his tie back over his head, his fingers fumbling as he settled the knot.

He put his hand on the stall door latch, but hesitated. He wanted to spend as little time in the restaurant under the effect of the drug as possible. Should he wait in the men's room until he felt the drug start to take effect? Would he even know when that happened? His heart was pounding, and he didn't know if it was from the drug or nerves. He put his fingers to his wrist, feeling for his pulse, but what would that tell him that he didn't already know? He raised his hands and scrubbed them up and down his face, then flipped the latch on the stall door and stepped out, right into a man headed for the urinals.

"Hey, watch it!" The man was in his early thirties, sporting a Caesar haircut and a slightly more flashy suit than most of the conservatively dressed men in the restaurant.

"Sorry," mumbled Mitchell. He tried to step around the man, but they both sidestepped in the same direction, and he ended up bumping into him again.

"Jesus," muttered the man. "Already drunk, and it's not even seven."

"I'm not drunk," said Mitchell.

"Whatever you say," said the man, stepping around Mitchell and unzipping his fly.

"I'm not drunk!" said Mitchell, louder.

The man rezipped his fly, turned back to Mitchell, and stepped to within a foot of him. "If this is how you behave when you're sober, I'll bet no one wants to be around you when you're drunk. If you're done in here, why don't you step outside and find someone else to declare your sobriety to. Unless hanging around men's rooms is your thing." He began to turn back to the urinals. "Asshole," he muttered under his breath.

Mitchell felt his fist draw back and piston forward into the side of the man's head. It happened so fast that the man had no time to react, no time to hit back, not even time to duck or twist away.

But Mitchell knew it wasn't really his arm that was striking out—it was the steroid-boosted power of his mind. He could almost hear the blood vessels in the man's brain burst as the blow landed.

The man dropped without a sound, his head hitting the tile floor with a sickening thud.

Mitchell turned and stumbled out the door.

He made his way toward the bar, his thigh hitting the corner of a table on the way and setting up a clatter of plates and silverware and a muffled squawk from the table's occupants. He saw Erik notice him, register alarm, and rise from his barstool.

With a little thrill of elation, Mitchell realized that if he cut across the restaurant directly toward Erik, they would meet up almost exactly next to the two women Erik was going to chat up to give Mitchell time to use the crush on the target. He felt a wave of almost manic glee rise above the churning anger of the encounter in the men's room. This would work out after all.

He reached the women's table and noticed the occupants at both tables—theirs and the target's—leaning warily away from him. Erik came up beside him just as Mitchell bent toward the woman.

"My friend thinks he knows you," Mitchell said. He had meant it to be a discreet whisper, but he realized he had said it much louder than he intended.

Erik grabbed his elbow, then dropped it and stepped back as Mitchell wheeled on him. "Don't you think you know them?" Mitchell almost yelled at him.

Erik glared at Mitchell, then turned toward the women. "My apologies, ladies, my friend has perhaps had more to drink than he should have."

Mitchell turned toward the other table. The target had put

his napkin aside and was rising, evidently to intercede on behalf of the two flustered women.

"Perhaps you just need some fresh air," the man said, and reached his hand toward Mitchell's arm.

The force in Mitchell's mind was growing. Now it wasn't a mere piston on some chugging machine, it was a whirling maelstrom, a supercell, a gigantic tornado touching down and flinging trees and trucks and whole houses into the air. The tornado of Mitchell's thoughts reached out and touched the target's brain.

The man clapped his hands to his temples and doubled over. A noise that started as a groan and then crescendoed to a shriek ripped from his throat. He staggered, crashed into the table where the two women were cowering behind their shopping bags, and collapsed to the floor.

The restaurant erupted in pandemonium. The closest diners shrank back, several jumping to their feet and heading for the door. Others, further away, were standing at their tables, straining to see what was going on. A woman turned her young daughter away from the scene. The daughter twisted in her arms, trying to see.

Several servers and the maître d' converged on the target's table.

Erik grabbed Mitchell's arm. "Kom igen!"

Erik steered them toward the front door. Mitchell was afraid he would have trouble moving through the crowd, but he felt like he had suddenly become tremendously tall, a giant stepping over Lilliputians. He jerked his arm out of Erik's grip and stumbled into one of the barstools.

Erik grabbed Mitchell's arm again and tried to keep him moving toward the entrance, but an authoritative man in a suit was turning people back.

"Please return to your tables, ladies and gentlemen—every-thing is under control."

"Like hell," Erik swore under his breath as they turned back toward the dining room. "We'll find a back door," he whispered in Mitchell's ear.

The door to the kitchen was near the restrooms, and as they neared it, they could see that it was blocked by a gaggle of kitchen staff trying to see what was going on without venturing into the dining room itself.

Erik swore again and scanned the room for alternatives.

"This way," he said.

The restaurant adjoined a hotel, and Erik led them to a glass door etched with the name of the establishment. It opened onto a short hallway that ended in a cavernous lobby.

They had just stepped into the lobby when a cheer went up from a boisterous crowd near the big screen TV at the packed lobby bar.

Erik started toward the crowd, then hesitated. "It's a good place to hide in case someone comes looking for us," he said, "but we can't have any more casualties. Can you control yourself?"

"I can control myself," said Mitchell, trying to convince himself as much as Erik.

Erik led him across the lobby. Mitchell no longer felt as if his legs were stilts, raising him above the petty concerns of ordinary people. Now each step shuddered up his spine, as if his feet were encased in concrete. It took all his concentration to keep moving in a generally straight line.

They skirted the crowd, putting it between them and anyone who might emerge from the hallway leading from the restaurant. A couple who had been seated at a table on the periphery of the action got up just as Erik and Mitchell reached it, and Erik pushed Mitchell into one of the seats.

"Take your tie off, we look too dressed up," Erik said, as he loosened his own tie.

Mitchell's fingers felt swollen, and he fumbled ineffectually at the knot.

Erik jammed his tie into the pocket of his jacket. "Here, let me," he said, and leaned toward Mitchell.

"I can do it!" cried Mitchell. "Don't treat me like a child!"

"Then don't act like one," Erik shot back and reached for Mitchell's tie.

Mitchell's hand swatted Erik's away just as Erik winced, then put his hand to his head with a groan.

"Fy fan, Mitchell," he said, his eyes squinted in pain. "I'm trying to help you."

A thread of reason began to worm its way into Mitchell's overheated brain. He fell back in his chair, trying to catch his breath and slow the hammering of his heart. He could feel the storm in his brain fading, the power gradually leaking away to be replaced by a gray fog of helplessness and hopelessness.

Erik looked at Mitchell with a combination of revulsion and fear. "Are you done?" His voice was slurred.

Mitchell nodded.

Erik dropped his head into his hands and stayed that way for half a minute, then straightened and fumbled a phone out of his pocket. He pressed a speed dial and after a moment said, "Jag behöver hjälp. Sakerna gick inte enligt planen. Skicka någon för att hämta oss." Mitchell heard him give the name of the hotel. Then he ended the call.

"Shouldn't we get to the car?" asked Mitchell.

"I can't drive," said Erik. "Can you?"

Mitchell shook his head.

The crowd at the bar turned as an ambulance moved past the lobby windows and toward the restaurant's main entrance, its lights spattering the night with blue and white. It was followed a moment later by two police cars. People craned to see what was happening, then a cheer from the hardcore fans nearest the TV drew their attention back to the game.

Fifteen minutes later, Erik roused Mitchell from a half-sleep, half-faint and guided him to the hotel entrance where a limousine idled under the awning. Mitchell's head was pounding, and the ache he dreaded was already settling into his bones.

37

Louise and Theo stood in the lab, eyes on a monitor displaying the bedroom of Mitchell's suite. Mitchell lay on the bed, a pretty young woman pressing a damp cloth to his forehead. She said something—they had the sound turned off and so couldn't hear what it was—and Mitchell gave a barely perceptible shake of his head. She sat down on the chair next to the bed and glanced self-consciously toward the monitor, then turned back to Mitchell.

"You gave him the dose I specified?" asked Louise, her voice tight.

"Yes, exactly what you specified," he replied angrily.

Louise crossed her arms. "Perhaps the effect is magnified with multiple administrations. Maybe some residual amount stays in the system longer than I anticipated."

Theo turned from the monitor to Louise. "I have an employee who is now having difficulty using his right hand and walking. He was a promising young man—I'm not pleased that he's been incapacitated."

"I'm not pleased either," Louise shot back. "It seems as if the situation you sent Mitchell into was almost certain to result in some undesired consequences."

"It seems very much like the situation you sent him into when you had him kill the attorney general."

"Don't be ridiculous. I was with him from the time he received the injection until right before the attack, and George was there to get him away afterwards."

"Unfortunately, since you're wanted in connection with an arson and a murder, we couldn't very well send you with him this time, and thanks to your inability to control the situation with Ballard and Castillo, Mr. Millard is no longer available to us."

"I didn't create a situation that resulted in a completely innocent bystander being killed."

"You tested Pieda out on a random individual in Philadelphia."

"It was a homeless man."

They glared at each other, then Louise continued, her voice tight with anger. "We might possibly have gotten away with having the congressman's death deemed to be a medical anomaly, but the fact that another man was found in the men's room dead of a massive stroke eliminates any possibility of that. The DC police, the FBI, Homeland Security—they're all going to assume that it was caused by man-made forces, maybe even that it was a terrorist attack. At some point, someone's going to tie this event to the death of the attorney general, and they're going to compare the video of Russell Brashear's news conference and security camera footage from the restaurant and realize that Mitchell was right next to all three victims when they died."

Theo folded his arms and glared at the monitor.

"You've rendered him useless for any other assignments," continued Louise. "Every security organization in the country—

and probably outside of it—will be looking for him. And for me."

"I believe we've agreed that you won't be anywhere the authorities will be able to find you, at least for the foreseeable future."

They were silent for a half minute, looking at the monitor, then Louise asked, "What about Mitchell?"

"What about him?"

"I have a stake in his well-being."

Theo looked up at her, his eyebrows raised. "You do?"

"He's my patient."

A bitter smile tugged at Theo's lips. "I would argue that you relinquished your doctor-patient relationship when you violated the Hippocratic Oath in your work with him. *Primum non nocere.*"

"Fine. Then if you do not consider him to be my patient, you should consider him to be my subject."

"Dr. Mortensen," said Theo, "to you goes the credit for developing the drug. But Mr. Pieda has passed from being the subject of your experimentation to being the mechanism of my own agenda."

"And what is that agenda now?"

"For you, the agenda is to continue your research and to bring me the results. The agenda for Mr. Pieda is no concern of yours."

"The scope of topics you consider to be my concern seems to be shrinking. And I don't relish the thought of having you and Edmund Rinnert comprise the entirety of my human interactions."

"You must not be missing the outside world too much—it took you three days to realize your mobile phone was gone."

"There's a difference between a refuge—which is what I thought you were offering—and a prison."

Theo's eyes narrowed. "Louise, if you find the arrangement unacceptable, by all means, leave and contact the authorities. I will be curious to find out if the *prison*, as you call it, that I am providing for you here is worse than the prison that awaits you outside my compound."

After a beat, Louise said, "That is the quintain—the punishment for me not toeing the line?"

"That is one option open to me."

"And what are the others?"

"I would suggest that you not put yourself in a position to find out."

Theo looked back at the monitor for several moments, then glanced at his watch. When he spoke again, his voice had resumed its normal modulated tone. "Please continue monitoring Mr. Pieda. Elsa can provide you with information about his condition, and she can administer medication if needed. You can convey any messages through Maja." He tilted a slight bow to Louise, then strode to the door. Before he stepped out, he turned back. "I must admit I am having to rethink my agenda. But I believe Mr. Pieda can perform one more valuable service for me. And I am counting on you to ensure he can do that."

38

The next day at noon, Philip knocked on the connecting door to Rey's room. "I'm hungry," he called through the door. "Can we grab some lunch?"

"Can't we just order room service?" she called back.

"I'm getting cabin fever."

"Okay," she said, sounding resigned. "Step back from the door."

Philip stepped back. "Okay."

She unlocked the door and gave him plenty of clearance when he entered her room. They always left from her side so she wouldn't have to disarm the alarm on Philip's door.

They went to one of the resort's restaurants. The hostess led them to a booth, the high backs of the benches creating a private space.

"Can we get a table instead?" asked Philip.

"Sure," said the hostess, and changed direction toward a table.

"Better people-watching," he said to Rey.

She sighed. "Okay, fine."

When they reached the table, Philip beat Rey to the seat facing the dining room.

They placed their orders, then Philip leaned back in his chair. "So, Viklund's your uncle. Going into the family business?"

She raised an eyebrow at him.

"As far as I can tell," he said, "your uncle is basically asking me to go into business with him. I like to have a little more information about any business relationships I'm considering entering into."

"Considering?" she asked.

"Should I interpret that to mean that I shouldn't view it as an optional choice?"

She shrugged. "I believe my uncle already explained the consequences of choosing not to cooperate with him. He just needs to let the authorities know where to find you, and they'll take care of you for him. At this point, they assume you were responsible for the fire and murder in Pennsylvania. It wouldn't be difficult to help them fill in any gaps in their case."

"How did your uncle get himself into the position of being able to get police investigations closed?"

"Perhaps if you earn his trust, he'll tell you himself." She took a sip of water. "But you can think of it as a barter economy. He does favors for people or organizations and can ask for favors in return."

"He did a favor for the Lenape Township Police Department?"

"The connection doesn't have to be that direct. It might be a favor for someone who has some control over what a particular police department investigates. Or someone who has control over that person. In fact, in many cases, the more links in the chain, the better it is for my uncle—harder to trace things back to him. But no matter how long the chain is, quid pro quo is still the best way to pave the way to the desired outcome."

"Yes, that's true," he said.

"As true in prison as in the business world?"

He looked at her sharply. "Yes."

"And what kind of bartering did you do in prison?"

"You don't expect me to tell you my secrets if you won't tell me yours, do you?"

She smiled. "Even a quid pro quo when it comes to sharing information."

"Absolutely."

The conversation switched to more innocuous topics—weather and current events—while Philip surreptitiously scanned the dining room. As they were finishing their entrées, Philip spotted the scenario he had been watching for—a young Native American man sauntering into the men's room which, as far as Philip could tell, was otherwise unoccupied.

"Excuse me," said Philip, standing. "Need to use the restroom."

Rey folded her napkin and glanced around the restaurant, no doubt to flag down their server to sign for the meal. "We'll go back to the room."

"Come on, I was looking forward to dessert. I won't be a minute." Philip hurried away before she could protest further.

The young man, who was wearing a baseball hat sporting a King Ropes logo, was just zipping up as Philip entered.

"Hey, buddy," Philip said, "can you do me a favor and let me make a call on your phone?"

King Ropes looked at him suspiciously.

"I'm here with my girlfriend," continued Philip, "but I was supposed to meet this other girl for lunch, and I've got to get a message to her. My girlfriend is always asking to borrow my phone—I think she's looking at the calls I make—so you'd do me a big favor if I could just make the call on yours."

King Ropes sniggered. "Sure. Just make it quick."

Philip was only going to be able to make one call. He pressed in a number he hadn't called in a long time, hoping he remembered it right, hoping it still belonged to the same person—and that that person was still alive.

"Hello?" came the greeting, the voice deep and raspy.

He heaved a sigh of relief. "Hey, it's Philip."

The tone lightened noticeably. "Philip Casal? Haven't heard from you in a dog's age. How the hell are you?"

"I need a little help extricating myself from a situation."

"You need extricating, you came to the right place," came the response, accompanied by a hoarse laugh.

Philip, aware of the increasingly impatient young man behind him, talked fast, hoping the person on the other end of the line was getting it all.

He ended the call and handed the phone back. "Thanks, I really appreciate it."

"That didn't sound like a call to a girlfriend."

"You don't know my girlfriend."

Philip waited a half minute after King Ropes left, then stepped out of the restroom. Rey was standing just outside the door.

"We're going back to the room," she said.

"Whatever you say," he replied.

At a table across the restaurant, King Ropes was saying something to a table of buddies and laughing. He looked up, caught Philip's eye, and gave him a thumbs up.

Philip was glad that Rey was already headed for the restaurant entrance and didn't see it.

39

By the morning after the attack on the congressman, Mitchell's condition had improved, and Theo told Louise she could return to the lab. Maja would summon her if advice concerning Mitchell was needed. Louise bit back a retort that she didn't appreciate the implication that she could only return to the lab with his permission. She knew it would have been a vain retort—it was becoming clear that if Theo wanted her in the lab, then it was to the lab she would go.

That morning she had also discovered that the glass doors that led from her suite to the outside were locked.

She spent a few hours at the lab, although she accomplished very little. When the door clicked open to admit Maja bringing Louise and Rinnert a late-morning tea service, Louise's flinch snapped the end off the pencil with which she had been pretending to make notes.

By early afternoon, Louise was finding the lab claustrophobic and Rinnert's silent presence unnerving, and she called Maja to request an escort back to the main house. She ate lunch in her suite, then sat at the table next to the floor-to-ceiling windows, gazing out at the wooded grounds. A casual observer would have assumed she was daydreaming.

A casual observer wouldn't have known that Louise Mortensen never daydreamed.

Eventually, she picked up the phone and called Maja.

"Hello, Dr. Mortensen," Maja answered. "Shall I have your lunch dishes cleared?"

"At some point, but I'd really like to take a tour of the grounds. Could you bring my coat? And would you accompany me?"

There was a pause, then Maja said. "I will need to check that Herr Viklund … doesn't need me at the house."

"By all means. I wouldn't want to take you away from something Theo might need."

"Very good," said Maja, sounding relieved. "I will check and then come to your suite."

Maja arrived in a few minutes, her assistant in tow, Louise's coat draped over his arm. Maja took the coat from him, then gestured to him to clear the table.

"Herr Viklund was happy to hear that you wanted to take a walk," said Maja, holding the coat up for Louise. "It's not healthy to spend too much time indoors."

Maja went to one of the doors leading outside and, her body hiding the keypad, pressed in a code. She stood aside to let Louise step out.

Louise turned to the left, toward what she assumed was the other wing of Theo's compound, but stopped at the sound of Maja's voice.

"This way, Dr. Mortensen."

"Of course. I'll let you lead the way."

The grounds were not manicured, but the paved paths that led through them were swept clean. They walked in silence for a time, the main building eventually disappearing in the trees, then Louise said, "My shoes are perhaps not the ideal footwear for walking."

Maja glanced down at the Louboutin pumps. "Flat shoes would be more comfortable," she said. "And perhaps slacks."

"Yes, that would be better than a dress." The air of the March afternoon was in fact cold on her legs.

"I could get you such clothing."

"Thank you, Maja, that would be very helpful."

"Do you have any preference regarding the clothes? Style? Color?"

"I will rely on you to choose—you did so well with the dresses you provided."

"Thank you," said Maja, obviously pleased.

Louise turned the collar of her coat up. "I appreciate you taking time away from your duties for this walk."

"It's my pleasure, Dr. Mortensen."

"You've worked for Theo for a long time—I recall meeting you many years ago."

"Yes, I have worked for him for many years."

"And obviously hold an important role in his household."

An odd expression flickered across Maja's face. Louise couldn't tell if it was embarrassed pride or something else. "Yes, Herr Viklund knows I will ensure that things run according to his needs."

"And the other members of Theo's staff obviously look to you for direction."

"Yes. The household staff, in any case."

They continued along the path, which was clear of leaves and dirt even at this distance from the house. Louise did feel better for getting some fresh air.

Eventually they came to a body of water, perhaps a quarter of a mile across, no other buildings visible along its perimeter.

Louise looked around. "Is this all Theo's property?"

"Yes, everything you see belongs to Herr Viklund."

"No need to worry about bothersome neighbors," said Louise, trying for a lighthearted tone.

Maja glanced over at her. "No."

"Is the lake natural or man-made?"

Maja smiled. "In Sweden, we would not refer to such a small body of water as a lake."

"Pond?"

"Yes," said Maja, "perhaps 'pond.' It is natural. There are streams running through Herr Viklund's property and they run to this pond."

"Large streams? Big enough for fish? I might—" She hesitated at the enormity of the lie, but then forged ahead. "I might enjoy fishing."

Far from exhibiting disbelief, this revelation seemed to cheer Maja up. "I myself enjoy fishing very much. When I was a child, my father would take me and my brother fishing." She shook her head. "But no, the streams on Herr Viklund's property are not big enough for fishing." She hesitated. "Perhaps if you let him know this is of interest to you, he could arrange a trip to a more suitable location."

"Yes, I will certainly ask him about that," said Louise. "But I know he has a lot on his mind, no need to bother him about that right now."

"There are several places not far away," said Maja contemplatively, and lapsed into silence, looking out across the pond.

"Do you have a chance to get back to Sweden to fish with your family?"

"No. My father is dead."

"You no longer fish with your brother?"

"No." Half a minute ticked by, then Maja said, "He used to work here. You might have met him on one of your previous visits. He used to help with the dinners when Herr Viklund had guests. His name was Nils." She glanced at Louise.

"I'm sorry, I don't specifically remember a Nils," Louise said. "Perhaps I will get a chance to meet him now."

Maja clasped her hands and rubbed them, as if the cold had penetrated the mittens she was wearing. "He no longer works here." Maja turned away from the pond. "Perhaps it is time to go back now."

When they got back to the suite, Maja took Louise's coat with her when she left, and returned a short time later, her assistant following her with a mug of hot chocolate on a pewter tray. Later in the afternoon, she reappeared with wool pants, a cashmere turtleneck, coordinating cashmere socks, and lace-up leather walking shoes. She displayed them to Louise with shy pride and, when Louise congratulated her on her good taste, blushed and hurried off to put them in the closet.

"Let me know how they fit and I'll bring you more of a selection," said Maja.

"I will. Thank you."

Maja headed toward the door, then turned. "Oh, I almost forgot. Herr Viklund sends his apologies, but he will not be able to dine with you this evening. Would you like to eat here or in the dining room?"

"Here would be fine, thank you."

Louise turned back to the windows, where the woods were now darkening in the dusk. She was relieved not to have to face Theo tonight. She hoped, in fact, not to have to face him at all.

40

Daisy's desire to get to Los Angeles as soon as possible combined with her driving stamina enabled them to make good time on the trip.

The morning they passed from Texas into New Mexico, Lizzy told Daisy, "We're getting near where I'm going. I'm going to have to drop you off tomorrow."

"Where are you headed?" asked Daisy.

"Winslow," said Lizzy, naming another town she knew of in Arizona that wasn't Williams, Sedona, or Phoenix.

"Too bad you don't have a flatbed Ford," said Daisy, laughing.

"What?"

Daisy waved her hand. "Never mind. It's from a song my grandmom used to play a lot. What are you going to do in Winslow?"

"I promised a friend I'd do something for them."

"What's that?"

Lizzy blushed. "It's a secret."

～

LIKE BAD KARMA, just before they crossed the state line into Arizona, Lizzy's stomach began to roll with something more than just nerves. Since Daisy was fine, Lizzy suspected it was the tuna salad sandwich she had had for lunch. The pavement markings flashing by the windows and the vibration of the road made her feel worse. She saw a sign: *Rest Area 1 Mile*

"Can we stop for a little bit?" she asked. "I think if I could just take a nap in back without us moving, I'd feel better."

"Sure," said Daisy. She pulled off the highway and navigated to a remote corner of the parking lot. "I'll park here. Less noise. Easier for you to rest."

"Thanks."

Lizzy climbed into the back of the van and began unfolding the mattress. "Just a quick nap," she said.

"No problem," said Daisy. "I'll take a walk." She thunked the driver's door shut, but after a few moments, opened it again. "Listen, why don't you give me your phone number and I'll call you in a little bit and see if you're ready to go."

"Sure," said Lizzy, and gave Daisy the number. "If you give me your number, then if I wake up and you're not back, I can call you."

Daisy gave her the number and Lizzy added it to her Contacts list.

"Don't rush your nap," said Daisy. "I'm happy to walk around a little bit, stretch my legs."

Lizzy unrolled the sleeping bag and climbed in—the day was a little cool—and lay back gratefully on the pillow. She already felt better than she had when they had been on the road. She closed her eyes, calculating the date. It was hard to keep track when there weren't those ordinary commitments that helped anchor a week, and she realized that it would have been her father's birthday. Uncle Owen had always come out to Parkesburg and taken them out to dinner. He had only missed one year, when he was at a conference, and that year he had arranged to have a restaurant in Kennett Square deliver a fancy dinner to the house.

She rolled restlessly to her other side, and a memory of her seventeenth birthday, just a few months before, drifted into her mind.

She was with Uncle Owen, Andy, and Ruby in the Florida Keys, where they had fled after the death of Louise's husband, and before Lizzy and Owen had continued on to Sedona. Andy had given her a snorkel, mask, and fins as a birthday present that morning, and she had gotten a bad sunburn on her back while gazing at the aquatic life off Sugarloaf Key. Uncle Owen had loaned her an enormous William Penn University T-shirt to wear, and Ruby had made a trip to the drugstore to get some aloe vera.

They had planned to go into Key West for a celebratory dinner, but when dinnertime rolled around, Lizzy was still feeling uncomfortable and out of sorts. Owen and Andy ventured out and returned with a large pepperoni pizza topped with seventeen candles—plus a medium pizza "as back-up," as Uncle Owen explained. They got out the game of Scrabble that Owen had picked up the day before in a thrift store, and Owen and Andy had gotten into an extended debate about whether *CABG* was allowable.

It had been so ... normal. Sitting in that hotel room, eating pizza and drinking a Dr. Pepper, she had a view of what her life might be like if they could only figure out a way to get back to Pennsylvania without incurring Louise Mortensen's vengeful wrath and George Millard's fatal attention. As Owen and Andy bickered good-naturedly, she thought that perhaps her life was now on an upswing, and that, with care and planning, she could leave the traumas of her past behind her.

If only it had turned out that way.

She had just started to drift asleep when she realized she needed to use the restroom. Pretty quick. She scrambled out of the sleeping bag and looked around for Daisy. She didn't see her, but she wasn't going to spend any time looking. She realized that she didn't know where the keys were—not in the ignition. Daisy must have taken them with her. She swung the door shut and pantomimed locking it, just in case anyone was watching. Then she hurried across the parking lot to the service plaza.

She was in the bathroom for quite a while, and when she came out, she bought a ridiculously expensive box of Pepto-Bismol pills from the gift shop.

As she walked back to the van, she scanned the area again but still didn't see Daisy. She decided she'd wait at the van for a little while to see if her system had settled down, then call Daisy if she hadn't come back to the van by then.

She climbed into the passenger seat, then glanced into the back, thinking that perhaps she should roll up her sleeping bag.

The sleeping bag wasn't the way she had left it. She had exited the van in a hurry, pushing the bag to one side, and she remembered thinking that she'd straighten it when she got back. But now the bag was pulled up—not completely straight, but not the way she had left it. She twisted in the seat and scanned the back of the van.

Daisy's backpack was gone.

Lizzy jumped out of the van, looked frantically around the parking lot, then climbed into the back. With a sick feeling, she shoved everything to one side and pulled up the stowed back seat under which she had hidden the money.

Only one envelope was there.

With trembling hands, she counted the few bills that were still in the envelope. Two hundred and fifty dollars. Daisy had taken over three thousand dollars and left her two hundred and fifty dollars to get to Williams, do what she had to do, and get home again.

And that wasn't the only thing she had taken. She had taken the keys to the van.

"Dammit!" She threw the envelope back into the well, tears of anger springing to her eyes. Then she remembered that she had Daisy's phone number—if it was the real number, she thought bitterly. But not having any other option, she got out her phone and tapped the entry in her Contacts list.

"Hello." Much to her shock, it was Daisy's voice.

Had she jumped to the wrong conclusion? Was there another reason Daisy's backpack was gone?

"Where are you?" she asked. Then she remembered the other thing that was gone. "Where's my money? And where's the key to the van?"

"I don't have it. It's still at the rest area. I'll call you in a little while and tell you where it is. I just needed to make sure that you wouldn't follow me."

"I can't follow you—I told you I can't drive on the highway. I can't even get on the highway!"

"You'll work it out. I'll bet you have people who would be all over themselves to help you out if you let them know you needed help. There's someone back home who cares enough about you to make you promise to text them every day to let them know you're okay. You're driving all the way across the country to do a favor for someone, and I'll bet that person would help you out. You know who I have to call if I get in trouble? Nobody."

"I'm sorry about that, but that's not the point," said Lizzy, trying to marshal her argument. "And even if it was the point, it's not true—I can't just call my friends and run home. Plus," she said, hating the fact that her voice was high and cracking, "it's my money."

"I left you some," said Daisy. "You'll be fine. In a couple of years, this will just be a story you tell your friends, part of your teenage cross-country adventure."

Lizzy balled her hands into fists, her heart pounding with rage, and with self-recriminations for not being more careful with Uncle Owen's money.

She heard a male voice in the background, and Daisy's sharp reply, directed away from the phone. "None of your business."

"Who are you with?" asked Lizzy.

"Some guy." There was a pause, then Daisy said, "Tracy, when I hit it big in LA, you come out there and bring along those folks you've been texting with, and the person you're doing the favor for, and I'll pay you back with interest. I'll take you all out to dinner at a fancy restaurant and introduce you to all my celebrity friends. I'll text you in a little bit and let you know where the key is."

And Daisy ended the call.

Lizzy slumped back against the wall of the van.

She had the two hundred and fifty dollars left in the envelope, plus about forty in her knapsack. The stock of food was getting low—she had planned to do some grocery shopping this evening. She would need to pay tolls. She would need to get gas before she got to Williams.

And when she had finished her business in Williams, maybe she'd have enough money left to drive to Los Angeles and look for Daisy. But she knew she wouldn't do it.

She went into the service plaza and asked if anyone had turned in a key. No luck.

She was trudging back to the van when her phone buzzed with a text. She pulled it out of her pocket: Ruby.

Dr McNally doing well, sneaking food, sends his love. How are things with you? Having a nice break?

Lizzy climbed into the back of the van. She thought of the

text she could send: *Almost to Arizona to kill a man but money stolen, van key gone, trapped in rest area*

She leaned against the inside wall of the van and took a deep breath ... and another ... and another. Then she thumbed in a response.

Everything's good—glad to hear Uncle Owen is feeling better. Take good care of him.

Ruby sent back a thumbs up.

An hour later, her phone chimed with a text: *the key is under the dumpster behind the building*

Fifteen minutes after that, Lizzy was rolling down the ramp to the highway, her teeth gritted with determination, the horn of an irate motorist blaring behind her.

41

───────

It had been twenty-four hours since the attack on the congressman, and Mitchell was still suffering the inevitable aftermath of using the crush. His head throbbed, his eyes burned, and a bone-deep ache pounded in his arms and legs.

He was sitting in a deeply cushioned chair pulled up to the wall of windows, his hands clasped around a mug of tea that Elsa had brought him, when he heard the chime of the video monitor. With a groan, he pushed himself out of his chair and made his halting way to the desk. Theo gazed out at him from the monitor.

"Mitchell, how are you feeling today?"

Mitchell lowered himself into the chair at the desk. "Better than I felt yesterday."

"I'm glad to hear it. I must thank you again for your assistance with the congressman. You have done me a great service to have removed him from the equation, and work is in progress to take advantage of the power vacuum he's left behind."

Mitchell nodded, then asked, "Why did you want him killed?"

"He was pushing through some legislation that would have interfered with my colleague's plans to expand his business."

Mitchell waited, hoping that Theo would elaborate, but he was silent. Mitchell cleared his throat. "I didn't mean for there to be another victim."

Theo waved his hand. "Please don't worry about that. I've done some research into the man who accosted you in the men's room, and I haven't been able to find any information about him that would lead me to regret the outcome."

Mitchell was silent.

"I know it is asking a great deal of you," continued Theo, "but I have another important assignment for you."

"Oh?" asked Mitchell dully. "What's that?"

"The same colleague whose business endeavors were being hindered by the congressman is also being impacted by some industrial saboteurs. You could take care of them for him."

"How would I do that?"

"They arrive as a group and set up their operation right outside my colleague's business."

"They're protesters?" asked Mitchell.

"They are vigilantes."

"You want me to give strokes to a whole bunch of protesters?" asked Mitchell, some horror at Theo's request making its way through his crush-induced lethargy.

"I wouldn't say 'a whole bunch.' There are never more than a dozen of them—usually a half dozen—and you wouldn't need to give them massive strokes, just enough to incapacitate them, and to deter others from taking their places. In fact," added Theo brightly, "it might be sufficient to give only a few of them strokes."

"What are they protesting?"

"They are protesting my colleague's completely legal use of his business and property," said Theo, his voice taking on a tinge of impatience.

Mitchell didn't have the energy to press the topic. "I don't know how many more times I can do this."

"I know I'm asking a great deal of you," replied Theo. "There's a limited window in which we can demonstrate our worth to my colleague, and I believe that taking care of the congressman and the protesters will make our point. Once we have done that, you will have as much time as you need to rest and recuperate."

After a long pause, Mitchell spoke. "How come you never come see me in person?"

"Because I am unwilling to put myself at your mercy," said Theo promptly.

Mitchell laughed humorlessly. "You're afraid I'm going to crush you?"

"It's possible, if you became angry with me for some reason. But I must admit that the primary reason for our virtual meetings is your mind-reading ability."

"You don't want me to read your mind?"

"Certainly not. Knowledge is power, and the knowledge of someone's thoughts is the ultimate power. I would not want to subject myself to your power."

"What are you thinking that you wouldn't want me to know?"

"It's not a specific thing. I am merely uncomfortable with the idea of my mind being probed by someone with your talents. It's a disconcerting concept for those of us not blessed with that ability."

"It's ..." Mitchell's voice trailed off.

"Yes?" Theo prompted.

"It's lonely here," Mitchell replied, a bit reluctantly.

Theo nodded. "Yes, I imagine it is. I believe I might be able to provide a solution to that situation, as well as a well-deserved thank you for the work you are doing on my behalf. I have a home in California that would provide much more appropriate accommodations than the guest suite here, and is staffed with two of my most tenured employees."

"You're not afraid I'd read their minds?"

"I feel certain that you'd read their minds, but neither of them knows anything particularly important—except perhaps to themselves—and neither of them will know about your skill, so they won't be aware of any forays you may make into their thoughts."

"You're not afraid that I'll use the crush on them?"

Theo smiled. "I feel confident that neither of them will do anything that would lead you to want to crush them."

42

———

Louise went to bed at her accustomed time of ten o'clock. She watched the clock on the bedside table tick through the minutes until midnight, then climbed out of bed.

She went to the bathroom and opened the closet. There was not the tiny strip of light at the back of the closet that had first alerted her to the presence of the service door. That was good— it might mean that the room or corridor behind it was not in use. Louise pushed the clothing hanging on the rod to one side, stepped into the closet, and pressed her ear to the back wall. She could hear no sound from the other side of the door. After a minute, she pushed lightly on the door. There was a tiny bit of play, but it didn't open.

She got the Theo-provided phone and shone its light on the back wall. She could see on one side the heads of two small screws, such as might be used to secure the latch of a cupboard. She went to the vanity drawer that Maja had stocked with toiletries and found a metal nail file. She returned to the closet and inserted the tip of the file into the screw head. It turned easily.

She went to the bathroom door, intending to lock it, but discovered that the door did not have a lock. She considered using one of the dining table chairs, the back slipped under the doorknob, as an alternative. If Maja arrived in the room after Louise had left through the closet doorway, it might give her an extra minute or two before the method of her escape was discovered. However, if someone came to the room, a barricaded door would certainly alert them to an issue.

Then she had another, more disturbing, thought.

She scanned the bathroom for anything that could be a camera. But she knew it was a useless effort—she had no doubt that if Theo had such cameras installed in the complex, they were unlikely to be of a type that would be easily spotted. She would have to take her chances.

She unscrewed the two screws with the tip of the file and heard a clatter as the latch on the other side of the door fell to the floor. She held her breath, listening for footsteps. A minute passed. Silence.

She pushed the door open and stepped out of the closet into a linoleum-floored service hallway. A dim light at the end of the hallway illuminated shelves holding neatly arranged cleaning supplies and other household items.

She retrieved the latch hardware from the floor, stepped back into the closet, and pulled the door closed as best she could. She hurried to the bedroom and arranged several pillows under the covers in a rough approximation of a human form. She had no illusion that the ploy would fool anyone for more than a few seconds, but every second she could buy herself was valuable.

She returned to the bathroom and swapped her pajamas for the walking clothes Maja had provided. She had tried them on earlier and found that the shoes were half a size too small, but they still seemed a better choice than her pumps.

Lacking a coat, she pulled one of the wool dresses on over the sweater.

After a moment of consideration, she left the phone in the room. She would have liked to have had its flashlight app, but she didn't want to risk the possibility that Theo could track her movements with it.

She stepped back into the hallway, pushed the door shut again, and headed toward the dim light at the end of the corridor.

This floor, which must be under the main floor of the complex, housed the facilities that supported Theo Viklund and his guests—a room with an industrial-sized washer and dryer, racks holding linen tablecloths, a hallway along which a dozen dining room chairs stood in two rows on either side of the hallway like a phalanx of soldiers standing guard. A professional grade kitchen looked, with its stainless steel appliances and counter tops, more like a surgery. The corridors and rooms were all lit by dim nightlights, all were deserted, and none contained a door to the outside.

At one point she heard two voices in conversation, and she stepped into a utility room, her heart thudding, until the voices faded as the speakers moved away from her.

At last, in an alcove that must have been used at one time as a small greenhouse, she found a door whose glass-paned panels revealed the dark woods of Theo's estate. There were cobwebs in the corners of the greenhouse, and the windows were grimed with dust. She peered at the edges of the door, searching as best she could in the dim light for any wires or other indication that the door was alarmed, but could see nothing. Finally, she flipped the latch on the deadbolt and, ready to run if an alarm sounded, eased the door open.

The only sound was the shush of wind through the treetops, which swayed in the light of a gibbous moon.

She pulled the door closed behind her and walked away from the house as fast as the dark night, uneven ground, and pinching shoes would allow.

43

bout fifteen minutes and two ankle-twisting falls after Louise had left Theo's home, she came to the fence, stretching away into the darkness in both directions. She turned in the direction she judged to be away from the main entrance and followed it.

She picked her way along the fence for what she estimated was another fifteen minutes before she found what she had been looking for. One of the small streams that Maja had mentioned flowed under it, and although the pickets had been extended to the stream bed, the water had evidently made them deteriorate—one had already broken off, perhaps when debris had washed up against the fence in a storm. She waded into the water, which was shallow but bitterly cold, and pulled on the adjacent picket. It, too, must have been weakened by its exposure to the water, and after several tugs, it broke off.

After several minutes of pulling and pushing—fingernails breaking and tearing, her feet in her now-sodden cashmere socks numbing to the point that maintaining her balance was difficult—she was able to break off enough pickets that she could squeeze through the fence. She climbed up the stream bank on the other side and continued walking.

In less than a minute, she saw headlights a hundred yards away, moving beyond the trees and then disappearing in the distance. She made her way toward what must be the two-lane road that she had taken on her trip to the compound.

When she reached the road, she followed it, keeping to the shadows of the trees. If someone at the complex had discovered her disappearance, they would no doubt send cars out to search for her.

A few minutes later, she saw a box truck parked by the side of the road, *AJ's Plumbing* stenciled onto its back doors. Its lights were on, its engine running. She picked up her pace as best she could, trying to ignore the stabs of pain from her cramped and frozen toes. As she approached the truck, she could see that the light in the truck's cab was on. Still hidden in the trees, she drew even with the truck and could see the driver, who was wearing a baseball hat with *AJ's Plumbing* across the crown. He was bent over a paper map he had unfolded across the steering wheel.

She removed the wool dress, balled it up, and stuffed it under some leaves. It left her even colder than she had been, and still bedraggled-looking, but at least she was less eccentrically dressed. She limped toward the passenger door and tapped on the glass.

The man continued to examine the map.

She tapped again, harder.

Still no response.

She opened the door and the man glanced up, then jumped when he saw her.

"I'm sorry to startle you," she said, "but I need your help."

The man shook his head and pointed to his ear, then pulled a small spiral notepad and pen from his pocket and handed it to her.

Louise pointed to herself and then to the passenger seat, and the man nodded.

Louise scrambled into the cab and locked the door behind her. With a shaking hand, she wrote, *Swerved to miss a deer and ran into a ditch. Can you drive me to a service station?*

She handed the notepad and pen back to the man. He read the message and nodded. He stuffed the map into the space behind the seats, put the truck into gear, and pulled onto the road.

She caught her breath when she saw the gate leading to the drive to Theo's house coming up, its metal dully illuminated in the truck's headlights.

And she was not altogether surprised when the truck slowed and turned in at the gate.

Although they were still moving, she grabbed the door handle and tried to open it, but the door stayed closed despite her frantic tugging.

She turned back to the driver, thinking that her now-jagged fingernails were her only remaining weapon. Lucas was leaning forward from where he had been hiding behind the seat, a gun pointed at her neck.

"It's locked," he said.

"And even if it wasn't," said the driver in an equally heavy accent, "there's nowhere to run."

She turned back toward the road, her body humming with fear.

None of them spoke further as the truck wended its way through the woods to the front door of the main house.

When they reached the entrance, Maja was standing on the flagstone terrace, her arms crossed over the front of a bulky cardigan against the cold of the night.

Louise heard the back door of the truck open and close, then Lucas appeared at her door and opened it.

"Step out," he said.

Louise climbed out and stumbled.

Lucas grabbed her arm and jerked her upright.

"Släppa henne," said Maja sharply, and Lucas dropped his hand from Louise's arm.

Maja stepped forward and took Louise's elbow, far more gently than Lucas had done.

"Come with me, Dr. Mortensen."

Louise climbed the steps to the door, her feet leaden.

With Lucas following them, Maja led her down hallways to what must have been the very back of the main building, to a room Louise had never seen before. On one side of the room was a gray metal desk with a chair on either side. The other side of the room was blocked by a folding screen. It was impersonal to the point of sterility, more like a doctor's office than a room in a residence.

Maja gestured toward a chair. "Please have a seat, Dr. Mortensen."

Louise lowered herself into the chair, her knuckles white where her fingers lay interlaced in her lap, her body setting up a rattling shiver that she was incapable of controlling.

Maja removed her sweater and draped it over Louise's shoulders. "Herr Viklund is on his way."

Maja stepped out of the room and closed the door behind her.

Louise thought back to a time when she was ten and her mother had taken her to the pediatrician. Her ear was very painful, and the doctor had peered into it with an instrument he told her, when she asked, was an otoscope, and had probed her neck with his heavy fingers. He had washed his hands, then said to her mother, "Mrs. Mortensen, may I speak to you in the hallway for a moment?"

Her mother and the doctor had left, and the young Louise

had spent a miserable five minutes wondering what could be so awful that the doctor couldn't say it in front of her.

Eventually, her mother and the doctor had returned to the room, her mother looking more annoyed than traumatized, and the doctor explained to Louise that she would need to have an operation on her ear. Louise loved doctor shows—in fact, with the exception of this particular doctor, she loved everything having to do with doctors—and was actually quite excited at the prospect of an operation.

She suspected that the surprise that awaited her now was not going to be exciting in quite the same way.

The door opened and Theo Viklund stepped in. He circled to the other side of the desk and remained standing, his hands clasped behind his back.

"I'm surprised and disappointed, Louise."

She was silent.

"What made you try to leave?"

"I saw what you did to Mitchell. I have no reason to assume you will show me any more consideration."

"I'm deeply hurt, especially in view of our long-standing relationship. Your time here has offered some compensations, has it not?"

"I have no desire to serve as your lackey. If I found a way out once, I can find a way out again—only this time I will be more careful."

Theo laughed, but there was no amusement behind it. "Louise, surely you don't think you ever actually escaped. It was all quite carefully laid out—the ineffectively masked service door in your closet, your path through the lower level, guided by lighting and strategically placed staff, a conveniently unsecured exit door, an otherwise impregnable fence breached by a small stream. Even my approval for Maja to provide you with more suitable clothing for your adventure. In fact, if all the other arrangements failed, we would have been able to locate you by the tracking device embedded in the sole of one of your walking shoes." He pulled out the chair and sat. "I must admit that your fortitude in the face of the physical challenges was impressive."

"You expected me to try to leave."

"I suspected you might. I was curious if you would."

"You can't control everything, or control it forever."

Theo leaned back and steepled his fingers.

"Did you notice anything unusual about Edmund Rinnert?" he asked.

Louise shifted. "No."

"Really?"

"Well, he was missing a thumb."

"Yes. He had all his digits when he got here."

Louise felt the blood drain from her face.

Theo reached into his inside jacket pocket and pulled out a long, narrow packet. He opened the packet and removed a scalpel. He turned it contemplatively. "And can you guess the circumstances in which he lost his thumb?"

Louise slowly shook her head.

"He tried to leave the compound." He looked up at her, waiting for a reply.

"Oh?"

"Yes. I wasn't happy about his attempt to leave."

Louise stared at him, her eyes wide.

"I don't want you to think we're barbarians. We didn't hack off his thumb like some gang of Italian mafiosi." He paused, then continued. "No, it was all very civilized—a simple operation in our little dispensary." He nodded toward the screen behind Louise. "He was completely anesthetized the entire time."

Louise felt the jagged edges of her broken nails digging into her palms. She willed herself not to faint.

"We removed his left thumb, believing that to be a more humane option than his right. Unfortunately, we learned after the operation that he is left-handed." He looked up at Louise. "I wouldn't like to have to repeat the operation, but it could be easily done if necessary."

The silence spun out.

Finally, he said, "Will it be necessary?"

She licked her lips. "No." It came out as a whisper.

"No," he said. He picked up the scalpel, folded it into its wrapping, and slipped it back into his jacket pocket. "I didn't think so."

44

———————

Philip and Rey ate dinner in the same restaurant the next day, Rey having extracted a promise that if Philip needed to use the restroom, they would return to their rooms.

Philip took his time choosing an appetizer and an entrée. When he ordered dessert, despite his stomach's protestations, Rey glowered but didn't countermand the order. He wanted to make sure there was plenty of time for his instructions of the previous day to be put into effect.

When he had finished his pie and suspected that Rey wouldn't put up with him ordering another cup of coffee, they headed back to their rooms.

As usual, they entered through Rey's room, and Philip passed through the communicating door to his own room. Rey swung the door shut behind him and he heard the click of the lock on her side. He pressed his ear against it.

He heard her steps cross the room, a long silence, then the steps recross, headed toward the bathroom. Then heard a gasp, a grunt, the sounds of a brief struggle, then silence. In a moment he heard the lock turn and the door swung open.

"If it ain't Philip Casal in the flesh." Wayne Watchman stepped into Philip's room and enveloped him in a bear hug. "Good to see you, Casal."

Philip muffled a yelp. "Watch it—I got shot in the shoulder a week ago."

Wayne stepped back, looking sheepish. "You should have said."

Philip looked over his shoulder into Rey's room.

"How'd it go?"

"Smooth as silk."

They crossed to where Rey's pantsuit-clad legs protruded from the bathroom door. She was lying on her back and her jacket had fallen open, revealing an empty shoulder holster. A syringe lay on the floor next to her.

"There you go," said Wayne, handing Philip a gun.

"It would be handy to have the holster, too," said Philip.

They got Rey into a sitting position and Wayne slipped off her jacket, then Philip unfastened and removed the shoulder holster.

"Don't knock her head on the floor," he said as Wayne lowered her back onto the ground.

Philip resized the holster, slipped it on, and holstered the gun.

"I brought ties and tape," said Wayne.

"Did you get the dose from Doc?"

"Yup."

"Then we don't need to tie her up—she should be out for a couple of hours."

They searched the room and found about a thousand in cash, but nothing else of interest. Philip handed the cash to Wayne. "Here you go. Although I may need to ask for a loan until things get straightened out."

Wayne pocketed the money. "You're a stand-up guy, Casal. Want me to put out the *Do Not Disturb* sign?"

"No. She requested no room service, so no one's going to come by. I figure when she comes around she'll call back to the mother ship for instructions, but by that time, we'll be long gone."

THEY TOOK Wayne's Pontiac Sunbird south from Flagstaff, then turned west toward Jerome, stopping along the way to pick up a burner phone for Philip and, as they neared Wayne's trailer, a pizza and six-pack for dinner.

Wayne normally shared his trailer with his girlfriend, but, conveniently for Philip, they had just had a falling out, and she had moved in with friends in Prescott. Unfortunately for Philip, if the trailer had ever been clean, it had been the girlfriend who had kept it that way. There was a fog of cigarette smoke in the air and dirty dishes overflowed the trailer's small kitchen counter onto various other surfaces.

"Jesus, Watchman, you're a pig," Philip said as he picked up a couple of crusty plates from the kitchen table. He glanced around the kitchen. "Do you have a sponge I can wipe the table down with?"

"I don't know. Use a T-shirt from the laundry."

"I'm not wiping the table down with one of your dirty T-shirts," said Philip. He located a box of Brillo pads under the sink. "I wouldn't normally use these on a kitchen table," he said, removing one from the box, "but in this case I think it's not a bad idea."

After pizza and two beers, Philip stepped out of the trailer, happy to have a break from the cigarette funk and the boxing match that Wayne had playing at top volume on his big screen TV. He pulled out his phone. He was fairly sure he remembered Lizzy's cell number—he had had to retrieve it from his office answering machine when Mortensen's operatives had stolen his phone and wallet back in Sedona—but when he dialed it, he got a generic voicemail message. He wasn't sure enough that he had remembered the number correctly to leave the message he wanted to leave.

He tapped the phone on his hand. He did have Andy's number, which he had gotten from the phone that Viklund had given him. However, considering his current situation, he didn't necessarily want to open a two-way communication channel. Furthermore, it didn't seem out of the question that Viklund might be monitoring calls to Andy, or even Owen, and might be able to determine the caller's location. If Viklund could get police cases closed and attorney general investigations cancelled, Philip wasn't about to underestimate what data he might have access to.

However, Philip did want to know how Owen was doing. He called the main number at William Penn University Hospital, ready to hang up if they put him through to Owen's room. He was relieved to learn that Owen had been discharged several days earlier.

An hour later, he again tried the number he remembered for Lizzy, and again got voicemail. He sighed. He felt more confident of his assessment that Lizzy seemed like the kind of girl who would have a personalized voicemail message than of his having accurately remembered the number. In any case, from a practical point of view, he really had no need to talk with her—he was sure Andy would have been only too happy to convey the message to Lizzy that she was released from the promise she had made to Philip.

45

———

Lizzy sat in the back of the van, which was parked in the corner of an all-night truck stop. She didn't want to go back to a Walmart if she could help it. She didn't know what the rules were about parking at the truck stop, so she was trying to make the van look unoccupied. Not wanting to use the flashlight app, she groped around the back of the van when she needed to locate something: one of the gallon jugs to take a sip of water, a bruised banana from her dwindling supply of food for dinner.

She was sitting under the sheet tent, tapping listlessly on her phone. Like picking at a painful scab, she had been searching obsessively for an obituary for someone named Wilson living near the location of the Walmart back east. She was both frustrated and relieved that so far her search had not turned up any results.

Lizzy jumped when her phone rang. It was the same unfamiliar number from which she had gotten a call earlier. The caller hadn't left a message—she figured it must be a telemarketer. As she had done earlier, she hit *Ignore*.

Switching her attention masochistically to another painful

wound, Lizzy typed another search into her phone: *Daisy Flowers.*

The results displayed and Lizzy sat up, her breath catching in her throat.

Police Release Identity of Body Found in Bear Valley

She tapped on the first result, timestamped just a few hours before, with a shaking finger.

A homicide investigation is underway in Bear Valley following the discovery of a woman's body in a dumpster, police said.

Officers responded to the scene at a shopping center in the 2100 block of Victorville Road at approximately 7:30 a.m.

Police said the body was found by an employee of one of the businesses based in the shopping center.

In a nearby ravine, police found a knapsack containing a driver's license identifying the victim as Daisy Flowers, 21, of Levittown, Pennsylvania.

Bear Valley Coroner Jason Worthen confirmed the cause of death was strangulation.

Anyone with additional information that may assist the police in solving this crime are encouraged to contact …

The picture accompanying the article must have been Daisy's high school graduation picture—a formal shot, her chin resting on her softly closed fist. Her long blond hair was tucked behind her ears, just like when Lizzy had first seen her at the side of the road, her thumb out for a ride. Just like Lizzy used to wear hers. Just like Tobe Hanrick's victim Sarah Pearson had no doubt worn hers when she wasn't dressed up for her sister's wedding.

Lizzy switched her phone off and slipped deeper into her

sleeping bag, pulling it up over her head, her cheeks wet with tears.

It was impossible that Tobe Hanrick had been involved in Daisy's death, and nearly impossible that his gang had been, but whoever had wrapped his hands around Daisy's neck—whoever had squeezed the life out of her just as she had almost reached her destination—was no better than they were.

When she got to Williams and killed Tobe Hanrick, it would not only be to avenge his murder of Philip's prison mentor and of Sarah Pearson. He would stand in for Daisy's murderer as well.

And when he was dead, Lizzy might walk out of the prison and get in the van and just keep driving into the Arizona desert until the gas ran out, then get out of the van and start walking. One way or the other, it seemed as if terrible things always happened to the people whose paths crossed hers. Maybe out there in the desert, she would permanently remove that danger from the world.

46

———

Mitchell arrived at the site by helicopter.

When he first glimpsed their destination, miles from any other sign of human habitation, it looked like a railroad model. As they descended, the details of the complex became clearer: the bulldozers, backhoes, and dump trucks parked at the borders of the large cleared area toward which the helicopter was headed. The derrick-like construction that the pilot gave a wide berth. The piles of stone around the perimeter of the enclosure, which was bounded by a razor-wire-topped chain link fence. The sprays of water shooting out of pipes, the droplets glittering prettily in the early morning sun. The corrugated metal building, in front of which a group of a half dozen men, most wearing hardhats, were gathered. Lined up on the dirt road leading into the enclosure were two big rigs towing trailers carrying cylindrical silver tanks.

As the helicopter neared the ground, Mitchell could see what was keeping the trucks from entering the enclosure: a second group of a half dozen men, several wearing scarves across the lower half of their faces, stood in the road outside the fence. Two of them held a banner, but it snapped in the wash from the helicopter's blade and Mitchell couldn't read the rough lettering. A few signs that had been leaning up against the fence went skittering away across the scrub-covered ground, and one man broke away from the group to chase them down.

The men blocking the gate and the men inside the enclosure watched the helicopter descend.

When it touched down, the other passenger, Brad Fortin, said to Mitchell through the headset, "Stay here for a minute." Fortin, a stocky, dark-haired man sporting an impressive handlebar mustache, pulled off his headset and jumped to the ground. He strode to the group of men standing next to the building and spoke to them for a minute. With a few last glances toward the helicopter, they disappeared into the building.

Fortin jogged back to the helicopter and waved Mitchell out, then gave a thumbs up to the pilot. Mitchell followed Fortin to the building and heard and felt the thwack of the blades as the helicopter rose behind them. They stepped into the building, closing the door against the swirling dust.

Mitchell expected to see the men in the building—a cavernous space filled with equipment—but it was deserted as far as he could see.

"They're in a room in back," said Fortin. "Viklund said to keep them out of the way, unless there was trouble and we needed their help."

"Do you work for Theo?" asked Mitchell. Fortin's appearance didn't fit the mold of most of Theo's staff, and he had never heard anyone in Theo's employ refer to him so informally.

"No, I work for the owner of the mine," said Fortin. "Viklund's a friend of his. Or wants to be." He pulled a small earpiece from his pocket and handed it to Mitchell. "This is paired with your cell phone. Just press one and you'll be connected to Viklund. We'll send the drone up as soon as the turbulence from the 'copter dies down, and that will provide a video feed. We'll be able to see if you need any help."

Mitchell could tell by his look that Fortin thought it quite possible that Mitchell would need help.

"I'll be in back with the guys," Fortin continued. "You have everything you need?"

"Like what?" asked Mitchell, a thread of panic creeping into his voice.

"I don't know," said Fortin impatiently. "Viklund said you'd bring what you needed with you."

"Oh. Yes, I have what I need," replied Mitchell.

"Okay. Let's make sure the hook-up's working."

Mitchell fitted the earpiece over his ear, then got out the mobile phone that Theo had provided and pressed one.

"Hello, Mitchell," he heard. "Arrived safely, I see."

Mitchell nodded to Fortin, who gave him a thumbs up and then turned and strode off toward the back of the building.

"Yes. Can you hear me?" Mitchell asked.

"Yes, I can hear you. Did you enjoy Bennett Valley?" asked Theo.

Mitchell had spent the previous day at Theo's West Coast base—a rambling hacienda overlooking vineyards in Sonoma County—catered to by an old Swedish couple who evidently spoke no English. Among the many attractions of the location was its balmy weather—a good thirty degrees warmer than here in northeastern Arizona.

"It was very nice. Thank you."

"And I trust the caretakers did nothing that would have tempted you to subject them to the crush?" Theo asked, a smile in his voice.

"No, they were very accommodating."

"We'll send you back there when we're done here, and I can guarantee you plenty of time to recover. When you're feeling rested, you might want to make a visit to my home in Switzerland."

A movement in the sky caught Mitchell's eye, and he looked up to see a drone appear from over the building and then hover fifty feet above the dirt yard. The men at the gate turned to look at the drone, then drew together in consultation, glancing nervously back at the machine. The door of the first of the two trucks outside the gate opened and the driver stepped out onto the running board, his gaze more curious than concerned. Mitchell could see *Non-Potable Water* stenciled on the side of the tank on the trailer.

"The drone is in position and I can see the site," said Theo. "Can you see the targets from where you are?"

"Yes. I'm at a window at the front of the building." He hesitated. "I think one of them is a woman."

"Perhaps," said Viklund, "but it doesn't mean she's any less culpable—or any less dangerous—because of her gender. Give yourself the injection now."

Mitchell shrugged out of his coat and shirt, then removed the packet containing the vial and syringe from a jacket pocket. The quantity of liquid in the vial looked like less than what he had injected in the Washington restaurant. Perhaps the after-effects would be less, as well.

He filled the syringe, then rolled up the arm of his T-shirt. He wished Louise was there to give him the injection. It had never hurt when she did it.

"None of them are armed," said Theo. "The security detail made sure of that."

Mitchell pulled on his shirt and coat. "I thought you said they were dangerous," he muttered.

"Pardon?"

"Nothing," said Mitchell, louder than was necessary. He opened the door and stepped through it, his quick exhale pluming in the air. "Okay, I'm outside," he said.

"You don't need to tell me—I'm getting video from the drone," replied Theo. "Just go down there and pretend you want to talk with them, and when you feel the crush coming on, don't hold back."

Mitchell started down the road toward the gate. The protesters pulled together, the one Mitchell thought was a woman toward the middle. A couple of the men held up their signs: *Our People Our Water Our Future* and *Respect Mother Earth*.

His heart was thudding, and he felt as if his blood were turning to lava in his veins. There might have been half the amount of liquid in the vial, but it felt like ten times the strength. What assignment would Theo Viklund have for him next—an entire chamber of congressmen? A stadium full of sports fans?—and how much of the drug would Mitchell be given to discharge that assignment?

But there was a tiny portion of his brain that was watching the scene play out, like a movie that Mitchell dreaded the ending of—a movie made up of what he had seen when he raised the curtain on the privacy of others' thoughts.

He thought of Louise's housekeeper Juana, going through the motions of cooking and cleaning and caring for him and Louise, while mourning the death of her favorite, Gerard Bonnay.

He thought of his aunt, who, although she showed no apparent concern about her own appearance, had starched and ironed his dress shirts with never a sign of psychic irritation or resentment.

He thought of Philip Castillo, and that pure strain of love he had for the old man who had helped him survive prison, and whose death he was willing to risk a return to that prison to avenge.

Castillo. If Mitchell had killed him when he had the chance in Sedona, none of this would have happened.

He felt the drug-induced fury carrying him along now, only dimly aware of the shock and fear registering on the faces of the men—and, yes, one woman—on the other side of the fence. They shouldn't be here—Theo had explained it to him. They were interfering. They were obstructing. They were ... were ...

He was at the fence now, and he staggered forward, his clawed hands grasping at the chain link, the protesters less than a dozen feet away.

They were normal people trying to live normal lives. Trying, in fact, to lead good lives.

He had wanted to live a good life at one time—he was sure of it.

Louise Mortensen and Theo Viklund had torn that possibility away from him.

That boiling river of mental acid turned, like a boomerang, like the ricochet of an ill-aimed—or perhaps well-aimed—bullet, and Mitchell Pieda dropped to the ground.

For a moment, no one in the group moved, then one of the men took a few tentative steps toward the fence, on the other side of which the young man had fallen.

"Be careful, Bod," said the woman.

Bod bent toward the inert form on the other side of the fence, then squatted down. The others stepped up behind him.

"Did he faint?" asked the woman.

"I don't think so," said Bod. "I can't see that he's breathing."

The woman looked toward the building. "Where is every-one?" she asked, her voice taut with anxiety. "He needs help."

"I think he's beyond help," said Bod. "Look at him."

The group stepped closer.

The young man's eyes were open, staring sightlessly into the cloudless blue sky.

The whites of both eyes were blood red.

47

Louise stood next to Theo in the lab, watching with bile rising in her throat as the remote camera zoomed in on the inert body lying next to the fence, the protesters grouped on the other side. Then the view swung back toward the building, from which two men—one of them Brad Fortin—had emerged. They clambered into a pickup and drove the fifty yards to where Mitchell lay. They climbed out and approached the still form with some apparent trepidation, then Fortin lifted Mitchell's shoulders and the other man lifted his legs and carried him to the back of the pickup. Louise was illogically grateful that they lowered him with some care onto the bed of the truck.

Louise could hear the approaching chop of the helicopter over the audio feed, and the drone backed off from the scene and dropped behind the building.

"We've lost video," said Theo toward the mobile phone that lay on the table in front of the monitor on which the scene was playing out.

"We're switching to the security cameras," came a voice from the phone's speaker, and in a moment the scene showed a grainier view of the dirt yard, dust already kicking up from the rotors, then the helicopter descended into the frame.

The two men waited for the skids to settle, then lifted Mitchell out of the back of the pickup and carried him quickly to the 'copter. They disappeared inside for a moment, then the one who was not Fortin emerged and jogged back to the building.

A voice came from the phone. "Mr. Viklund, Brad Fortin here."

Theo picked up the phone, switched off the speaker, and put it to his ear. "Yes?" His face remained impassive. "How about the men at the gate? ... All right, men and woman. ... Are you sure? ... No, of course not. ... Yes. Thank you." He ended the connection and dropped the phone into his pocket.

They saw Fortin jump out of the helicopter and follow his colleague into the building. The helicopter ascended out of the frame, then appeared at a distance a few moments later, moving fast, until it disappeared behind a hill.

Theo continued to stare at the monitors, his arms crossed, his eyebrows drawn together.

"Is he dead?" asked Louise coldly.

"It appears that way."

"How much did you give him?"

"Half a cc."

"That's less than we gave him for the congressman."

"It was more concentrated."

"How much more concentrated?"

"Ten times."

Louise's head snapped around. "Are you insane? That's five times the dosage I recommended."

"We had five times as many targets as in Washington," retorted Theo.

"You sent him on a suicide mission!"

"I knew it might kill him—I didn't think he'd be the only victim."

Louise gaped at him.

Theo ran his fingers through his hair. "This is going to be difficult to explain to my colleague."

"You intentionally gave him a dose you knew would kill him?"

"He was useless—you must have known that, or you wouldn't have left him to burn in Pocopson. He was completely uncontrolled in his application of the crush—"

"I told you that!" yelled Louise.

"He was disposable," Theo yelled back. "We couldn't keep him here. I thought I'd at least be able to use his elimination of the protesters as a bargaining chip with my associate."

On the monitor, they saw the protestors resume their line at the gate. The driver who had been observing the proceedings from the running board of his truck threw up his hands and climbed back into the cab.

"You don't seem to have made much headway on that front," said Louise bitterly.

"Why didn't he kill them?"

"I have no idea. Perhaps he wasn't quite as uncontrolled in his application of the crush as either of us thought."

"What do you mean?"

"I doubt he went into that situation knowing you intended for him to die. In fact," she continued, her voice mocking, "he evidently went into that situation thinking that his reward was going to be a vacation in Switzerland. But maybe he decided it wasn't worth it. Maybe he killed himself. If he did, then I should have shown him a great deal more respect than I did, and you would have done well to show him that respect as well."

Theo wheeled on her. "I brought him here to help me advance my agenda," he said, his voice hoarse with anger. "I brought *you* here to help me advance my agenda. When I provide protection to a person, I expect them to throw their full support behind me. I would not like to have you come to grief the way Edmund Rinnert did, but if it comes to that—"

Louise slapped her hand onto the table, her fingers spread. "Go ahead, Theo," she hissed. "If you think amputating my thumb is going to solve the colossal mess you've gotten yourself into, go ahead. If you think that venting your frustrations by mutilating my hand is going to somehow be worth losing the tiny bit of gratitude I have left toward you for hiding me from the authorities, go ahead. If you're willing to eliminate any possibility that I will ever—*ever*—do any meaningful scientific research for you, or share any discoveries I make with you ... Go. Ahead."

Air whispered through the ducts above the dropped ceiling of the lab and a piece of equipment ticked off a regular rhythm.

Finally, Theo Viklund turned on his heel and strode out of the room, slamming the door behind him.

Louise Mortensen sank onto the stool next to the table, dropped her face into her hands, and cried.

48

Lizzy arrived in Williams under a gray March mid-afternoon sky. She was exhausted, and if she had had any money, she would have been tempted to splurge on a motel room, take a long, hot bath, climb into a real bed, and sleep for a day. With most of her money gone, she could have been tempted to find somewhere to park the van, take what her mother used to call a bird bath using the water from the refilled gallon containers, climb into her sleeping bag, and sleep for a day.

But more than any of that, she wanted to have what she had come to Williams to do behind her.

Before she had left Philly, she had filled out an Arizona Department of Corrections visitor application online and had also reviewed the visitor rules. She found the dress code for visitors to the prison both funny and alarming. With the length of her hair, there would be no question about her violating the rule against hair extensions. And complying with the code for clothing—no tube tops, no mesh, no cleavage, no spandex— would be no problem. Even before her confrontation with Gerard Bonnay, she had never gone in for clothes that would be considered revealing. After that confrontation, she always wore long-sleeved, back-covering tops to hide the scars from the bullet wounds. But what did the need for this code say about the place she was about to visit?

The prison was a few miles outside of Williams, single-story, desert-tan buildings looking more like warehouses than human habitations. She followed the signs to the visitor parking lot and locked up the van, taking only her license and the van key with her. Then she joined three other visitors in a bus stop-like shelter. According to the information on the prison's website, the bus arrived on the hour to ferry visitors to the prison.

A few minutes before the designated time, a bus appeared from between two of the prison buildings, stopped at the entrance as the gate rumbled open, then pulled up at the shelter. A guard stepped out.

"IDs, please."

Lizzy stepped forward and handed the Tracy Coates driver's license to the guard. She hoped that Philip's friend hadn't exaggerated his claim that he was giving her a premium product.

The guard looked between her and the license once. Then a second time.

Lizzy's heart pounded.

"Got a trim, I see," said the guard.

"What?"

He nodded toward her brutally short hair.

"Oh," said Lizzy, her hand going to her head. "Yeah. Dyed too."

"So I see," he said, vaguely amused. He held the license up to a paper on a clipboard, then glanced back up at her, his expression now stern and disapproving.

"Tobe Hanrick?"

Lizzy nodded.

He shook his head and handed the license back to her. "Go ahead," he said, reaching for the ID of the next visitor in line.

When they had all boarded, the bus trundled back down the road and pulled up at the visitor entrance. She stepped off the bus and into a grim institutional room lit with buzzing fluorescent lights. Flyers and schedules pinned to gouged cork boards fluttered in the breeze from the door. The other visitors, obviously familiar with the routine, began placing purses and bags on a table next to which a guard stood.

The guard who had accompanied them on the bus waved Lizzy forward, toward a metal detector. "If you don't have any bags, you can go ahead."

The guard at the metal detector held out a plastic basket. "Everything out of your pockets," he said. Lizzy put the license and the van key into the basket.

"That's it?" asked the guard.

"Yes, that's it."

The guard took the license out of the basket and compared it to some information on a monitor behind the table. "You're here to visit Hanrick?"

"Yes."

He glanced at the other guard, then handed the license back to her. "Step through the detector."

She passed through the metal detector. Then, although there was no indication of the detector having tripped, a female guard on the other side gave her a brief pat-down.

When the other visitors had passed through the detector, a guard led them down a narrow hall to a metal door with a mesh-reinforced window. He keyed in a code, opened the door, and stepped aside to let them pass through.

They entered a large room, most of which was occupied by cafeteria-style tables and chairs. A plastic dollhouse stood in one corner next to a laundry basket holding a selection of battered toys. The three other visitors immediately went to a bank of vending machines along one wall and began feeding coins into them and retrieving snacks and sodas.

Lizzy started uncertainly toward one of the tables.

"Miss," said the guard.

She turned back to him.

"Hanrick?"

"Yes."

He gestured toward the side of the room opposite the vending machines, to a row of seats facing scratched and smudged Plexiglas.

"Number three."

She crossed to the chairs and sat in the one labeled 3. Her hands were clammy, and the metal arms of the chair were cold in her grip. On the other side of the glass was a small enclosed room with a single chair, at the back of which was a metal door with a mesh-reinforced window.

She sat for a minute, her stomach rolling, thinking she might need to ask to use the restroom, when the door in the back of the room opened and Tobe Hanrick stepped through.

This was the Tobe Hanrick of the photo from the news article—the one where some buddy had had an arm draped over his shoulders. His face was tanned. His arms, where they extended from the short-sleeved orange shirt, were corded with muscle. His expression was open and curious. If she had had to guess his occupation just from his appearance, she might have guessed farmer—maybe at some fancy organic farm—or, more fancifully, cowboy. She could understand how he could have lured Sarah Pearson into his van.

He broke into a grin at the sight of her. He sat down and, despite the fact that the chair appeared to be bolted to the floor, managed to slouch back comfortably in it. He examined her for a moment, then sat forward and picked up the phone handset.

She stared at him, hands still gripping the arms of the chair. With an amused smile, he gestured to the handset on her side of the glass. It clattered against its cradle as she picked it up.

"Well, who have we here?" he said.

"I'm Tracy."

"Tracy, I can't imagine we've had the pleasure of meeting already—I'm sure I would remember you."

"We haven't met before."

She tried to summon the emotions she had felt when she had squeezed Lucia Hazlitt—anger—and Anton Rossi and Gerard Bonnay—panic and fear—but she could hardly be panicked and fearful with a sheet of Plexiglas between her and Hanrick, and she was having trouble summoning anger in the face of his charm offensive.

"And what brings you to Williams this fine day?" he asked. When she didn't respond, he leaned forward. "Read about me, did you? Curious about old Tobe Hanrick?"

"No. I mean yes." She should have thought this through before she was sitting across from him. She tried to rearrange her features into a semblance of interest—even infatuation. "I wanted to meet you."

She let him talk, trying to make sense of what was happening, trying to marshal her emotions. He at first tried to engage her in the conversation, but when that wasn't successful, he chatted unconcernedly about a movie he had seen and a band he thought a teenager would like.

"How old are you, anyway?"

"Eighteen."

He grinned. "Glad to hear it. Going to college?"

"No. I don't think so."

"Kicking around on your own a bit first? Smart move. That way when you go to college, you know the ropes. Know who to look for. And who to look out for."

She thought back to the three days he had had Sarah Pearson in the remote cabin, and tried not to think of what he had done to her, but images flashed through her mind nonetheless.

Tobe continued to gaze at her, seemingly unconcerned—and certainly unsqueezed. If the thoughts of the cabin and Sarah Pearson didn't enable her to summon the squeeze, nothing would.

She stood up abruptly, her chair skittering back. "I better be going."

He looked up at her. "Am I going to be seeing you again, sweetheart?"

Lizzy swallowed. "Yes, you'll see me again."

"Don't make it too long."

"Maybe tomorrow."

He grinned, and she had to look away from those eyes. "Yeah, tomorrow would be perfect."

49

The next morning, Lizzy sat in the back of the van behind a bowling alley a few blocks from the prison, since shooting up in the prison's parking lot didn't seem like the best idea. She knew she could only bring herself to go into the prison one more time, and when she did, she had to be sure she could squeeze Tobe Hanrick. If she didn't, she would be leaving the job for Philip to do, and she couldn't imagine he'd be able to kill Tobe without ending up back in jail himself—or worse.

She held the vial she had taken from Mitchell Pieda when they were in Pocopson and that she had been carrying with her ever since. He had said that Louise Mortensen had developed the drug to increase his squeeze—or, as Mitchell called it, the crush. Since her attempt to squeeze Tobe Hanrick on her first visit to the prison had apparently been a complete failure, she figured she needed all the help she could get to make sure she could fulfill her promise to Philip today.

She propped her phone up to rewatch the video of how to inject yourself—you could learn anything on YouTube. She'd inject it into her muscle, since she certainly wasn't going to try injecting the drug directly into a vein. She gingerly inserted the needle, purchased with surprising ease from a drug store, into the vial and drew out about half the contents. She also wasn't going to risk giving herself a full dose—plus, it might be good to have some left for Uncle Owen or Andy to analyze when she got back to Pennsylvania.

She winced as she inserted the needle into her arm and depressed the plunger, then quickly bundled the syringe and the vial back into the case and returned them to their hiding place in the seat wells. Then she climbed out of the back of the van and began walking quickly toward the prison. She didn't want to be behind the wheel of a large vehicle when the drug kicked in.

She had timed it so that she would arrive at the bus stop in the visitor lot just a minute or two before the bus was scheduled to pull in. Since she didn't know how long the effect of the drug would last, she hoped the bus was running on time. Her heart was beating harder than normal, but no more than could be explained by her hurried walk and the fact that she was on her way to kill a man.

She had expected something dramatic, but she felt pretty normal, although her surroundings did seem unusually noisy. A jarring screech from next to the sidewalk made her jump, but when she searched for the source, she could see only a wren-like bird. It opened its beak and screeched again.

She reached the shelter just as the bus was loading its one other passenger. The two-minute ride seemed to take ten times as long, and she was aware of every squeak of the van's suspension, every ping of a rock off the undercarriage, the slight groan from the wheel as the driver made the last turn to the visitor entrance.

As before, she had brought only the van key and her license.

She placed the key in the plastic basket at the guard's desk and handed over her license.

The guard looked down at the monitor on his desk. "Don't know why a young girl like that wants anything to do with that bastard Hanrick," he said.

Lizzy started. She glanced around, trying to see who the man was talking to, but there was no one nearby. Was he talking into an intercom?

"No telling what's going to turn them on, I guess," continued the guard.

Lizzy reddened. "I'm not turned on," she said.

The guard looked up, startled. "What?"

"I said I'm not turned on," Lizzy repeated. "And I don't think you should talk about me like that when I'm standing right here."

The guard glanced around, then looked back at Lizzy, his eyes narrowing. "I'm not talking about you. And you'd best be careful what you say to me if you're so intent on visiting your friend Hanrick." He imbued *friend* with special venom.

"He's not my—" began Lizzy.

"Little miss smart ass," said the guard.

But his lips hadn't moved.

Lizzy gawked at the guard. "What?"

He put his fists on his hips. "Are you giving me lip?" he said, in the normal manner. But at the same time Lizzy heard, *Do I need to put up with this crap?*

She realized she was staring at him with her mouth hanging open. "No," she stammered. "No, sorry, it's just, well, stressful, you know, to come here like this. And I'm really no friend of Mr.

Hanrick, I know the terrible things he's done. I just ..." She trailed off.

The guard dropped his fists from his hips. "You come visiting him an awful lot if he's not your friend," he grumbled, and simultaneously she heard, *Poor screwed up kid.* He handed her her license.

She followed another guard down the hallway and even though she couldn't see his mouth, she knew he hadn't said out loud what she heard: *Hope Maybelle packed ham and cheese today.*

A thought drifted over to her from the other visitor walking beside her, a woman not much older than Lizzy. *Thank God I'm only going to have to be making this stupid drive for another month.*

Her head whirling, Lizzy stepped into the visiting room. The guard inside the door checked his clipboard. She heard *Four* and started toward the chair facing the Plexiglas window.

"Four," she heard the guard call after her.

She lowered herself into the chair, her heart pounding and her fingers twisted together in her lap. What was happening? She heard the buzz of a conversation behind her and resisted the urge to turn and see if anyone in the room was actually talking.

A minute ticked by and she had almost decided she would leave when Tobe stepped into the room on the other side of the Plexiglas, followed by a guard. He sat, grinning, and picked up the handset. She stared at him through the glass.

Good thing Spacy Tracy didn't wait any longer to start her fangirl visits.

She jumped, then grabbed the handset on her side.

"Hello there, gorgeous," he said out loud. *She might be dumb but she sure is cute.*

"Hello," she replied.

Her thoughts were whirling. She shouldn't have taken so much of the drug—if that was less than one dose, what must

Mitchell Pieda have gone through when Louise Mortensen administered it? Thoughts careened through her mind like the silver ball in a pinball machine. She struggled to focus, and to concentrate this energy toward Tobe.

Can't wait until I get out of here.

He had only thought it, but she couldn't help responding. "You're never going to get out of prison, right?"

He looked momentarily surprised, then smiled a smile that held no joy, only cruelty. "Never say never," he said, but over that she heard, *Any minute now, sweetheart. And then I'm going to find you and—*

She wished she could clamp mental hands over her ears to block out his thoughts, but they were only too clear. She hoped she was keeping her horror from showing on her face ... but maybe this hatefulness was what she needed to make the squeeze work.

But *any minute now*—what could he mean by that? According to everything she had read about him, there was no way the justice system would ever let him go.

"Maybe," she said, trying for an encouraging tone, "there's some sort of appeal you can make."

He leaned back as far as the metal cord of the phone allowed and scratched his stomach. "There's something appealing right here in front of me." She could hear in her head a more vivid version of what he found appealing.

This time she couldn't keep her expression neutral, and he laughed. "Hey, sweetheart, you're the one who came visiting."

"Maybe ..." She swallowed down her disgust. "Maybe if you ever get out, we could meet up."

Clemson best get his ass in gear, thought Hanrick, *because I want to be sure that this piece of ass is still around when I get out.*

"You bet, sweetheart," he said with a grin. "I can't wait."

Won't have to wait too long, if Clemson didn't screw up the plan.

He had a plan for getting out. And it was a plan that was going to go into effect soon.

So Tobe Hanrick was not just a threat to the men in prison with him—if this plan worked out, he would be out there among the Sarah Pearsons and the Daisy Flowers of the world again. And what would he do to the next young woman that caught his eye? Actually, based on his mental monologue that was still boring into her brain, she had a pretty good idea.

If ever she needed to squeeze someone, now was the time.

She tried to summon the power she had used on Lucia Hazlitt, on Anton Rossi, on Gerard Bonnay, on George Millard, on Wilson at Walmart. She tried to focus on the emotions she had felt during those times and direct them toward Tobe.

But her thoughts kept dissolving into some horrible fun house distortion, with maniacal clowns shrieking with laughter from one side and ghoulish demons screaming from another. She clamped her hand over her mouth, trying to hold back a sob. Tobe grinned at her, enjoying her obvious distress.

Then his eyes shifted to over her shoulder, and the grin changed to a scowl. Lizzy yelped and dropped the phone as a hand touched her shoulder. She turned to see the guard standing at her side.

"You okay, miss?" he asked, his eyes concerned. *You okay, miss?* she heard.

Lizzy stared at him, trying to clear her head.

"I think it's time to go," he said, and took her elbow, gently. *Poor little thing.*

"She's an adult," said Tobe, raising his voice to be heard through the Plexiglas. "She can decide for herself when it's time to go."

The man at Lizzy's side gestured to the guard in the room with Hanrick. "Hanrick's going back to his cell," he called. *Hope the bastard rots there.*

Tobe stood, looking mildly annoyed, but mainly amused. "See you around, darling. Soon, I hope." *Real soon.*

"CAN I just walk back to the parking lot?" she pleaded with the guard when they reached the visitor entrance.

"No, sorry, can't let you do that." *Who knows what this nut case would do.*

"I can't wait here for an hour," Lizzy said, barely holding back another sob.

The guard sighed. "Sit there," he said, motioning to a molded plastic chair. "I'll see what I can do." *Frank's probably just sitting on his ass in the break room—* The mental voice faded as he went to a desk behind the metal detector and picked up a phone.

She huddled in the chair, her arms crossed, trying to ignore the voices around her. She had failed. Even with the help of the drug—or maybe because of it—she not only couldn't help Philip avenge his friend's death, she couldn't even find a way to make sure this despicable excuse of a human stayed behind bars. She couldn't tell the guards. How would she explain how she knew?

In a few minutes, the guard was back. "Okay, your ride's outside."

She followed him to the door where the van idled, the driver looking at her curiously. *Wonder what happened—they never tell me anything.*

"There you go, miss, he'll take you back to the gate."

"Thank you," she said gratefully.

She stepped out the door, then turned at the guard's voice.

"Miss, don't come back. We're putting you on the no-visit list." *Can't imagine she'd want to anyway.*

"No, I won't."

She rushed onto the bus and endured two minutes of listening to the driver sing an odd two-part accompaniment—the one inside his head in perfect harmony, the other hummed out loud and off-key.

When the bus pulled up at the stop in the visitor lot, she scrambled off with a gasped "Thank you," and ran for the bowling alley parking lot where she had left the van. The wren screeched as she passed its nest.

She didn't even bother with the balky driver's door lock, but scrambled in on the passenger side and clambered across the passenger seat into the driver's seat. She turned the key in the ignition, wanting to put as much distance between her and Tobe Hanrick as possible. Then she thought better of trying to operate the vehicle in her current condition and switched the engine off. She gripped the steering wheel and took deep breaths until her heartbeat had slowed to a near normal rate.

What should she do? She had to make sure Hanrick didn't get out of Williams—or, if he did, that he didn't get far.

There was nothing she could tell the guards that they would believe. She couldn't claim that Tobe had told her about his plans during her visit—there had been a guard standing right behind him the whole time. She thought back to their conversation. They had talked about him getting out of prison. Maybe she could claim that one of his answers had been some sort of coded message that his escape was imminent.

But she realized that was a bad idea in at least two ways. One was that it would put her right in the middle of an investigation into some conspiracy to break Tobe Hanrick out of prison, and that wouldn't turn out to be good for anyone. The second was that they already thought she was crazy and probably wouldn't believe anything she told them.

She cast about for other options. She couldn't call Uncle Owen and risk upsetting him while he recovered from his heart attack. She didn't want to get Andy and Ruby involved. If only she could get in touch with Philip.

Then she thought of the unidentified calls she had received—the calls that she had assumed were telemarketers. Maybe Philip was trying to get in touch with her. Maybe he didn't have his phone and was using someone else's. It couldn't hurt to try—if it really was a telemarketer, she would just hang up.

She got out her phone and hit *Call Back*.

50

Philip walked down the dirt road that led from the trailer to the highway, hoping to clear his lungs of the acrid cigarette smoke that seemed to hang in the air of Wayne's trailer even when he wasn't actually smoking. Above him, the stores and houses of Jerome proper clung like mountain goats to the side of Cleopatra Hill.

He was about to turn around and head back to the trailer when his phone buzzed with an incoming call. He glanced at the caller ID: it was the number he had used to try to contact Lizzy. He stabbed *Accept*. "Hello?"

He heard a deep, gulping breath. "Philip, it's Lizzy." And she burst into tears.

He pressed the phone to his ear, as if its proximity would bring her closer. His heart thudded. "Lizzy, are you okay?"

"Yes, I'm okay." He heard another breath, smoother this time, and a sniff. "I'm okay," she repeated, as if trying to convince herself.

"What's wrong?"

She laughed tremulously. "Where should I start?"

Then she fell silent, and after a few seconds, Philip asked, "Where are you?"

"Can I tell you?"

"Yeah. If you're referring to my advice to Andy not to let me know where you are, that's not a concern anymore—or at least not at the moment."

"You're not with whoever got you away from the hospital?"

"No—I can tell you about that later, but I'm footloose and fancy free at the moment. Where are you?"

"I'm in Williams, not far from the prison. I was going to—take care of Tobe Hanrick, like you asked me to."

"Jesus, I thought you were in Pennsylvania! I told Andy to tell you that you didn't have to do that—" he began, his voice angry.

"Andy told me. But I had told you I'd take care of him—"

"You promised that you'd *think* about it—"

"I know. But then I read about what he'd done, and I thought that if anyone ever deserved to be squeezed, he did."

Philip stepped off the road and sat down on a rock. "Lizzy, I can't believe I asked you to do that—it was so wrong of me. I was so angry and I didn't see any way I could take care of him myself. I'm taking it back. I'm not sure how, but I'm going to take care of him. It's important to me that I do it myself."

"You might have to."

"What do you mean?"

"I went to the prison like a visitor, just like you suggested—"

"Lizzy—" Philip dropped his face into his hand.

"—but I couldn't do it. The first time I think it was because I couldn't be scared of him because there was nothing he could do to me."

"The first time?"

"Yeah. I went there twice."

"What happened the second time?"

She hesitated. "Are you sure no one's listening in?"

"As sure as I can be," said Philip.

"I wanted to be sure I could squeeze him, so I took some of that drug that Louise had given Mitchell."

Philip shot upright. "Lizzy—"

"Don't worry, it didn't hurt me," she interrupted him. "But ... I can read minds."

"You can ... what?"

"I can read minds, like Mitchell. He needed the drug to make his squeeze stronger, for me it made me be able to read minds. I could hear what the guards were thinking—just like they were talking, but their lips weren't moving. And that made it even less possible for me to squeeze Tobe Hanrick. Not only did I still have a wall of Plexiglas between us, and guards everywhere, so I couldn't feel scared of him, but the experience of being able to hear what people were thinking was so disorienting—I couldn't concentrate. I could hear what he was thinking, too. He's going to try to escape."

"Escape?"

"Yes, and he seemed pretty sure that it's going to work out."

Philip tried to process what he was hearing. "Could you tell when?"

"Not exactly, but soon, I think. Very soon."

Philip stood up and paced back and forth across the deserted dirt road. "This might actually work in our favor. If Hanrick's going to get out of Williams, I really can take care of him myself. Or," he added with a sardonic laugh, "the guards will take care of him for us when he tries."

"How will you know when he's out?"

"Oh, I think it will be clear to everyone when Tobe Hanrick is a free man," said Philip grimly. "He's someone who likes to leave his mark." He thought for a moment. "You go somewhere else—anywhere else—and check into a hotel. I'll wait for news, and then when I've taken care of Hanrick, we'll meet up."

"I don't think I have enough money for a hotel. Someone stole most of the money Uncle Owen gave me."

"Unfortunately, I'm not exactly flush with cash myself." He considered and discarded options, Lizzy silent on the other end of the line. Then he said, "Hey, I know. You can stay at my place, and Eddie can keep an eye on you."

"Do you think it's safe to go to your house?"

"I'm not sure anymore what's safe and what isn't, but I know I'd feel better with Eddie right next door to you. Plus, the guy who sprung me from the hospital and the minder he sent to Arizona with me probably expect both of us to be headed to Williams, so anywhere away from Williams is a good idea." He paused. "Hanrick doesn't have anything that would tie you to Sedona, right?"

"No. As far as he's concerned, I'm Tracy Coates from Wisconsin. That's the ID your friend sent me."

"And you didn't mention me to Hanrick?"

"No, Philip," said Lizzy, and Philip smiled at the hint of truculent teenager in her voice.

"Perfect. I'll give Eddie a call and let him know you're coming. I don't see any reason not to use your real name, but I'll think of some story to tell him about why you're staying there. I'll also ask him to give you some money, for groceries or whatever." He was feeling more optimistic as his plan took shape. "You lay low, I'll take care of Hanrick when he ventures outside of Williams, then I'll take you back to Philly and you can nurse Owen back to robust health. How does that sound?"

She was silent for a moment, and Philip was afraid she was going to protest, but then he heard a sigh. "That sounds good." Then, concerned, "You're sure you'll be all right?"

"Me? Absolutely. I have someone helping me—someone I

trust—and I'm somewhere where it would be tough for anyone to track me down."

"Where are you?" asked Lizzy.

"I'm in Arizona, too."

"You are?" Her voice took on a brightness that made Philip's heart ache. "Maybe we can meet up!"

"We will—I promise. Not quite yet, but as soon as we can."

"How did you get out here, anyway? And how did you get out of the hospital?"

Philip gave her an abbreviated rundown of events since he had been driven away from Mercy Hospital in Theo Viklund's limousine.

"Jeez, it makes Louise Mortensen sound like small potatoes."

"Yeah. In fact, it sounds to me like Mortensen's gone from being queen of the board to a pawn. She's definitely still in the game," he added hastily, "but I don't think she's the one calling the moves."

"The fewer pieces we have to worry about, the better," said Lizzy with a weak laugh.

"Don't forget that Mitchell's working for Viklund, too."

"Yeah. Poor Mitchell."

"I know you can feel an empathy for him that the rest of us can't, but you can't let down your guard about him."

"No, I won't."

"You must have a story of your own to tell," said Philip. "Getting all the way out here on your own."

"I wasn't on my own. I met someone ..." her voice trailed off.

"Someone ...?" he prompted.

"A girl I met helped with the drive."

"Is she still with you?"

"No," she said, a hitch in her voice. "I can tell you later. Can I call you after I get to your house?"

He hesitated. "I think you better not. I'm ninety-nine percent sure that the guy who brought me out here won't be able to find me, but just in case my phone falls into the wrong hands, we should probably limit contact with each other."

"Okay."

He gave Lizzy the address of his casita in Sedona. "I'll be in touch as soon as I can."

"Okay. Be careful, Philip."

"I will. You too."

He waited for a moment for her to break the connection, but when she didn't, he reluctantly ended the call.

As Philip turned back toward the trailer, he searched for the number for Eddie's house flipping and rental business, then dialed the number.

"Hey, Phil, what's up?" boomed Eddie. "You been on vacation?"

"Yeah, sort of," said Philip. "Listen, I have a favor to ask you—"

"What's new?" said Eddie with a laugh.

"A young lady is going to be coming by my place shortly, and I'd like you to let her in and give her a key."

"You sly dog."

"I'm not a sly dog—she's the goddaughter of a friend of mine."

"Okay, okay, keep your pants on."

"Her name's Lizzy. In fact, she's Owen McNally's goddaughter. You remember Owen?"

"Sure. Owen who was concerned about a tripped security alarm in a house that didn't have a security system. How could I forget?"

"Someday I'll buy you a beer and explain that. Anyhow, can you keep an eye on her? Her boyfriend's looking for her," he improvised, "and it would be best if he didn't find her."

"Gotcha."

Philip expanded on the improvisation. "Keep an eye out for the boyfriend," he said, and gave Eddie a description of Mitchell Pieda. "And his mom might be tagging along with him," he added, trying to keep the grin out of his voice. He described Louise Mortensen. "Also, any chance you could give her the money I gave you for next month's rent? I should be able to repay it within a couple of days—a week or two at the most."

"Hey, now you're hitting me where it hurts."

"I know—I wouldn't ask if it weren't an emergency."

"Yeah, I know." Eddie sighed. "Okay."

"Thanks, Eddie—I owe you."

Philip reached the trailer as he ended the call. Wayne sat on the couch, a beer dangling between his knees, a boxing match playing on the TV at a room-rattling volume.

"Mind if we turn it down a little?" Philip yelled.

Wayne picked up the remote and muted the sound.

"I just got some news." Philip went to the refrigerator, got a beer of his own, popped the cap, and sat on the couch. "You have any interest in meeting up with our old friend Tobe Hanrick? Just you and me and him? No guards. No bars."

"You fucking kidding me?" said Wayne, sitting forward. "I've been dreaming of that for years. And I know a couple of other guys who have the same dream."

"No one else, just you and me."

"Sure, sure." Wayne snickered. "But there's going to be one hell of a party when that bastard's gone. So, how do you plan to manage the 'no guards, no bars' part?"

"I hear that Hanrick is going to try to escape."

"No shit—how did you find that out?"

"Can't say, but I think it's legit."

"How's he going to do it?"

"I don't know."

"When's it going to happen?"

"Don't know that for sure either—but my source says soon."

"So what are we supposed to do?" asked Wayne irritably. "Surround the jail and wait for him to come out, hope we notice him before the guards do? Just the two of us?"

"I don't think we need to get to him the minute he gets out, we just need to wait for him to surface and then go find him. And he's not going to slip away unnoticed. There are some scores he's going to want to settle, and he'll be sure to do it in a way that everyone knows it was him."

"So, we wait for him to smoke someone?"

Philip shrugged. "Like you said, if he's under the radar enough to slip out of Williams, he's likely going to be too under the radar for us to find him."

Wayne considered while he drank more beer. "Makes sense. And I guess if I've waited this long to have some fun with Hanrick, I can wait a little longer. We going to go to Williams to wait?"

"Actually, I like your trailer better. Who knows where he'll surface—I don't know that being there would give us any advantage."

"You just like the free room and board."

"Hey, if you want to give me half the cash we found in the hotel room in Flagstaff, I'd be happy to pitch in for food and beer."

Wayne waved his beer bottle. "Nah. Mi casa es su casa."

They both turned to the television. Wayne unmuted the sound but dropped it to a bearable level. After a couple of minutes, he said, "So ... you seen Olivia since Oscar died?"

Philip didn't take his eyes off the screen. "Just at the funeral."

"Yeah. She didn't look too good," said Wayne morosely. "Well, you know, *good*, but not happy."

"Yeah, I knew what you meant."

"Haven't seen her since then?"

"That's what I said."

Wayne took another swallow of beer. "I'm surprised, because I thought you two—you know ..." He trailed off when he noticed Philip's expression.

They drank in silence for a minute, then Wayne said, "I told you what I plan to do when Hanrick's dead—have a big party to wish that bastard good riddance. What about you?"

"I've got a delivery to make to Pennsylvania. Then? No freakin' idea."

51

Lizzy pulled into the driveway of the address Philip had given her. The main house was a modest rancher, and she could see a smaller detached building in back.

As she climbed out of the van, a large bald black man stepped out of the side door of the rancher.

"You Philip's friend?" he asked in a friendly voice. *This Philip's friend?* she heard in her head.

"Yes." She held out her hand. "Lizzy."

He shook her hand, more gently than she had expected based on his size. "Pleased to meet you, Lizzy. I'm Eddie. Welcome to Casa Castillo. Or Castillo Castillo," he said with a laugh. *Castillo Castillo* she heard, accompanied by a psychic chuckle.

He led her to the door of the casita, unlocked it, and stepped aside for her to enter.

If Lizzy had imagined Philip's home, she wouldn't have been far off. She stepped out of the tiled entrance area into a living room with a comfortable-looking couch, a pair of cushioned chairs, and several large ceramic pots topped with copper trays serving as side tables. One wall was taken up with shelves holding books, CDs, and small pieces of pottery.

"I'm sure I speak for Philip when I say make yourself at home," said Eddie. He went into the kitchen and Lizzy could hear him opening the refrigerator door. "Well, as much at home as possible," he continued. "Not a lot of supplies in the fridge, I have to say." *Wonder what a teenage girl would want?* She heard cupboards open and close. "There's some soup and crackers."

"That's okay," she said. "I have some food in the cooler in the van."

Eddie stepped back into the living room. "I'm going to the store later today, want me to pick anything up for you?"

"No, that's okay—I can run over to the store later."

Eddie looked skeptical. *Thought she was supposed to be laying low.*

Lizzy wondered what story Philip had told him. "Actually, if you could pick something up, that would be great. Probably best if I just stay here."

Eddie nodded. "I'll pick up some stuff—if it's not something you like, I can use it."

He popped his head into the bedroom and bathroom. "Everything else looks in order." He came back into the living room and got out his wallet. "Philip asked me to give you his rent money—" he glanced into the wallet "—but I'm going to have to stop by the ATM first." He held out two twenties. "Here's an advance."

Lizzy blushed and took the money. "Thanks."

Eddie stuffed the wallet into his back pocket. *Seems like a sweet girl.* "Don't thank me, it's Phil's money." He glanced around the casita one more time, checking that everything was ship-shape, then handed her a key. "Lock up behind me, and don't open the door without checking to see who's out there. I'd also recommend keeping the windows closed and locked—if it gets stuffy you can put the AC on. Keep the blinds closed so no one can see in. It's a pretty secure little house—I don't think you'll be bothered. And if anyone shows up, they're going to have to walk by my kitchen window." He grinned. "And I see everything that comes by my kitchen window. Want to get your stuff out of your van?"

He helped her unload, surveyed the room once more, then stepped out the door.

"Don't forget to lock up."

"I won't. Thanks again."

He waved a hand. "No problem."

He pulled the door closed behind him and she sensed him waiting on the other side. She flipped the deadbolt, and then heard his footsteps recede toward the main house.

She pulled up her contact list—she had updated it with Philip's new number since, based on what he had told her, the phone attached to the old number was probably a melted lump in Pocopson. Despite Philip's caution to her, her finger hovered over his name, but then with a sigh she tucked the phone into her pocket.

She transferred a few items from the cooler to the refrigerator and threw out a couple of items from the refrigerator that were clearly well past their use by date. Then she returned to the living room and looked over the offerings on the bookshelf, pulling out a book about the history of Sedona. She took it to the couch, which proved to be just as comfortable as it looked. After a few minutes, she levered off her boots and lay back. Doors and windows locked, blinds drawn, and Eddie just a driveway away, she closed her eyes and slept.

52

———

Lizzy was microwaving some soup for dinner when her phone rang. She had already gotten Ruby's daily text—*Everything good here—how are you doing?*—and had sent off her reply—*I'm fine too. Missing you guys.* Maybe Philip had decided it was okay for them to keep in contact. She snatched up the phone and checked the caller ID: *Uncle Owen*

She stabbed *Accept*, her excitement veering toward fear. Why was Uncle Owen calling her?

"Hello?"

"Hello, Pumpkin. How are you doing?"

The wave of homesickness that swept over her was almost more than she could bear. She dropped into a chair at the small kitchen table. "I'm so glad to hear from you."

"I'm glad to be talking to you."

"How are you doing?"

"Much better. I'm at home now."

"Yeah, I hear Ruby is taking care of you."

"Yes, she has been, but she had to leave today. Her brother-in-law passed away."

Lizzy felt tears fill her eyes. "Oh, no. Poor Ruby."

"Yes." He was silent for a moment, and Lizzy pulled a paper napkin from a holder on the table and blew her nose.

"I know we said we'd try to limit contact," said Owen, "and Ruby told us you preferred not to talk with us because it would make you homesick, but I didn't want you to worry if you didn't hear from Ruby."

Lizzy gave a watery laugh. "I did hear from her. She sent me her text today, just like always."

"I should have known she wouldn't let that slip," said Uncle Owen. He paused while Lizzy blew her nose again, then said, "How are you doing, Pumpkin? Really?"

"I'm ..." She was going to say *okay*, but then everything that had happened to her since she had left Pennsylvania swept over her: squeezing Wilson at the Walmart, having her money stolen by Daisy, learning of Daisy's death, meeting the horrible Tobe Hanrick and having to listen to his even more horrible thoughts. She thought back to that night in the truck stop parking lot when she had thought she would walk into the desert and never come back—would rid the world of a life that seemed to curse not only itself but everyone else whose lives it touched—but she didn't want that anymore. She just wanted to go home.

Just click the heels of her Ruby Slippers and go home.

"I'm lonely," she said with a sob.

"Pumpkin, did something happen?"

"Yes. No. I don't know." She gripped the sodden napkin and took a deep breath. "I'm all right. It's just—there's been a lot going on."

Lizzy could hear Andy's concerned voice in the background. "Is she okay?"

"She's upset," said Owen. "Pumpkin, I don't like the idea of you being all alone—wherever you are."

The sound of that familiar voice extinguished any desire she had to continue keeping her location secret from her godfather.

"I'm in Sedona."

"Sedona?" Owen's voice was nearly a squawk. "What are you doing there? I thought you were somewhere in western Pennsylvania!"

"It's a long story, and I'd rather not tell it over the phone."

"Well, then, we need to bring you back home so you can tell us in person."

And just like that, the pain that had gripped her heart since she had left Pennsylvania—had, in fact, gripped her heart ever since Uncle Owen had had the heart attack, ever since her father had been shot in a Philadelphia alley—seemed to drop away. She knew it couldn't be that easy. Louise Mortensen was still out there, now working for the mysterious man who had gotten Philip away from the hospital and away from the police, and evidently Mitchell was working for him as well.

But at least she didn't have her promise to kill Tobe Hanrick hanging over her anymore. She had done what she could. She had told Philip that Hanrick was getting ready to break out of prison, and beyond that, what could she do? She felt like she should be helping Philip in some way—or maybe trying to talk him out of his plan—but in this matter she felt completely out of her depth. Staying out of his way was probably the best she could do for him.

And as for the others? She'd rather deal with them in Pennsylvania along with Uncle Owen and Andy than hiding like a fugitive alone in Arizona.

"Yes," she said with a hiccup of relief. "I would love to tell you in person."

She heard an indistinct voice—Andy whispering something—and Owen said, "One sec, Pumpkin."

"What's he saying?" she asked impatiently.

Owen was back in a moment. "He says he'd like to go to

Sedona and accompany you back, and I agree with him. I don't want you to have to be by yourself anymore."

"What about you? Will Ruby still be staying with you?"

"We haven't had a chance to talk about it, but I think she has other things to worry about at the moment. Maybe I'll go stay with my parents, or to a friend's house. I could hire a bodyguard."

Lizzy began to protest on general principles, then stopped. She really had no wish to make a return journey in the van by herself, and Andy could do all the driving. He probably wouldn't have a problem getting onto an interstate, she thought ruefully.

"That sounds good," she said.

"Oh. Good," said Owen, obviously surprised at the ease with which she had agreed to his plan. "Where in Sedona are you?"

She got up from the kitchen table and wandered into the living room. "I'm staying at Philip's house."

"At Philip's house?" His voice spiked again, this time with a different type of concern.

"Yes, Uncle Owen," she said, "at Philip's house, but he's not here. He thought it would be a good place for me to stay because his friend Eddie, the ex-cop, is right next door."

"Oh, right, that makes sense." He paused. "Where is Philip?"

"He's back in Arizona, too."

"Really? How did he get there?"

"I don't know all the details, but he got away from the person who got him out of the hospital."

"What's he doing in Arizona if he's not in Sedona?"

"He has some things he needs to take care of here."

Lizzy heard Andy's voice again. "I say let's leave Philip to take care of whatever business he has in Arizona, and get Lizzy back here ASAP."

Lizzy flopped down on the couch in relief.

"Yes, let's do that," she said. "I can't wait to see you guys."

53

———————

When Lizzy got up the next morning, she saw the news that she had been expecting: Tobe Hanrick was missing from the Williams Correctional Facility. She checked the locks on the doors and windows and peered out the small glass panes in the front door, comforted by the sight of Eddie's big pickup parked on the street.

She spent the day napping, snacking on the food that Eddie had dropped off, and compulsively checking the status of Andy's flight into Phoenix.

Around noon, the news reports flashed an update:

The body of Ivan Crane, a former associate and later rival of prison escapee Tobe Hanrick, was found by his wife in the basement of their home near Kingman, Arizona, at eight o'clock this morning. Crane and Hanrick, who escaped from the Williams Correctional Facility sometime between lights out last night and the wake-up call this morning, were locked in a struggle for control of the drug trade in Kingman when Hanrick was arrested in connection with the torture killing of

University of Arizona student Sarah Pearson. Police are withholding the cause of Crane's death.

Lizzy entered *Kingman* into her map app—almost three hours away from Sedona.

Her fingers itched to contact Philip—to find out where he was and what he was doing—but she remembered his caution to her as he had prepared to enter Louise Mortensen's Pocopson home: not to call or text him. Maybe he was in just as dangerous a situation right now as he stalked Tobe Hanrick.

That evening, a former Hanrick associate turned informant was found hanging in a hotel room in Las Vegas. Two hours from Kingman, and in the opposite direction from Sedona.

As she made her tenth check of Andy's flight status within the previous hour, she noticed that the phone's battery icon was red, showing just a tiny sliver of remaining life. She sighed and went to where she had left her knapsack by the door. The power cord wasn't in the pocket she usually kept it in. She checked the other pockets and inside the knapsack. No cord. She went through her other bags and even checked inside the Styrofoam cooler. Still no cord.

Maybe she had left it in the van. She went to the door and looked out. The sun had set, but the driveway was well lit by a floodlight and the van was only about thirty feet from the door of the casita. More important, she could hear the sounds of a party at the house next door, and some of the partiers had spilled out into the back yard just on the other side of a hedge, probably to have a smoke. If she could hear them chatting and laughing so clearly, they would certainly be able to hear her if she ran into trouble and called out.

And if someone actually attacked her, there was the squeeze. If she ran into someone in the driveway, she wouldn't have to worry about a protective pane of Plexiglas keeping her from experiencing the emotions that would enable her to use her inborn weapon.

She stepped outside and scanned the area, but the floodlight didn't illuminate much beyond the driveway itself. She locked the casita door behind her so that no one could slip in while she checked the van, then scurried to the vehicle.

She looked everywhere she could think of—between and underneath the seats, under and inside the sleeping bag, even in the space under the stowed back seats where the last of her dwindling supply of cash was hidden—popping her head up periodically to make sure no one had appeared from the darkness.

Finally convinced that the cord was not in the van either, she went to the door of Eddie's house and knocked. Maybe he would have a cord she could borrow.

She waited a minute and knocked again, but there was no answer. Not that she should have expected one, she thought. As far as she knew, it wasn't like Eddie had promised to stand guard over her around the clock.

She'd have to run to the store to get a cord—she couldn't afford to be out of touch with Philip or Uncle Owen or Andy at this point. She went back in the house to get her knapsack.

Much to her annoyance, her phone died as she pulled out of the driveway, so she didn't have a way to search for where to go to buy a power cord. She wasn't aware of any Targets or Walmarts near Sedona, and a slow drive up the main tourist drag didn't reveal any likely looking sources. After some pondering, she drove to one of the hotels just a few blocks from Philip's house, pulled into a parking space in the lot in back, and went to the main desk.

"Excuse me, I lost the cord to my iPhone."

"You came to the right place," said the young man behind the desk with a laugh. *Cute*, she heard, and blushed. "We could open an electronics accessory shop if we wanted to." He went into the back room and emerged a minute later with a box overflowing with cords. "Will one of these do the trick?"

Lizzy sorted through the cords. "Yeah, this one is like mine." She glanced up at him. "I can't tell for sure if it's mine. Is it okay if I take it anyway?"

"Sure," he said. "Not doing anyone any good sitting in our lost-and-found box."

She returned to the van humming, pleased at her inventiveness and consoling herself that she hadn't actually lied to the guy at the desk.

The night was dark, but the parking lot was well lit, and her nerves were soothed by the fact that she could hear the murmur of conversation from a car parked a few spaces away from the van. Perhaps someone speaking on their phone, since she could only hear one voice.

She slipped the key into the lock and was jiggling it to get it to turn when she heard the voice moving away from the car. She stopped the jiggling to listen more closely. The voice was approaching the van from the other side.

Her heart beating harder, she renewed her efforts to turn the key in the door lock. The voice—definitely a man—was getting closer. She would see him through the van windows in a second or two.

There was another sound as well—a faint thrumming sound —the source of which she couldn't identify.

She glanced around, realizing that a lit lot was no safer than an unlit one if there was no one there to see her. But did she really need to be nervous? If someone were trying to sneak up on her, he would hardly be talking as he approached.

She tried to force the key to turn, but it remained stubbornly unmovable. Her heart was hammering now, the man just on the other side of the van.

"This should be fun."

Her fingers froze on the key as a sickening realization dawned on her. She turned toward where the man was stepping around the front of the van.

"Hey there, sweetheart," said Tobe Hanrick.

Looking even better than I remembered, he thought.

She drew in a breath to scream, but two instincts stopped her. One was a lifetime of programming—by her parents, by Uncle Owen—to avoid attracting attention. The other was the idea that in a moment Tobe Hanrick was going to meet the same fate as her other victims.

Maybe she would be able to discharge her promise to Philip after all.

She stepped backwards, wanting to postpone the inevitable, and Hanrick stepped after her. The thrumming sound grew louder—actually more like a mutter.

"I've been looking forward to seeing you again," he said with a grin.

She saw a movement out of the corner of her eye. An object flashed in front of her face and suddenly there was something around her neck.

"Don't scream," a voice hissed in her ear.

She couldn't have screamed if she wanted to. The van key and power cord fell to the ground as she tried to get her fingers under whatever was around her throat, but it was too tight.

Tobe stood grinning at her, enjoying her panic.

Her heart was hammering from the shock of the encounter, but at any moment Hanrick and the man tightening the noose around her neck would collapse as blood vessels burst in their brains.

But the noose didn't loosen.

On the contrary, it tightened as the man behind her used it to lift her to her toes.

Tobe bent to pick up the key and cord. Lizzy kicked out toward him, but she was too far from him, and the movement put more pressure on her neck. She kicked her heel back into the leg of the man who was strangling her.

"Goddamn!" he yelped and cinched the noose tighter. "Hurry up, Tobe!"

Tobe turned to the van door and inserted the key.

Her blood pounded in her ears. Her lungs strained in vain for oxygen. The darkness started to take on a dancing sparkle that wasn't from the parking lot lights.

"Can't get the goddamned key to turn," she heard Tobe say, then, *A car isn't quite as good as a van for what I have in mind.*

The last thing she heard before the sparkles turned to black was, "I'm not jacking around with this lock anymore—get her in the car. We'll come back for the van later."

54

The plane from Philadelphia landed in Phoenix about seven in the evening.

"Thanks for the restaurant recommendations," said Andy to the flight attendant as they waited for the door to the jetway to open.

"Too bad you won't be in Phoenix long enough to try them out," she said.

"But I'll have them for my next trip out here."

She gave him a brilliant smile. "Yes—maybe it will be on one of my flights."

Andy returned her smile. "I certainly hope so."

The door opened and the passengers began filing out.

"Why do you bother flirting with women you're never going to see again?" asked Owen, puffing slightly as he followed Andy up the jetway.

"You're such pessimist," replied Andy. "I might decide that Arizona is my new favorite vacation destination."

Owen rolled his eyes.

"Seems like it's your favorite destination," continued Andy, "considering that you got all fired up about coming along."

"I will be quite happy not to be making any return trips to the desert southwest once we get Lizzy back home."

They arrived at Philip's casita around ten o'clock. They were walking up the drive, past the main house on the property, when the rancher's side door opened and Philip's ex-cop landlord, Eddie, stepped out.

"Hi there, Eddie," said Owen. "Owen McNally. You helped me out a couple of months ago when the security alarm went off at the house I was staying in off Coffee Pot Drive."

"Sure, I remember you, Owen," said Eddie, crossing the driveway and shaking his hand. "And this must be your brother."

Andy put out his hand. "Andy McNally."

"I don't suppose you gentlemen know where Lizzy is?" Eddie asked tentatively, his forehead creased with worry.

Owen and Andy exchanged alarmed glances.

"We thought she was here," said Owen.

Eddie shook his head and rubbed a hand over his head. "I expected her to be. I had to run out for a little while. Some renter was grilling on the deck and caught it on fire. When I came back, her van was gone, and she was gone, too."

"You checked the casita?" asked Andy.

"Yeah. When I knocked and didn't get an answer, I went in."

"Can we see inside?" asked Owen.

"Sure." Eddie led them into the casita. "I tried calling Philip's cell but it went to voicemail."

They made a quick search of the casita.

"No sign of a struggle," said Andy with strained hopefulness.

"Jeez, I feel terrible," said Eddie. "I figured she'd be fine as long as she stayed inside with everything locked up tight."

"Certainly a reasonable assumption," said Owen, who had his phone pressed to his ear. He looked at Andy and shook his head. "It's going to voicemail." In a moment, he said, "Lizzy, it's

Uncle Owen. Please call me as soon as you get this message. Love you."

Andy ran his fingers through his hair. "Maybe she ran out for something?"

"Maybe," replied Owen. "Why don't we drive around, see if we can find her." He turned to Eddie. "I'm sure it's nothing, but if you see her before we do, can you ask her to give us a call?"

"Sure thing," said Eddie. "Unless you'd like me to help look. I did it for a living for a lot of years."

"I think it will be better if someone stays here in case she comes back," said Owen.

They left Eddie standing in the door of the casita, his expression sober, his hands jammed in his pockets.

"Do you know what the van she's driving looks like?" asked Andy as he unlocked the rental car and they climbed in.

"More or less—it's pretty generic, as I recall. Hold on." Owen got out his phone and pressed the speed dial for Ruby.

"Hello, Dr. McNally," she answered.

"Hello, Ruby. How are you doing?"

"I'm doing well. I'm at my sister's house, we're preparing for the funeral. How are you?"

Owen gave her a brief rundown of the situation. "We're going to drive around and see if we can spot the van," he told her. "If you can give us the make and model, we can look it up and at least have a better idea of what we should be looking for."

"I can do better than that. Lizzy had a little encounter with a guard rail after we left Philly, and I took a picture of it in case I needed it for the insurance. I'll send it to you."

Owen opened the photo, which showed the long silver streak down the side of the van.

"That should be easy to spot," said Andy, looking at the photo over Owen's shoulder.

They drove first to Philip's office in Uptown Sedona, just a few blocks from the casita, then over to West Sedona where Owen and Lizzy had stayed. They checked the parking lot of the Sugarloaf Trail, and even went to both trailheads of the Thread-the-Needle Trail, although Owen found it hard to believe Lizzy would choose to go there, considering her encounter with the rattlesnakes at the Needle. Owen continued to try to reach Lizzy on her cell phone, with no luck.

"I guess we have no way to get in touch with Castillo," said Andy.

"No."

"Anyplace else we should check?" Andy asked.

"I can't think of any place to stake out other than Philip's house or his office."

"We have Eddie keeping an eye on his house, so why don't we go back to his office and you can keep trying to call her."

"What if she's not the one deciding where she goes?" asked Owen, his voice unsteady.

"It would be hard for someone to kidnap her, or to hurt her, without coming to grief himself," said Andy.

Owen nodded, unconvinced.

As they approached the office, Andy said, "On the off chance that there *are* bad things afoot, we should probably park somewhere we can keep an eye on the office, but not right in front of it where we'd be easy to spot."

"That makes sense."

They parked about fifty yards from the office and settled in to wait.

55

P hilip was cleaning the gun that Wayne had taken from Rey Viklund when his phone rang. He glanced at the caller ID, although he hardly had to, since Lizzy was the only one who had the number.

"Hey, Lizzy," he answered. "What's up?"

"Lizzy? So her name isn't Tracy Coates … or is 'Lizzy' just a little pet name you have for your girlfriend?"

Philip felt as if all his blood had been sucked into his heart.

After a moment, the familiar voice said, "What, cat got your tongue, Casal?"

"Hanrick," he said, his voice leaden.

"You guessed it. And not behind bars anymore, as I'm sure you've heard. I had to make a quick trip up to Kingman to visit my good friend Ivan Crane, then I sent some buddies on to take care of some business in Vegas, but I had business of my own back in Arizona. I want to thank you for sending your friend Lizzy to me. We had such a nice chat when she visited me in prison, and now I'm so pleased to be able to meet her in the flesh." His tone lingered horribly over the last word.

"How did you find her?" Philip asked.

"Some pretty young thing comes visiting, I'm curious who she is. I got a message to a guy on the outside—Clemson, maybe you remember him—and when she left after the second visit, he followed her. Turns out Miss Lizzy has a lot of people interested in her comings and goings. Clem noticed that he wasn't the only person waiting for Lizzy when she left the prison—there was also a pretty blonde dressed all businesslike."

Rey. Philip could barely hear Hanrick for the blood pounding in his ears.

"They all made a happy convoy to Sedona—Lizzy and then the blonde and then Clem—and Lizzy holes up in a casita guarded by the world's nosiest landlord. The blonde makes like she's going to stake out the casita, but I told Clem I wanted to find out why she was interested in my visitor. I was feeling pretty protective of my girl, I don't mind telling you." There was a pause, and a sucking sound. Philip hoped it was a draw on a cigarette. Hanrick coughed, then continued. "The pretty blonde —Clem sent me a picture, said she must have been from Sweden or Norway judging by her accent—told him pretty quick that she worked for someone back east and had come out here with Philip Castillo looking for someone named Elizabeth Ballard. He tried to find out more about this Philip Castillo from the blonde, but he was a little too ... overenthusiastic. I'm going to have to give that boy some coaching on questioning techniques."

"Let me talk with Lizzy."

"So, with the blonde dead," Hanrick continued, "and that scum in Kingman taken care of, I decided I needed to see my pretty visitor again without a big slab of Plexiglas in between us. And pretty soon, she ventured out of the casita. You'll never guess why."

Hanrick paused, waiting for a response.

"Why?"

"My guess is her phone was dead and she'd lost her power cord, and what teenage girl can stand having a dead phone? So she ventures out to get a power cord, and we met up with her in a hotel parking lot in Sedona."

"Let me talk with her."

"Once we got the phone plugged in, it was chock full of interesting information," continued Hanrick. "Actually, I was surprised that she only had six entries in her Contacts list. *Andy. Daisy. Philip. Philip Work. Ruby. Uncle Owen.* I don't know much about teenage girls—at least not about what contacts they store in their phones," he said with a leer in his voice, "but six entries was a lot less than I had expected. But fewer contacts was better —easier to find the one I might want to contact myself. Get a little cash to start my new life in exchange for the girl."

"How do I know you have her unless I talk to her?"

"*Uncle Owen* seemed promising. *Ruby* and *Andy* might be friends, although Ruby seemed like an unusual name for a girl her age. But *Philip* was interesting because there were two entries—and *Philip Work* at least suggested an adult. I thought I'd give *Philip Work* a call, see if I could find out a little more about him. And you know what I heard?"

Hanrick paused again.

"What?"

"Philip Castillo, psychic counselor, inviting me to leave a message. You can just imagine how tickled I was. Philip Castillo. Philip Casal. I'd recognize the voice of Oscar Riva's Indian sidekick anywhere. I thought to myself, Tobe, old boy, your re-entry into civilian life is going to be even more fun than you had anticipated. What do you think about that, Casal?"

"I think you better give me a reason to think you actually have her."

"Oh, I have her, but she's not in a talking state at the moment. Clothesline around the neck, courtesy of Clemson—

although unlike with the Swede, I made sure he stopped in time with Lizzy."

"You better be sure no harm comes to her."

Hanrick gave a rough laugh. "You're talking a big game considering you have zero leverage in this situation. Although," he continued, "I might be willing to consider a swap. Miss Lizzy for Philip Casal. You and I could chat about our mutual friend Oscar Riva."

"Where are you?" Philip asked.

"I'm surprised you need me to tell you, if you're so psychic."

"I'm not that kind of psychic."

Hanrick snorted. "Too bad for you. You know the abandoned trailer park up 89A from Sedona?"

"Yeah, I know it."

"Go there."

"I'm an hour away."

"What are you doing so far away on a school night? Lizzy might have needed help with her homework."

Philip bit back a retort. "I had business to take care of."

"Philip Castillo, psychic counselor, does house calls? That's perfect. I think I need some psychic counseling, and I need it quick. You better start driving now. If I'm here with Miss Lizzy for too long, I might rethink the swap." said Hanrick. "And you better be alone."

The call disconnected.

56

───────

Lizzy woke to a grating pain in her throat. Her head was tilted at an awkward angle, and when she tried to raise it, a hot bolt of pain shot from her neck down her arm. She groaned, and heard a soft sound that she realized was a chuckle.

"Crick in your neck, sweetheart?"

She jerked at the voice. She tried to raise her hands to block the presence she could sense but not see, but they were immobilized—tied or taped to the arms of the chair in which she sat. Her ankles were bound, too—one to each chair leg. Something was tied over her eyes, and a wad of cloth was stuffed in her mouth.

And she was so cold. She could tell from the echo of Tobe Hanrick's words that they were inside, but there must have been a door or window open because she could feel the icy fingers of a breeze across her raw neck. She was still wearing her coat, but her body was seizing with shivers.

She jumped again when she heard Hanrick's voice just a couple of feet away from her.

"Guess you won't need this way down here in the canyon."

She gasped and tears sprang to her eyes as the tape that had been holding the gag in place was ripped from her cheeks.

"Can't wait until Casal gets here."

"Philip's coming?" she said, trying to sort through the confusion of thoughts in her head.

"What makes you think that?" he asked, and she realized he hadn't spoken the comment about Philip out loud—she had heard it in his thoughts. She clamped her lips together. In the parking lot behind the hotel, she had perceived his thoughts as spoken words—that had been her downfall. Now she had fallen into the same trap again, and that could be Philip's downfall. If she couldn't tell the difference between what Tobe said out loud and what he said only in his mind, she would stay silent. What danger had she put Philip in by mentioning his name?

"What's the matter, sweetheart? You were so chatty when you visited me at Williams. Gotten shy all of a sudden? That would be quite a disappointment."

He continued to talk, his tone more than his words filling her with dread, but it was his thoughts that made her stomach churn. She tried to turn her attention away from them, as she might turn away from the sight of a twisted deer carcass by the side of the road. But she couldn't block the poisonous monologue that filtered from his brain to hers.

Eventually, she thought she could distinguish his thoughts from his speech by a slight fuzziness attached to the unspoken words.

As he talked, she tried to piece together what had happened. He and the person who had choked her must have followed her from the casita to the hotel. She remembered Tobe trying to get the van door open, then making a reference to using a car for their getaway instead. Was the van still sitting behind the hotel on Sedona's main drag? Once Andy got to the casita and realized she was gone, he would go looking for her, and there was a tiny possibility he would find it, although she couldn't imagine what good that would do her.

"What did you do with my van?" she asked.

"Don't you worry about your wheels, my man Clemson's taking care of it," he said, and then she heard, *and then he's going to come back here and make sure no one bothers us.*

Clemson must have been the person whose thoughts she had heard as the muttering sound right before the noose slipped around her neck.

She had to keep Tobe talking. Not only was there a chance she'd hear something that would help her or Philip, but talking with him—odious as it was—was preferable to the other activities she could see passing through his thoughts.

"Do you know Clemson from prison?" she asked.

"Yeah. He's dumb as a concrete block, but faithful as a beaten dog."

"Do you know Philip Casal from prison?" She had already given away that she knew Philip, she figured that asking about him couldn't make things worse.

"Indeed I do," he replied, "Phil and I were like brothers." He gave a nasty laugh. "Cain and Abel."

"I can't remember which was which," she said.

"Oh, I'd say I'm Cain and he's Abel," he said. "And I don't much mind a life of wandering."

"Wandering?"

"Not much of a Bible scholar, are you, Lizzy."

Somehow the fact that he knew her real name broke her resolve, and she gulped back a sob.

"Poor little Lizzy," murmured Hanrick. "You and Phil must be pretty ... tight. You asked before if he was coming." She flinched at the sound of the click of a lighter, then smelled the tang of cigarette smoke. She heard a long exhale. "Oh, yeah. He's coming. And it'll be just like the old days when he arrives." He gave a rough cough. "Except for you, of course. We didn't have pretty girls like you at Williams." He laughed again. "It will make a nice change of pace."

57

The speedometer of Wayne's battered Sunbird hovered near ninety, and Philip prayed there weren't troopers patrolling tonight—or that the car didn't spontaneously disintegrate, as a chorus of rattles and squeaks suggested it might.

"I don't know why you're doing the driving," said Wayne, bent over his work.

"I'll get us there faster."

"I'll say." Wayne glanced up at the road. "I hope some cow doesn't pick now to cross the road—we'd be cooked if we hit one at this speed."

"You're going to be cooked if you don't shut up and let me concentrate," growled Philip.

Wayne was holding Philip's left boot and picking a seam out of the top with a small pocket knife. After a few minutes, he retrieved a much larger knife from the glove compartment and slipped the blade into the opening at the top of the boot. He held it up for Philip's inspection.

"How's that?"

Philip glanced over. "Looks good."

Wayne pulled the knife in and out of the boot a few times. "You don't think he'll find it?"

"I'll have the gun in the shoulder holster—I'll throw that one away when he tells me to disarm. If someone pats me down, they'll find the one in the ankle holster, and I'm hoping they'll think that's it and won't look further."

"If they pat you down, they'll find the knife, too."

"If they see I'm right-handed, they'll likely pat down my right leg first, and if someone is close enough to pat me down, they'll be close enough to get a knife into."

"You won't be able to get to the knife fast if you have your pant leg pulled over it."

"Thanks, Wayne," said Philip tightly. "You let me know when you have a better idea."

They were silent for a few minutes, Wayne fussing with the knife and boot. Then Philip asked, "How well do you know Sedona?"

Wayne put the boot on the floor and pulled his gun out of its holster. "Not really my neck of the woods."

"The trailer park where he says he has her has been abandoned for years."

"I'm surprised anywhere around Sedona would be abandoned with all those tourists."

"It's about a mile north of town, and it's pretty deep in the canyon. It's shaded for most of the day, and tourists come for the sun."

"Anything nearby?"

"No." Philip's first thought had been that the trailer park would provide the privacy Hanrick no doubt wanted for the evening's events. His stomach rolled and he took a deep breath. "The only flat piece of ground in that section is the highway. Cliffs straight up on one side, and then just a little strip of land between the highway and the creek that the trailer park sits on."

"Might not have needed my silencer," said Wayne, fiddling with the mechanism attached to his gun.

"Better safe than sorry." After a moment, Philip added, "It won't be quiet in the canyon—the water's running high in the creek, and that makes a lot of noise. That will be in our favor. Easier for you to sneak up on him. I'll let you out near my office in Sedona, then you hustle up there."

"You want me to walk along a road that's cliffs on one side and a river on the other in the dark?"

"You're willing to help me kill Tobe Hanrick, but you're not willing to walk along a country road at night?"

Wayne sighed. "Okay. Fine."

"In any case, you should stay in the woods, or along the creek." Philip pulled into the left lane to pass a car doing seventy. "You might get to take out Hanrick all by yourself."

"What about Clemson?"

"Take them all out."

"Do we need to call in reinforcements?"

"There's no time."

They drove in silence for several minutes, then Philip said, "If Hanrick says he'll let the girl go in exchange for me, do you think he'll do it?"

Wayne snorted. "Hanrick? That bastard?"

"He's a bastard, but think about it—have you ever heard of him going back on something he said he'd do?"

Wayne thought for a few moments, then said, almost reluctantly, "No, can't say I've ever heard that."

"It's like that story about Manny Ortega and his wife. Hanrick promised Ortega he'd leave his wife alone, and he did."

"Yeah, but look what he did to Manny."

"Yeah. I remember."

They were silent again, then Wayne said, "So, what, you're

just going to walk into his hideout, watch the girl walk away, then let Hanrick do whatever he wants to you?"

"That's not how I'm hoping it goes down."

"But if it comes down to that?"

Philip blazed past another car. He felt his stomach roll again and hoped he wouldn't have to pull over to be sick.

"Yeah, if it comes down to that, that's what I'll do."

58

———

The Uptown Sedona streets were largely deserted, so the man jogging painfully toward the center of the tourist strip stood out. He was tall and thin, and as he drew nearer to the car in which Owen and Andy sat, he passed under a streetlight and they could see the sores spotted across his face and the rotting teeth in a mouth gasping for air.

"Methhead marathon?" said Andy.

Owen shook his head. "Who knows."

Ten minutes later, Andy, who had been watching the oncoming traffic in the driver's side mirror, sat forward. "Here comes a white van."

The van passed them, a silver scrape clearly visible on the passenger side.

"That's her!" exclaimed Owen.

Andy turned the key in the ignition.

"She's not stopping at Philip's office," said Owen.

"Maybe it's not her driving," said Andy.

Owen fidgeted with the fringe on a maroon scarf draped around his neck. "Let it get a little bit up the road before you follow it. We won't lose it—once it's out of town, there aren't any turns you can make off the highway."

They waited about thirty seconds, then Andy pulled out.

They could see the van ahead of them, its taillights appearing and disappearing as the road wound along the edge of Oak Creek canyon. After about a mile, the van slowed and pulled off the road.

"Keep going," said Owen.

As they passed, a man got out of the vehicle.

"Shit," said Andy. "That's marathon man."

Owen watched in the passenger side mirror as the man unhooked the chain that crossed the rough gravel drive. "What in the world is going on?" he said, his voice thready with panic.

About a hundred yards further on they came to a turnout which, in the daylight, was no doubt a scenic overlook.

"Turn the lights off so they don't see us pulling over," whispered Owen.

Andy turned off the headlights and pulled into the turnout. "You don't have to whisper," he said.

They climbed out of the car. Through the trees that lined the banks of the canyon, they could see the car lights below them, flickering as the intervening branches moved in the slight breeze. A moment later, the lights went off.

"What's down there?" asked Andy.

"An abandoned trailer park, if I remember correctly."

"I'm going to sneak down there and see what's going on," said Andy.

"No, it's too dangerous," said Owen.

"Do you remember if Lizzy has her phone set to ring or just to vibrate?"

"She usually has it set to ring. Why?"

"Wait a few minutes and try calling her number again. If I'm close enough, maybe I'll hear if it's ringing in the van. That would suggest that she might be in there, too."

"But you and I should stay on the line so I can hear if you need help."

"That would be great if we had multiple phones."

"I should come with you," said Owen.

"You shouldn't even be out here, let alone slogging through the woods. Plus, who's going to call in the cavalry if things go tits up? I'll open a call if there's trouble, and even if I can't talk, you can hear what's going on."

"Maybe we should call the cavalry now."

"Let's play the scenario out," said Andy. "Let's just say Lizzy's down there. We call the cops and tell them that we think your goddaughter is being held against her will in some abandoned trailer park. In the worst case scenario, they dick around until it's too late anyway. In the best case scenario—a heavily caveated 'best'—they come roaring in in force with guns drawn, and there's Lizzy, the Queen of Squeeze, right in the middle of the most stressful situation you could imagine. Seems like we're setting up a scenario that could result in a whole lot of cranial carnage."

Owen was silent, gazing miserably into the dark woods toward where the van had disappeared.

"Or," Andy continued, "let's say Lizzy's not down there at all. Maybe she went to the grocery store to pick up some supplies to greet the arrival of her favorite godfather-once-removed and these guys stole the van. Now the cops are pissed—and have a whole lot of awkward questions for us—because they rolled the big iron thinking they had a kidnapping on their hands and all they got for it was a car thief."

"That seems like an unlikely scenario," said Owen.

"This whole situation is an unlikely scenario. In fact, Lizzy's got the unlikeliest defense of all—the ability to squeeze anyone who tries to hurt her."

"Maybe they knocked her out—maybe she's unconscious."

"If she's unconscious, maybe it means we have a couple of minutes to figure out what to do. And if she regains consciousness before we get there, heaven help the people who grabbed her."

Owen prepared to mount a counterargument, but then deflated. "Okay, fine. But please let me know what's up as soon as you can."

"Will do." Andy stepped over the guardrail that marked the edge of the turnout and disappeared into the woods.

Lizzy heard the approaching rumble of an engine and the crunch of tires on gravel. Then the engine died, and she heard the thump of a door and footsteps outside.

She heard Tobe moving away from her.

"Clem, take a swing through the woods," he called. "Make sure we don't have any midnight hikers exploring the canyon."

"Goddammit, Tobe," a whiney voice from outside called in reply. "I just ran all the way from here to town, and it's cold as hell out here. Can't I come in for a minute and warm up?"

"What do you think, we're running a heater in here? It's just as cold in here as it is out there, you moron."

Lizzy heard a grumbled response, then steps receding from the shack.

Casal better haul ass if he wants to see her in one piece.

59

———

Philip pulled off the highway onto the dirt and gravel road leading deeper into the canyon, to the trailer park and Oak Creek. He was alone in the car now, having dropped Wayne Watchman off just outside of Sedona.

Eventually his headlights picked out the dilapidated wooden structure that had once housed the trailer park's office. A nondescript tan sedan and a white van were parked next to it. He coasted to a stop and got out of the car.

"Turn the engine off," came Hanrick's voice from the dark hole of the shack's doorway. "But leave the lights on."

Philip reached into the car and turned off the ignition.

"Step to the front of the car."

He stepped to the front, the headlights throwing his shadow across the broken concrete of the parking area and into the trees beyond the shack.

"Got a gun?" asked Hanrick.

"Yes."

"Drop it."

Philip pulled his gun out of the shoulder holster and put it on the ground.

"Kick it away."

Philip kicked it in the direction of the shack.

"Strip."

"Why?"

Hanrick's horrible laugh came from the shack. "Don't get your hopes up—probably not for the reasons you think. Probably," he added, a grin in his voice. "But just because you dropped one gun doesn't mean you're not carrying another one."

Philip shrugged out of his jacket and unbuttoned his shirt as slowly as he dared, his mind racing to try to accommodate the developing situation. He pulled his T-shirt over his head.

"Got yourself in a little trouble, did you, Casal?"

It took Philip a moment to realize that Hanrick was referring to the bullet wound on his shoulder, the skin still discolored and puckered around the stitches.

"You should see the other guy," replied Philip.

Hanrick laughed again. "Philip Casal, always the joker."

Philip pulled his boots off, angling his body to keep the knife protruding from the left boot out of Hanrick's line of sight, and dropped the boot knife-side down.

No comment from Hanrick.

He pulled off his socks, then unzipped and dropped his jeans, revealing the ankle holster.

He heard another laugh from the shadows. "Nice try."

He unfastened the ankle holster and tossed it toward the shack.

"Quite an arsenal you've got there."

Philip hooked his fingers into the waistband of his briefs, his heart hammering.

Hanrick stepped out of the shack, a gun in his hand. "That's enough. I can see you don't have anything in there."

Philip took a deep breath, trying not let his overwhelming

relief that he didn't have to face Tobe Hanrick naked show, trying not to shiver in the near-freezing air.

Hanrick picked up the two guns and, keeping his own gun trained on Philip, went to the tan sedan, popped the trunk, dropped them in, and slammed the trunk closed.

"What's with this *Castillo* shit?" asked Hanrick. "Building castles in the air?"

"Where's Lizzy?" asked Philip.

"The driver's license is good," said Hanrick. "Kamy?"

Philip remained silent.

Hanrick shrugged. "It looks like a Kamy product. I'm guessing you called in a favor to get your girlfriend a fake ID."

"She's not my girlfriend, she's a client. Where is she?"

Hanrick ignored his question. "You're going to an awful lot of trouble for a client."

"She's in the trouble she's in because of me."

"Not just a joker, but a man of honor. I always detested that about you."

"Where is she?" Philip said again.

Hanrick gestured with his gun toward the derelict office. "She's in there. Take a look."

Philip glanced toward the building. "Can I put my boots on?" The debris-littered ground between where he stood and the building made the request a reasonable one.

Hanrick snorted. "I'm surprised that the Philip Casal I knew turned into such a delicate snowflake after getting out of the joint. Sure, why not. Plus, the opportunity to see you in your skivvies and your fancy boots is something I can't pass up."

Philip pulled his boots on and walked toward the building. Hanrick was standing to the right of the door, so it was easy to keep the knife out of his sight. A flicker of hope lit in Philip's gut.

He stepped through the door of the office, Hanrick a judicious distance behind him. The inside was lit faintly by the

Sunbird's headlights. The room was largely empty, save for a wooden desk pushed into a corner and a metal filing cabinet lying on its side on top of it.

Then a flashlight, trained on Lizzy, lit the interior. She sat in the center of the room, her wrists and ankles duct taped to the arms and legs of a decrepit desk chair, a dirty bandana covering her eyes. Above the collar of her shirt, he could see an angry welt on her neck, and red patches on either side of her mouth where tape had no doubt been roughly pulled off. Her shoulders were hunched up to her ears, in either a defensive reflex or an attempt to keep warm. It was, if anything, colder in the building than it was outside.

"Jesus. Lizzy."

"Hi, Philip," she said, her voice unsteady.

He took a step toward her.

"What do you think you're doing?" said Hanrick.

"I need to see if she's okay."

"Forget it, Florence Nightingale. If I'd done anything to her yet, you'd be able to tell from where you're standing."

Philip turned from Hanrick back to Lizzy. "Are you all right?"

"Yes. So far."

He was wondering how Hanrick could have grabbed her without ending up with a brain riddled with bleeds when she said, "I don't think I've been causing Mr. Hanrick any headaches."

He was confused for a moment, then remembered what she had told him—the mind-reading ability that the crush drug had triggered in her.

"She's been a good girl," interjected Hanrick.

Could Lizzy read Hanrick's mind?

"I have a pretty good idea what he's thinking," said Lizzy a moment later, her voice breaking on the last word.

"I'll *bet* she has a pretty good idea," said Hanrick.

"So, what now?" asked Philip.

"You and I get ourselves straightened out," said Hanrick, "and then I drop little Miss Lizzy off behind some tourist shop in Sedona none the worse for wear, and I disappear again. Actually, though," Hanrick continued, "I might give Uncle Owen a call before that. Uncle Owen calls little Lizzy a lot. Once I'm done with you, I might see if Uncle Owen would be willing to give me some cash in exchange for Liz."

"You said you wouldn't hurt her."

"I did. But he doesn't know that."

At that moment, a muffled gunshot cracked out from the woods, followed by a shrieked "Goddammit!"

Hanrick's head turned toward the door of the office, and Philip pulled the knife from his boot and lunged.

Hanrick turned back and brought the gun up. Philip, frantic to avoid a replay of his encounter with George Millard, spun to the side. He expected to hear a gunshot, but then realized with self-loathing that he was so far from Hanrick that Hanrick hadn't even bothered to fire.

When he regained his balance, Hanrick had the gun pointed at Lizzy.

"I wouldn't do that again if I were you," said Hanrick, his eyes dead.

"Okay."

"Take the boots off."

Philip was still holding the knife, but had no intention of throwing it away before he was forced to. He pulled the boots off and tossed them away.

"Sit on the ground."

Philip sat.

Hanrick circled Philip, careful to stay out of the range of another lunge. Philip followed him with his eyes and, as Hanrick passed directly behind him, Philip turned his head to keep him in view.

"Philip, he's going to—" Lizzy screamed.

Philip felt an explosion of pain burst from his back, and barely heard Lizzy's "—kick you!"

Philip fell to his side, then rolled to the other side, trying to avoid another kick and sending a scream of protest up from his shoulder. Hanrick followed him. Philip tried to grab Hanrick's legs, but Hanrick jumped back again.

"Your head!" yelled Lizzy.

Philip managed to twist his head to avoid the full force of Hanrick's next kick, but even the glancing blow lit his vision with bright white. He tried to stand and Hanrick landed another kick, dropping him to the ground.

"Your wrist!" yelled Lizzy.

Before Philip could snatch his hand back, Hanrick's boot came down on his wrist and the knife was ripped from his hand.

Another shot cracked out from the woods, and another scream, then two more shots.

Then silence.

Philip lay on his side, gasping.

Hanrick stepped to the door of the office and peered out, eyes and gun scanning the woods. A minute ticked by, then two, Philip trying to control the shivers that wracked his body as the cold concrete floor sucked away his body's warmth. The only sounds were his own and Lizzy's ragged breathing.

Finally, Hanrick said, "I expected you to bring a knife, knowing your history. I see you brought along a friend as well."

"So did you," replied Philip hoarsely.

"Yes, but if you wanted to save your *client*, you should have played by my rules, and I told you to come alone."

"The shot will bring the cops."

"There's no one to hear it, way down here in the canyon."

Hanrick strode to Lizzy and shone the flashlight on her face.

"Can you see through that thing?" He grabbed her chin and jerked her head to one side and then the other, evidently looking for a gap in the blindfold's coverage.

"No," she sobbed.

"Little Miss Lizzy is quite an expert at street fighting," he said. "I might need to keep her around just for that."

"Or maybe you're just predictable," said Philip, trying to distract Hanrick's attention from Lizzy.

Hanrick stepped behind Lizzy and jerked the blindfold tighter.

Just then, they heard a cry from outside. "Tobe? Tobe!"

Hanrick grabbed Philip's arm and jerked him to his feet, twisting his arm behind his back and shoving him toward the door. Philip felt the sutures binding the gunshot wound tear. They stepped outside, Hanrick holding Philip in front of him as a shield.

There was a crashing from the trees and Hanrick swung Philip and his gun toward it. A tall, thin man appeared at the edge of the clearing, his hands clamped to his neck, blood running from between his fingers and down his arm. It wasn't Wayne.

"What the hell, Clemson," growled Hanrick.

Clemson staggered toward them. "I thought you said Casal was coming alone," he said, his voice almost a shriek. "He brought Wayne Watchman with him!"

"Where's Watchman now?" asked Hanrick.

"Lying back there," said Clemson, gesturing toward the woods with an elbow. "Dead," he added.

Hanrick stepped away from the door, still scanning the woods. "I thought *you* said you could make sure Casal didn't bring any uninvited guests."

"I can't watch the whole goddamned trailer park while you

play with him and the girl," whined Clemson. "I need a doc, Tobe. He shot me in the *neck*, for God's sake."

Hanrick hooked his foot around Philip's ankle and shoved him hard. Philip sprawled on the ground and rolled just in time to see Hanrick raise his gun toward Clemson. Another silencer-muffled shot thumped out, and Clemson dropped to the ground. "No excuse for sloppy workmanship," said Hanrick gaily.

He turned back to Philip and switched his gun to his left hand and pulled Philip's knife out from where he had slipped it into his own belt. The blade glittered in the headlights of Philip's car. Hanrick walked to him, put his foot on Philip's injured shoulder, and shoved, rolling Philip onto his back.

Philip bit back a scream.

Hanrick put his foot on Philip's other shoulder and shoved again, so that Philip was now lying on his injured shoulder.

Then he bent over and put the tip of the knife gently on Philip's left shoulder. "That's quite a tat you've got there, Casal." He traced the tattoo—an elaborate castle that stretched the length of Philip's bicep, with letters worked into the ornately rendered doors—with the tip of the knife. "*O-R*. That wouldn't be Oscar Riva, would it?"

"Yes," croaked Philip.

"That's so sweet that you got a tattoo in his memory. Or maybe you got it before he died?"

"After."

"How touching. And I recall you became quite good friends with old Oscar's granddaughter—what was her name?"

"None of your goddamned business," said Philip, and he tried not to cry out as the tip of the knife sank into his arm.

"Don't be difficult, Casal," said Hanrick conversationally. "Because when I send that tattoo to Riva's granddaughter, I want to make sure I address the package right."

"Stop it!" came a scream from the shack. "Stop hurting him!"

60

———

"Jesus," sighed Hanrick. He pushed himself off Philip and straightened.

Philip had turned toward the shack, and so he didn't see the kick coming. The air whooshed out of his lungs and he heard what he thought might be the snap of a rib. He drew his knees up, frantic for a lungful of air, trying to protect his ribs from another kick.

"Don't go anywhere," said Hanrick. He stepped away from Philip and toward the shack.

"You said you wouldn't hurt her," Philip gasped.

"Sure, but I didn't bank on her being such a goddamned pain in the ass," said Hanrick. "I'm having second thoughts."

"Leave him alone!" Lizzy yelled.

"Lizzy, be quiet!" Philip yelled back as loud as his breathless lungs would allow.

"I won't be quiet!" Over the rush of the creek, he could hear thumping noises, as if she were rocking the chair she was tied to. "Let me go!"

Hanrick crossed his arms and smiled. "Little hellcat, ain't

she? Are you really telling me that she was just a client? Maybe she's the one who gave you that boo-boo on your shoulder."

"You're a bully! You're a bastard!" she yelled. "You're a miserable excuse for a human being!"

Hanrick shook his head. "That's it. All bets are off. You expect me to just ignore such insults?" He turned back to Philip. "But don't worry, Casal—I'll take care of you first, so you don't have to be around to see what happens to Miss Lizzy." He bent over Philip. "Now hold still, I want it to be a nice clean cut for Riva's granddaughter."

He had failed. He hadn't saved Lizzy—he had condemned her to the same horrible fate that he himself was about to suffer. And gotten Wayne killed in the process.

He tried to roll away, hoping that he could at least do some damage to Hanrick before Hanrick started in with the knife, but Hanrick jerked him back and pinned him to the ground with his knees.

He couldn't get away, but he was damned if he was going to give Hanrick the pleasure of seeing him shut his eyes.

"Now!" Lizzy screamed from the shack. "He's going to hurt Philip! Do it now!"

From the corner of his eye, behind Hanrick's back, Philip saw a form barrel out from behind the corner of the shack and crash into Hanrick.

His first thought was that Wayne must have survived the encounter with Clemson after all, but the person wrestling with Hanrick looked too tall. And too red-haired. It looked, in fact, like Andy McNally.

Philip tried to extricate himself from the pile of humanity on top of him, triggering another bolt of pain from his shoulder. He tried to figure out where the knife was, to see if he could grab it, but as far as he could tell, it was trapped between Hanrick and

McNally. He tried to see where Hanrick's gun was, but he couldn't see it in his waistband.

The two men rolled off Philip and out of the pool of light cast by the car's headlights, accompanied by a barrage of grunting and swearing. Philip dragged himself to his feet, the pain from his ribs doubling him over, and looked around frantically for something to use as a weapon. His right arm was out of commission again, and Hanrick would barely notice a kick from his bare feet. There were rocks by the water—if he could get a rock and get behind Hanrick—

There was a yelp from the shadows. Definitely not Hanrick. If Hanrick had stabbed McNally, Philip didn't have much time to make sure the scene didn't end with Hanrick having three people at his mercy instead of two.

He staggered toward the water and banged his foot into something hard and round. He dropped to his knees and scrabbled at the ground with his left hand.

He had managed to pry the rock out of the frozen ground when suddenly the sounds of the struggle stopped, and he heard a whoosh of expelled air. He knew that sound only too well—the sound a man makes when he's been stabbed. The sound Oscar Riva had no doubt made when Tobe Hanrick had sunk a knife into his guts in the Williams lunch line.

But which one was it—Hanrick or McNally?

Philip stood in the shadows, his heart pounding, waiting for the victor to emerge.

Then Hanrick stepped into the pool of light.

Philip was about to turn and run. Maybe he could lead Hanrick into the woods, maybe he could get Wayne's gun, maybe he could circle back to check on McNally and free Lizzy.

Then he saw the red stain spreading down Hanrick's shirt from just below his ribcage. Hanrick's hands were wrapped around the handle of the knife that protruded from his stomach.

Hanrick took a few weaving steps toward Philip's car. He had almost made it when, with a horrible gasping rattle, he fell to his knees. Philip stepped out of the shadows and advanced on him. Hanrick reached for the hood of the car, missed, and went tumbling onto his side.

Philip crouched down beside him, grabbed the knife, and wrenched it out of Hanrick's stomach. Hanrick shrieked and tried to roll away, but Philip dropped to his knees on Hanrick's torso.

"Look me in the eyes, you bastard," he said.

Hanrick looked up, his eyes wide. He tried to say something, but only brought a froth of blood to his lips.

Philip plunged the knife into Hanrick's carotid artery, then rolled off him to avoid the arc of blood that pulsed out of his neck and, after a few seconds, slowed to a dark red trickle.

Philip heard a sound and whirled back toward the van as a tall, red-haired figure staggered out from behind the open van door, a maroon scarf grasped in its hand.

"Philip?" called the figure. "My God, what did he do to you?"

Then Owen McNally crumpled to the ground in a very large heap.

61

———

Philip spun at the sound of someone approaching—none too quietly—from the woods. How many people were out there? He had the knife, but he would have preferred to have a gun.

"It's Andy!" called Lizzy from the shack.

A moment later, Andy McNally emerged from the woods.

"How're you doing, Philip?" he said as he made a beeline for Owen.

"I'm okay," Philip replied. "I'll check on Lizzy."

He limped to the shack as Andy bent over Owen.

The interior of the shack was still illuminated by the flashlight, which Hanrick had set on the desk. "Lizzy, are you okay?"

"Yes, I'm fine," she said. "Put on some clothes before you freeze to death."

"How do you know I'm—" he began, somewhat embarrassed, then stopped. "Never mind."

Philip set aside the knife and scrambled into his clothes, trying to ignore the stab of pain from his ribs. He was slowed by the shaking of his hands that was equal parts cold and adrenaline. When he was dressed, he went to Lizzy and pulled off the blindfold.

Despite the souvenirs of her encounter with Hanrick—the welt on her neck, the angry marks on her cheeks from the tape from a gag, and her trussed state—she looked relieved, even calm.

It seemed wrong to use the knife he had just used to kill Tobe Hanrick to cut the tape that bound her to the chair, and he was trying to think what else he could use when Lizzy said, "It's okay, you can use that knife."

This was going to take some getting used to.

He wiped the blade on his pants and cut the ties at her wrists and ankles. When she was free, he took her by the upper arms and looked in her eyes. "You're sure you're okay?"

"Yes, he didn't do anything to me. Although he would have if you hadn't shown up and rescued me."

Philip gave a bitter laugh. "I'm pretty sure I would have ended up doing more harm than good if you hadn't helped me out, but let's save that argument for later. We need to make sure there aren't any other friends of Hanrick around."

"There aren't. It was just him and Clemson."

"None other that you know about—" he began, then stopped. "If they had been thinking about another accomplice, you would know, right?"

"Right."

"Then let's check on Owen."

"He's okay, he's waking up."

"He's coming around," Andy called from outside the building.

Philip helped Lizzy up and they stepped outside to find Owen sitting up, pale and woozy-looking, supported by Andy. A rough bandage, evidently fashioned from Andy's shirt, was tied around Owen's thigh.

Lizzy ran to Owen, her gait a little uneven. She fell to her knees and wrapped her arms around him. "Uncle Owen, you saved us."

Owen gave a wobbly smile. "And then fainted dead away."

"I don't think the wound is too serious," said Andy.

"Thanks to my protective layer of fat," offered Owen gamely.

"Thanks to the fact that, much to my surprise, you turn out to be a pro at hand-to-hand combat," said Andy.

Philip waited for the snarky addendum, but it didn't come. Instead, Andy looked around the group and asked, "What now?"

"We should check on the guy who came with me," said Philip. "Clemson said he was dead, but he might just be injured."

"What if there are other people out there?" asked Owen, peering nervously into the woods.

"Lizzy says it was only Hanrick and Clemson."

"I'll go," said Andy.

"I'll come with you," said Philip. "Let me get the flashlight."

He retrieved the flashlight from the shack and Andy followed him into the woods.

It didn't take them long to find Wayne, his body slumped over a boulder near the creek. In the light of the flashlight, Philip could see a dark stain on the front of his coat, but Clemson hadn't wanted to count on that being fatal. He had also shot Wayne, execution-style, in the temple.

Philip stood over Wayne Watchman's body, feeling exhausted and useless and horrible. "Son of a bitch," he said. "Son of a bitch."

"We're leaving him here, right?" said Andy.

Philip took a shaky breath. "Yeah."

He turned and followed Andy back to the shack.

Andy checked the bandage on Owen's leg, then said, "I'll

take Owen to the ER in our rental car and you guys can leave in Ruby's van."

"How would we explain what happened to me?" asked Owen.

Andy ran his fingers through his hair. "I don't know, bro, but you got stabbed in the leg. It's not as bad as it could be, but it's going to need more than a Band-Aid."

"We've come this far without attracting undue official attention," said Owen. "I don't want to start now."

"I might have an alternative," said Philip. "A place with a well-equipped clinic that isn't likely to be making any official reports."

"Where's that?" asked Andy.

"I'd rather not say. It's a couple of hours away, but I can make a phone call and have people—and medical supplies—meet us halfway."

They looked at Owen.

"Philip, are you really all right?" Owen asked. "It looked like —well—" he broke off, casting a glance toward Lizzy.

"Uncle Owen, I know what he was doing to Philip, even if I couldn't see it."

"I'm fine," said Philip.

"You're not fine," said Lizzy.

"I'm fine enough."

"And Lizzy, you're really okay?" asked Owen.

"Yes, Uncle Owen, I really am. You guys showed up before he could do anything to me."

"And I'm fine as well," said Owen. "If someone can just help me up."

Philip, whose ribs were becoming increasingly bothersome, let Andy and Lizzy hoist Owen to his feet and get him seated on the floor of the back of the van.

Andy looked around the clearing. "How about the car you came in, Philip?"

"It belonged to Wayne. I'll wipe down anything I touched and we can leave it here."

"How about blood on the ground?" asked Andy.

"I don't think I bled onto the ground, and even if I did, at this point it would be so mixed up with Hanrick's blood that I don't see what we could do about it. How about Owen?"

"Not much blood," said Andy, "and even if he did leave some behind, they wouldn't be able to ID him with it, right? Unless," he said to Owen, "you did some time for street fighting that I'm not aware of."

Philip looked toward Lizzy. "Lizzy? Anything you might be leaving behind?"

She shook her head. "I don't think so."

"The ideal scenario," said Philip, "is that someone eventually finds Hanrick and Clemson and Wayne—might be tomorrow, might not be for a couple of days—and figures that it was an ex-con reunion gone wrong. They'll probably figure it was more than just the three of them, but there's nothing to tie it to any of us."

"It's pretty close to your office, and to where you live."

"Pretty close to Philip Castillo, but not to Philip Casal, who's the person who might have motive to kill Hanrick and Clemson. They could dig up the connection eventually, but I don't think I'm going back home or to work anytime soon. Let's get somewhere safe and then figure out the details."

Lizzy helped Philip wipe down Wayne's car, while Andy, at Lizzy's suggestion, unfolded the mattress in the back of the van for Owen. Philip gathered up the several guns and knives that Wayne had had in the trunk of the Sunbird, as well as the gun Hanrick had been carrying and the ones he'd put in the trunk of the tan sedan, and deposited them in the back of the van.

They piled into the van, Andy driving, Philip riding shotgun, and Lizzy in the back with Owen. When they got to the overlook where the rental car was parked, Philip said, "Andy, why don't I drive the car and you can follow in the van. Lizzy can stay in back and keep Owen company. If you need to stop for any reason, just flash your lights and we'll pull over. As soon as we're out of the canyon, I'll call to let them know we're coming."

"And the people you're taking us to—they're trustworthy?" asked Andy.

"I'd trust them with my life," said Philip. "In fact, I am trusting them with my life. And yours as well."

"Good enough for me," said Andy.

62

———

Louise, accompanied by Maja, pushed her hands deeper into the pockets of her coat as they walked to the lab. The temperature had plummeted the night before and she could see her breath.

She had had little appetite over the last few days, breakfasting only on tea and toast that morning, much to Maja's disapproval. The dozen tailored dresses now hanging in the closet were beginning to hang a bit loosely on her frame.

They arrived at the lab to find Theo and Edmund seated at one of the lab tables. The men looked up.

"Good morning, Dr. Mortensen," said Edmund.

"Louise," said Theo.

"Gentlemen," replied Louise.

She surrendered her coat to Maja and took a seat at the Mac, resuming her perusal of a cache of draft NIH policy guidelines.

Theo and Edmund turned back to what was evidently an argument about an article Theo had read in *Scientific American*. Actually, she could hardly call it an argument—Edmund clearly didn't agree with what Theo was saying but wouldn't respond with anything more definitive than "perhaps" or "if you say so." She blocked them out as best she could.

The conversation had turned to a piece of lab equipment mentioned in the article that Theo was considering acquiring when a cell phone rang. Louise glanced over at the pair.

Theo pulled his phone out of his pocket and glanced at the screen. "Pardon me," he said, and tapped the screen.

"Hejsan, Hugo," he said. "Hur är läget?"

Louise returned to her perusal of the NIH files, then turned back when Theo spoke again, his voice taut.

"Nej men, va? Vad hände .... När?"

Louise and Edmund exchanged glances.

Theo noticed their looks and rose from the lab stool and hurried toward the door. "Vem kunde ha gjort det åt henne? ... Nej, jag gjorde inte—"

The door closed on the rest of the sentence.

"What was that all about?" asked Edmund.

"I have no idea," said Louise.

She closed the NIH connection, pulled up a browser, and typed in a search: *online swedish lessons*. She couldn't very well ask Theo for a credit card number to purchase a course. She added *free* to the search.

She had completed a few of the online lessons, hurrying through those related to how to greet people or ask for directions, but she was distracted by her curiosity about the cause of Theo's outburst. Finally, she pushed back from the Mac, got out her phone, and pressed zero. Maja took longer than usual to answer.

"Yes, Dr. Mortensen?" she said. Her voice sounded unsteady.

"Maja, you were quite right, I should have had more than just tea and toast. Could you have breakfast sent to the suite, and come down to the lab to escort me back?"

"Certainly, Dr. Mortensen. I'll be there ... as soon as possible."

Louise ended the call and clicked through another lesson while she waited for Maja.

Nine minutes ticked by, then Edmund said, "Taking her longer than usual."

"Yes."

"Something's up."

"Yes."

Another four minutes had elapsed when Maja appeared at the door of the lab.

Louise rose from her seat. "I'll be back in an hour or so," she said to Edmund.

"I'll look forward to picking up our discussion," said Edmund.

Maja's eyes were red. As she stood back to let Louise pass through the door, she exclaimed, "Oj nej, I forgot your coat. Let me run back to the house to get it."

"That's not necessary," said Louise. "It's a short walk."

Louise walked with Maja up the path, resisting crossing her arms against the cold. The lapse seemed to have further rattled Maja, and it took her two tries to enter the correct code into the keypad at the door of the suite.

"Maja, are you all right?" Louise asked as they stepped inside.

"Yes, thank you," said Maja. She glanced distractedly around the suite. "Breakfast may be slightly delayed, but I'll bring you some tea to warm up."

"Maja, there's something wrong—what is it?"

"It's Rey ..."

"Theo's niece?"

"Yes. She's ..." Maja pulled a tissue from the pocket of her coat and blotted her nose. "She's dead."

"Dead? What happened?"

"Herr Viklund didn't tell me many details. But his brother—Rey's father—called to tell him. She was murdered." A tear trickled down her cheek and she blotted it away quickly.

"Murdered?" exclaimed Louise. "Good heavens."

"Rey worked for Herr Viklund," said Maja. "She was his ... sergeant?"

"Second-in-command?"

"Yes, second-in-command. Not yet, you understand—she was still so young," she blotted her eyes again, "but eventually. He is quite upset."

"Yes, I can imagine."

"We are all quite upset. We were all quite ... I can't think of the word ... förtjust."

"Fond?"

"Yes, fond. We were all quite fond of her."

"I only met her a few times," said Louise, "but I can imagine I would have grown fond of her as well."

"Yes, she would have been company for you." Then, perhaps feeling she had said too much, she glanced nervously around the room and returned the tissue to her pocket. "I'll check on the breakfast."

"Please don't rush. I know you and the rest of the household have other things to worry about at the moment."

"It is no trouble," said Maja. "It is good for everyone to have normal things to do. And to stay out of Herr Viklund's way."

She disappeared through the door and Louise could hear her steps hurrying down the hall.

Louise went to the window and gazed out at the woods. The wind tossed the tops of the trees and a cloud slipped in front of the sun, dimming the light.

So it was to be just her, Theo, and Edmund. There had been

few enough members in Theo's little coterie. Now there was one less.

Despite the warmth of the room, she shivered and crossed her arms.

63

The morning sun was slanting in the window of the clinic room as Andy wrapped up the story of his and Owen's trip to Sedona and their arrival at Oak Creek. Owen lay in bed, propped up against a mound of pillows, a faded quilt covering his legs. Lizzy sat in a chair next to his bed. Philip's chair was tipped back against the wall, his arm in a sling that one of the clinic staffers had insisted he wear.

"I got pretty close to the van," said Andy. "Close enough that I could have heard a cell phone ringing if it hadn't been for the creek being so close by, and so noisy. I not only couldn't hear a cell phone, but even though I could hear voices, I couldn't tell what they were saying, or who they were. I was going to open a call to Owen so he could listen in, but when I got out my phone I realized I wouldn't have heard a phone ringing even if it hadn't been for the creek—no reception in the canyon.

"Then it turned out I wasn't the only person sneaking through the woods that night. Philip's buddy and Hanrick's sidekick ran into each other—they were only about a hundred feet from where I was—and shot each other."

"I'm sorry about your friend," said Lizzy to Philip.

He nodded. "Yeah. I'm sorry about that, too," he said soberly. "He was a good guy. A good friend to me when I was at Williams."

Andy continued. "I thought maybe I could get a gun from one of them and save the day, but then the sidekick got up and staggered off and pretty soon there was another shot from near the shack. I figured there was still one person out in the woods —dead or at least injured—who had a gun, and was trying to find him in the dark, trying not to make too much noise moving through the brush—when suddenly a fight broke out in front of the shack. I was headed over there, trying to figure out what was going on, when I heard Owen asking Philip if he was all right."

They all turned to Owen, who blushed. "I came down to the trailer park when I realized there was no cell reception, and no other way to find out what was happening."

"And saw that Philip needed a bit of a hand and came to his rescue," said Andy. "And got a knife in the thigh for your trouble. My brother, the Lancelot of Lansdowne."

Owen's blush deepened. "It was really Philip. I just stumbled into the situation ..."

"Are you kidding me?" said Philip. "Owen, you got a knife away from the most badass guy in Arizona. No one else will ever know it was you, but as soon as news hits about what happened to Hanrick, you're going to become a hero to a whole lot of people."

"I really just meant to incapacitate him—"

Philip thumped the front legs of his chair down on the floor, a wince indicating it might not have been the best idea. "Let's argue this through another time—for now, just accept that you saved all of our lives."

Owen nodded with some embarrassment, then said, "I wouldn't have known when to tackle Hanrick if Lizzy hadn't alerted me that it was time."

"You could tell Owen was there because you could read his mind, right?" Andy asked Lizzy.

"Yes."

"Are you reading our minds now?" asked Owen.

"Not so much—it's fading. When I first took the drug, there really wasn't any difference between what people were saying out loud and what they were thinking. I couldn't tell which it was unless I could see their mouths. Now I can still hear some thoughts, but they're more ... whispery, I guess."

"Since it seemed like the squeeze wasn't working when you could read minds, do you feel like that's coming back?" asked Andy.

Lizzy shrugged. "I can't tell."

"What's it like, to hear people's thoughts?" asked Owen. "Is it disturbing?"

She considered. "No, it's not. It's not like I'm seeing into their innermost thoughts—it's more like I'm hearing what they're thinking that's one step away from being said out loud."

Owen shook his head. "Fascinating."

They heard steps approaching along the wooden floor of the clinic hallway. In a moment a woman appeared in the doorway. "Dr. McNally?"

"Yes?" said Owen and Andy.

She laughed. "I'm wondering if the younger Dr. McNally could give us a hand? A man just came in with a metal spike through his foot—our doctor will be here soon, but could you take a look at it until she arrives?"

Andy stood. "Sure thing."

"Thanks." The woman turned to Philip. "It's Sani's nephew."

Philip rolled his eyes. "Why am I not surprised." He levered himself carefully out of the chair. "I'll come along and do introductions."

Philip and Andy followed the woman out of the room.

Owen sighed. "I certainly am tired of lying around in bed."

"Andy says it shouldn't be too long until you're up and about again, but you have to take it easy for now."

"When I can drive, I'm going to McDonald's and ordering two Big Macs just to spite him."

Lizzy laughed. "I don't think that's what the doctor ordered. For anybody."

Owen smiled. "Yeah, I guess you're right." He patted her hand where it lay on the side of the bed, then looked around. "I wonder what this place is."

Lizzy hesitated. "They don't want us to know too much about it."

"Philip certainly has an unusual set of friends."

"A handy set of friends."

"That's for sure." After a moment, he continued. "Listen, Pumpkin—while they're gone, there's something I wanted to say to you." He cleared his throat. "When I stabbed Tobe Hanrick, I was so scared. I didn't know what I was going to do, just that I needed to do something. I couldn't see what was going on with him and Philip, and I couldn't hear much over the noise of the creek, so if you hadn't let me know that something had to be done—right then—I don't think I would have gotten there in time."

"I'm glad you understood what I was trying to tell you. I didn't want to say your name, so that if things didn't work out, he wouldn't know there was someone else there."

He nodded. "I figured if I tackled him, Philip would be able to take care of the rest."

"No, you weren't."

"What?" he asked, confused.

"That's not what you were thinking. You were thinking that Philip and I needed help, and you could help us."

"I don't know about that—"

She shook her finger at him. "But I do."

He laughed weakly. "This is going to make for an interesting relationship." After a moment, he continued. "I guess that when I stabbed Hanrick, part of me did it because I knew it had to be done to get you and Philip out of a pickle, but also because I didn't have any choice. I was thrown into this situation where something bad was happening, and I couldn't do anything but ... what I did."

She nodded sympathetically.

"Does that sound like anyone you know?" he asked.

"Oh." Her eyes widened. "Yeah."

"I've been telling you all your life that you shouldn't feel bad for what you did to Lucia Hazlitt and Anton Rossi and Gerard Bonnay because you didn't have any choice. Well, now I've killed someone—Philip may have struck the coup de grâce, but the stab wound to his gut would have been fatal. And even though I didn't have any choice, I know I'm going to feel bad about it for the rest of my life. I want to apologize to you for ..." He sighed. "For giving you some pretty useless advice. Now I know that feeling bad about it is unavoidable."

"It wasn't useless," she said. "It was good advice. You should take that advice yourself."

"Yes," he said. "I'll try."

They sat in companionable silence until Philip and Andy returned to the room. Philip eased himself back into his chair and Andy leaned against the wall next to one of the windows that overlooked the surrounding desert.

"So, Philip," asked Andy, "what about the guy who sprung you from the hospital? I did a search on *Theo Viklund*—he was in the news a lot a couple of decades ago, but then dropped off the radar, never came out of his compound in western Maryland."

"I think Louise Mortensen is a minor player compared to Viklund," said Philip. "He pulled strings in a lot of places, from small town police departments to the office of an attorney general. I get the impression that he has contacts in all the traditional halls of power—and probably some non-traditional as well—and I think he has even less compunction about wielding that power than Mortensen."

"And now she's working for him?"

"For him ... with him. It's hard to say, but I'll bet that he's the one calling the shots."

"So this is the person we need to be worried about now?" asked Owen.

"Not all of us," said Philip. "I think he's looking to expand his power in other areas, to expand his pool of ..." He searched for the right word. "Operatives? And in doing that, he doesn't want to attract attention to himself and put his existing base of power in jeopardy. That's why I think Owen and Andy are safe. You guys are visible members of a wide professional community, have family ties. That's going to make you less attractive to him as potential allies—whether willing or coerced." He turned to Lizzy. "But Lizzy and I are perfect for him: low profile, with our own reasons for wanting to stay that way, and we each offer something of value to Viklund. Obviously, Lizzy has the squeeze —and who knows what Viklund might know about your mind-reading ability. And I have contacts into a world that is currently closed to him."

Andy spoke up. "If Viklund is the kind of guy who could get murder cases and an AG investigation closed with no help from us, what is he looking to get from you?"

Philip shrugged. "Access to things like Indian casino operations or mineral rights on Indian lands would be a lot easier to manage with a person who looks like me than with the blond-haired, blue-eyed staff he's surrounded himself with. He might even be interested in contacts with first-hand prison experience —obviously it's a world he knows nothing about, since he was able to get the police and AG investigations closed easier than he could figure out how to get me a job at Williams."

"What are you suggesting?" asked Owen anxiously.

"I think you and Andy should go back to Philly and resume life as normal. And keep an eye on Ruby." He turned to Lizzy. "And I think you should stay here with me. In hiding."

"But Lizzy is anxious to get back to Pennsylvania," said Owen. "Right, Pumpkin?"

"I am," she replied, "but not if it's going to put you guys in danger."

"If we're all together, we could figure something out," he said, desperation beginning to creep into his voice.

Lizzy turned to gaze out the window. The three men were quiet as she thought.

Finally, she spoke. "I definitely don't want to be on my own anymore, and I would love to go home as soon as I can, but if I can stay with Philip—maybe just for a little while until we can figure out what's going on, I would be okay with that."

"I don't know ..." began Owen.

"It comes down to what will keep Lizzy safest," said Philip. "Does anyone disagree that she would be safer in hiding out here with someone who knows the area than she would be back in Philadelphia?"

After a moment, Owen shook his head. "No, I don't disagree," he said miserably. He looked to Lizzy. "If you are okay with it, Pumpkin, then I'll try to be okay with it. Hopefully not for too long."

She nodded. "I think it's the best plan."

"I have one more request, dependent on Lizzy's agreement," Philip said, his voice hesitant for the first time. "It sounds like the steroid drug that Mortensen developed to enhance Pieda's squeeze ability triggered the mind-reading ability in Lizzy, and it sounds like it's fading over time. Being able to read minds in specific circumstances would be a huge help in keeping out of Viklund's hands." He turned to Lizzy again. "Lizzy, would you be willing to have Owen analyze what's left of the drug? And would you be willing to take the drug again if he's able to replicate it?"

"Seriously?" "I hardly think—" said Andy and Owen simultaneously.

Philip held up his hand. "Let's hear what Lizzy has to say first."

They all looked at Lizzy.

She hesitated for only a moment. "Yes, I'd be willing to do that. It wasn't a bad experience. It was scary the first time because I didn't expect it, but it was ... interesting."

"You couldn't be on it all the time," said Owen, horrified. "Who knows what the long-term effects could be."

"I would never suggest that," said Philip. "But having that option for specific situations could prove very helpful. Could prove to be a life saver." He turned to Lizzy. "You're up for it?"

She nodded. "I'm up for it. Let me get the bottle." She jumped up and left the room.

A moment later, the woman who had solicited Andy's assistance earlier popped her head in the door. "Philip, there's someone who wants to see you."

The three men tensed.

"Who is it?" asked Philip, his hand drifting to the handle of the knife in a sheath at his belt.

The woman raised an eyebrow. "No one you're going to want to use *that* on."

Philip glanced at Owen and Andy with a look of mild confusion. "Stay here, I'll be right back."

He stood and left the room.

"I'll just check to make sure everything's okay," said Andy, and followed him out of the room.

FROM THE WINDOW-LINED hallway of the building that housed the clinic, Andy saw Philip step into the rose-tinted light of the desert sun. A woman was standing next to a pickup truck parked in the dirt yard of the clinic. She was tall and slender, with black hair pulled back in a long braid. The door of the clinic faced east, and Philip's eyes must have been adjusting to the light, because he didn't appear to see her at first.

The woman pushed herself away from the truck and began crossing the yard to where Philip stood. As she did, Philip saw her and the slight hunch he had exhibited, no doubt caused by his injured ribs, disappeared as he straightened. He walked toward her across the yard, pulling the sling over his head and dropping it to the ground as he went.

They met in the center of the yard, straight into each others' arms, Philip's face buried in the woman's hair, she with her arms wrapped around him, her hands on his shoulder blades.

Andy turned away and walked back to Owen's room. Owen was alone.

"What happened?" asked Owen.

"Were you thinking what I was thinking when Philip was describing his plan—that you weren't thrilled about leaving Lizzy alone with a thirty-something ex-con who we actually don't know all that well?"

Owen glanced nervously toward the door. "Well, yes, a little—"

Andy grinned. "I feel pretty comfortable saying we don't have anything to worry about."

64

———————

Louise hit zero on the mobile phone.

"Maja, Edmund and I have something we'd like to show Theo, could you ask him to come to the lab at his convenience? And could you bring us tea for three?"

"Certainly, Dr. Mortensen."

A few minutes later, the door to the lab opened and Theo entered, followed by Maja and her assistant with the tea tray.

"You already have something to show me?" he asked. "How gratifying." His usual good humor was subdued.

"We do," said Louise.

Maja's assistant put the tray on one of the lab tables. Maja gestured for him to leave, then reached for the teapot.

"Thank you, Maja," said Louise. "I can do that."

"Certainly, Dr. Mortensen."

Maja bowed slightly and stepped out of the lab, closing the door softly behind her.

Louise poured tea into the three cups. "Theo, I know you like milk and sugar," she said, pouring from the creamer and dropping a sugar cube into the cup. "Edmund?"

"Just sugar for me, thanks."

Louise handed cups to the two men. "Theo, there's something we'd like to show you. Just let me pull up the results." She sat down at the Mac and tapped at the keyboard while Edmund and Theo sipped their tea. Louise clicked through lists of files for a minute. "Edmund, I thought you put the documents out on the server."

"Oh, no," said Edmund, "they're on my laptop. Should I copy them to the server?"

"Yes. Please." She stood as Edmund opened his laptop. "More tea, Theo?"

Theo held out his cup. "Thank you."

She took his cup to the tray, poured tea and added milk and sugar, then returned the cup to Theo.

He cleared his throat as he took the cup. "Air's a bit dry in here."

Louise crossed to where Edmund sat at his laptop and looked over his shoulder. A minute ticked by.

"Edmund ...?" she said, the annoyance clear in her voice.

"I'm sorry, Dr. Mortensen, I must have saved the files somewhere else. I'm sure it won't take me more than a few more minutes to find them."

Louise waved her hand. "Later. We don't need it now." She turned to Theo. "I'm happy to report that we have had some very promising developments related to the work that Dr. Rinnert and I have been doing. I can't speak highly enough of the benefit of having someone of Dr. Rinnert's caliber to work with. It has enabled us to achieve results we couldn't possibly have achieved individually."

"I'm intrigued."

"We've been able to use the ion torrent sequencer for deep sequencing to discover some gene regulatory elements that govern embryonic developmental trajectories."

Theo coughed, then asked, "Could you simplify that for me a bit?"

"I believe our work is providing new strategies for successful cloning of non-human primates."

Theo raised his eyebrows. "Cloning?"

"Cloning is a fascinating study. There are extraordinary possibilities in terms of control over physical attributes like sex, strength, speed ... even cognitive abilities."

"Just for non-human primates?"

"To begin with."

Theo coughed, more violently this time, and tugged at the collar of his shirt.

"Is everything all right, Theo?"

"Yes, I'll be fine, I just—" His sentence was cut off with another bout of coughing. His face reddened alarmingly.

"Are you *sure* everything is all right?" she asked again, her voice taking on a frosty finality.

Theo looked at her, irritated, then his eyes widened. He gasped for breath. "Did you ..." He looked down at his empty tea cup, then swept it off the table with his arm. It crashed into the side of the sequencer and fell to the ground in shards.

A small, somewhat insane smile played on Edmund Rinnert's lips.

Louise put her own cup aside. "Oh, yes, Theo, we did. Dr. Rinnert has been such a help."

Theo fumbled in his pocket and pulled out his mobile phone.

Louise stepped to his side. "Let's not call for Lucas just yet," she said, and pulled the phone from his shaking hand.

Theo swayed, and she took his elbow and guided him toward one of the lab stools. He tried to push her away but stumbled. He grabbed for the stool as he fell and brought it down on top of him. Edmund pulled the stool off Viklund and set it aside.

Viklund's face was brick red, and his breath was coming fast.

Louise knelt next to Theo. "You missed the target, Theo. No iron ring for you. Just the quintain."

Theo's mouth gaped open as if to suck in lungfuls of air, but only a tiny whistle of breath passed through his throat.

Louise watched him, her face impassive. Edmund stood behind her, almost dancing in a frenzy of nerves.

The whistle became fainter and fainter, and in a minute, silence descended on the lab.

"Is he dead?" whispered Edmund with desperate glee.

Louise reached her fingers to Theo's neck and pressed them to his carotid artery for a full minute. "Quite dead."

"Do you think this will work?" asked Edmund. "Do you really think they won't suspect us?"

She stood. "Of course they'll suspect us. But what are they going to do—shoot us because we had the misfortune to be in the same room as their employer when he suffered an unexplained attack? I don't sense that Theo Viklund was someone who engendered tremendous love among his staff. And with Rey Viklund dead, there doesn't appear to be anyone else who is obviously second-in-command—or even someone who is jockeying for that position."

"Confusion about Viklund's death might protect us for a couple of days, but what then?"

"I feel confident that Maja will be happy to switch her allegiance to me, and I believe she will bring the rest of the household staff with her. We only need a few days to cement our position."

"And how do you plan to do that?"

"Theo himself provided all the tools we need—the lab, access to data. The threat to modify individuals' prescription medications—their own or their loved ones—could be effective. There are many options. I may test one of those options out on

Lucas." She got out her phone and pressed zero. "Maja, Theo has had an attack of some sort. Can you and Lucas please come down to the lab?" She ended the call.

"What about people outside the compound? The people Viklund was working with ... or working for?"

"With the reclusive life Theo led, it will take weeks—even months—for anyone to suspect that he's dead. Perhaps by that time, we can demonstrate to them that we are as formidable an ally as Theo was. And as formidable an adversary." She looked down at the body at their feet. "Theo may have been right that I wouldn't have sought out a position such as he has evidently built for himself, but he underestimated my willingness to step into that position if he made the alternative unpleasant enough."

She bent over Theo and returned his phone to his pocket.

"What about me?" asked Edmund.

"If I am successful in earning the loyalty of Theo's staff, I'll protect you. And if I am not successful, then I'll do my best to ensure I'm the one who pays the price, not you."

"You wouldn't need me anymore," he said tentatively.

"Edmund, you gave me your assurance that you would stay here, in exchange for me taking care of Theo. I expect you to adhere to that plan. And considering what you and I have been able to achieve in the short time we've worked together," she continued briskly, "just imagine what we will be able to accomplish over more time, and in an environment more conducive to careful study." She stepped to the door and pushed it open. Maja and Lucas were already making their hurried way down the path to the lab.

"You will be staying here, Edmund," said Louise. "I have great plans for you."

65

———

Owen sat at his dining room table in Lansdowne staring out the window, his laptop and a fan of papers spread before him. Andy and their parents had left several hours ago after a mid-day meal of lasagna and salad that his mother had prepared in Owen's kitchen. She seemed happiest and most like her old self when she was cooking.

He heard the front door open and the beep as the alarm was disarmed.

"Ruby?" he called.

"Yes, Dr. McNally," came her response. In a moment she appeared in the door. He began to push himself up with the cane that he was using while his leg healed, but she gestured him back into his chair. "Can I get you anything?" she asked.

"How was the service?" he asked.

She sighed. "It went as well as can be expected, I suppose. Opal held up pretty well."

"What now?"

Ruby took a deep breath. "Our cousin in Florida has asked

Opal if she wants to go down there to get away for a while, have a little vacation. I think it would be good for her."

"And how about you? You probably need a little vacation of your own—helping your sister on top of taking care of me must have been exhausting." He had seen the dark circles ringing her eyes, the droop of her usually resolute mouth.

"Florida really isn't for me," she said, some of her old briskness returning. "I can stay up here and get Opal and Tony's house straightened up. I wouldn't be surprised if she decides to stay down there, and she'll want the house looking nice if she decides to sell it."

"It sounds—" began Owen, then stopped himself. Any word he might use to complete that thought—sad? lonely?—would no doubt sound like pity to Ruby DiMano.

Ruby regarded him with an eyebrow raised in warning.

He sighed. "It's very thoughtful of you to do that for your sister."

"Well, I certainly won't start in on their house until you're up and about."

Ruby had been staying with Owen since his return from Arizona, since the combination of the heart attack and the stab wound to his thigh still made it difficult for him to get around.

"I would have been up and about days ago if I hadn't been taking advantage of your helpfulness," said Owen, more jovially than he felt. "I'm fine, really. You need to do what's right for you and your family."

She examined him with narrowed eyes, then said, "Well. All right."

"We can have a celebratory dinner—we have leftover lasagna—and then you can head back to Overbrook tomorrow," he continued, trying to maintain his cheerful tone.

"Oh. Yes. Well. All right." She glanced around the room. "Would you like some tea?"

"I just had some, thank you."

"I think I'll just have a cup myself." She turned and walked quickly down the hall toward the kitchen. In a few minutes, Owen heard the whistle of the kettle.

He pushed himself up from the table, retrieved the cane, and made his hitching way down the hall to the kitchen.

She was standing at the counter, her back to him, vigorously dunking a tea bag in a steaming cup of water.

"Ruby?"

"Yes, Dr. McNally?" she said, not turning around.

"Ruby, would you consider staying here with me for a little while longer? I miss Lizzy so much, and having company here makes it easier to take. You would be doing me a great favor if you would consider staying."

The dunking stopped. Ruby pulled a tissue from the pocket of her dress, dabbed her eyes, and turned around.

"Yes, Dr. McNally I would be happy to stay here a while longer."

66

———————

Two men stood in a conference room whose windows gave a view across downtown Phoenix to Camelback Mountain. The room was decorated in an odd mix of Western rustic and corporate sleek—longhorn steer horns mounted against raw silk wallpaper, a Remington sculpture of a bronco buster on an Italian mid-century credenza. Next to the sculpture sat a cowboy hat, brim up.

"They think it's for another solar farm?" asked a tall, barrel-chested man in a deep voice marked by a Texas drawl.

"Yes," said the shorter man. "They have no reason to think that we're ... diversifying."

"But the contract gives us an out?"

"Yes. They'd have to re-read the contract pretty closely to find the language that gives us the flexibility we need—it was a matter of changing just a few words."

"And the woman has the authority to sign for the allottees?"

"Yes. Once she signs, we're golden."

The taller man guffawed and adjusted his bolo tie. "We might have been 'golden' back in the day, but we'll be 'uranium' now."

The shorter man smiled humorlessly. "Clever."

The taller man swung open one of the credenza doors and removed a can of Red Bull from the refrigerated compartment that had been retrofit into its interior. He popped the tab and took a gulp. "They'll take the deal?"

The shorter man smoothed the lapels of his perfectly cut navy suit. "Cliff, that's what you pay me for—to make sure they take the deal."

There was a knock on the door.

"Yes," Cliff called.

The door opened and a handsome, rail-thin young man dressed all in black stepped into the room. "Are you ready for them?" he asked.

"Yes, Travis, send them in."

Travis nodded and withdrew back into the hallway.

"Let me do the talking," said the shorter man.

Cliff slapped him on the shoulder, eliciting a scowl. "I guess that's the other thing I pay you for, Jed," said Cliff jovially.

The party that entered the conference room looked out of place in the corporate setting. The first to enter was a Native American woman in her early thirties wearing a denim dress, a squash blossom necklace at her throat. Olivia Riva.

The second was a man of about the same age, also Native American. He wore neat jeans, polished boots, and a dark red shirt. At his waist was a belt buckle with a ladder design wrought in turquoise and silver, behind which the head of a snake, its eye rendered in red coral, protruded. Philip Riva. Their research hadn't uncovered any background on Mr. Riva.

The third was even more incongruous. A young white woman, deeply tanned, with short hair bleached gold by the sun but tipped with bright red. A turquoise, lapis, and onyx pendant in the shape of a Zuni bear hung at her throat. Elizabeth Owen. Like Mr. Riva, their searches on Ms. Owen had come up empty.

"Good morning," said Jed. He crossed from the windows to where the visitors stood near the door. "My name is Jed Grimwood, Cliff Ellerbach's attorney." He shook hands with Philip Riva and the Owen girl, then turned to Olivia Riva. "Miss Riva, such a pleasure to see you again," he said as he shook her hand.

The woman raised an eyebrow. "Mr. Grimwood."

Jed Grimwood waved the visitors toward the conference room table, into three chairs facing the window. "Please, have a seat."

The three sat down, Olivia Riva in the middle.

Grimwood and Ellerbach sat opposite them, the sun at their backs.

"Ms. Riva," said Grimwood, "I'd like to thank you and your colleagues for coming to Phoenix to finalize this deal. Mr. Ellerbach is very excited about the opportunity to expand his company's installations on your clients' land, and, as I'm sure you will agree, this is truly a win-win situation for all concerned. An opportunity for his company to continue to expand their presence in this vital industry, and an opportunity for your clients to reap significant financial benefits. We're pleased that you were able to review the contract with your clients, and that they have accepted our offer." He removed a Mont Blanc pen from his pocket, uncapped it, and laid it on top of the manila folder in front of his chair. "We've tabbed the pages where a signature is required." He slid the folder across the table to Olivia Riva and sat back.

Riva looked toward the girl, who shook her head.

Riva turned back to the men. "I won't sign."

Grimwood showed no response other than a slight tightening of his mouth. "What do you mean, you won't sign?"

"The agreement is unacceptable as it stands." She stood, and her two companions followed suit.

The two men stood as well.

"Wait a minute," said Ellerbach, looking between Olivia Riva and Grimwood, his face beginning to flush. "I thought we had worked out all the details. What could possibly make you tell us that our offer is unacceptable at this point?"

The man and the woman looked toward the girl, and the man gave her an almost imperceptible nod.

"You say you're going to build a solar farm," said Elizabeth Owen, "but you really want the land for uranium mining. This contract is different from what you sent to Olivia to review. This one is written in such a way that you can use the land however you want. The section that changed is ..." She looked at the lawyer for a moment, her eyes slightly squinted. "... Section H."

"What the hell—" said Ellerbach.

"Cliff, let me handle this," said Grimwood. He turned toward the girl. "What in the world makes you think that?"

"It doesn't matter. It's the truth, isn't it?"

Olivia Riva sat down, pulled the manila folder to her, flipped to the referenced section, and began reading.

Philip Riva and Elizabeth Owen sat as well.

After a moment, Grimwood and Ellerbach followed suit.

A minute ticked by. Grimwood sat with his hands resting on the table, fingers laced, watching Olivia Riva with narrowed eyes. Ellerbach snatched up the can of Red Bull from the table, and began squeezing and releasing it like a tin clicker toy. Grimwood looked at him with a raised eyebrow. Ellerbach banged the can down on the table and spun his chair to look out the window.

Finally, Olivia Riva flipped the folder closed. "That's not the same as the version you sent me as final."

"Perhaps there was some administrative mix-up," said Grimwood.

"There wasn't any mix-up," said Elizabeth Owen. "The guy who showed us in here, Travis, just changed the version number of the one you sent to Olivia, but now he's worried that there might be other copies he forgot about. He's also wondering if what Mr. Grimwood told him is true: that only the three of you know about the change. It is true. Mr. Grimwood made all the changes to the contract himself, so not even anyone else at his law firm knows about it, but Travis is mad that you guys involved him."

Ellerbach looked toward his lawyer. "Grimwood, you told me—"

"Shut up, Cliff," said Grimwood. He turned toward the three visitors. "If there was a change, I am certainly not aware of it." He turned back to Ellerbach. "Maybe Travis—"

"Don't blame this on Travis," Ellerbach shot back.

"Yeah, I don't think it's a good idea to try to blame Travis," said Lizzy, "because he and Mr. Ellerbach are—"

Ellerbach shot to his feet. "I said to leave Travis out of this!"

"Travis has been thinking about quitting."

"He has not!"

"Mr. Ellerbach thinks he would know if Travis was thinking about quitting because he and Travis spend a lot of time together."

"We do not!"

"Mr. Ellerbach is late home from work a lot, and he's worried that his wife is getting suspicious," continued the girl.

"What the hell—"

"There are some pictures that Mr. Ellerbach took of himself and sent to Travis, and now he's sorry he did that."

Ellerbach brought his fist down on the table.

"Shut up!"

The girl jumped, then continued, implacable. "If Mrs. Ellerbach gets the photos, Mr. Ellerbach is going to have to give her a lot of money in the divorce."

"She's never going to see those pictures!" Ellerbach yelled.

The room went quiet. Elizabeth Owen's face was flushed and she looked nervous but also satisfied. Olivia Riva raised an eyebrow. Philip Riva dropped his head, but not before Grimwood caught the grin breaking over his face.

Ellerbach stood and pointed toward the door with a shaking finger. "I want you out."

Olivia Riva sat back in her chair. "Mr. Ellerbach, for years your company installed very successful solar farms on Indian land—installations that have provided legitimate benefits to the allottees." She closed the manila folder and dropped it into a leather bag at her side. "I'm sure your attorney and your assistant can resurrect the version of the agreement that I reviewed with my clients. That's the agreement I came here to sign."

"I've changed my mind," said Ellerbach. "I have no interest in entering into any kind of agreement with you or your clients."

"Don't be hasty, Mr. Ellerbach," said Philip Riva. "I'm thinking that if Travis is starting to have second thoughts about his part in this deal, he might be willing to share whatever photos you sent to him. He'd have a legitimate claim of sexual harassment if his boss was sending him unsolicited photos of ..." He raised his eyebrows and looked toward Elizabeth Owen.

Ellerbach's face went from red to white.

"They were photos of—" said the girl.

"That's enough," said Grimwood. "Sit down, Cliff."

Ellerbach sat.

Grimwood turned to the three visitors. "So. A solar farm."

"Yes," said Olivia Riva. "Just as stated in the original agreement."

Grimwood turned to Ellerbach. "Another solar farm sounds like a capital idea, Cliff, don't you think?"

Ellerbach crossed his arms and glared at the three.

"I can just *picture* it," continued Grimwood.

The corner of Ellerbach's eye twitched. "Fine."

"It may take us a little while to identify the correct version," said Grimwood.

"We can wait," said Olivia Riva, sitting back in the chair and resting her laced fingers in her lap.

"Well, I can't sit around here while you straighten up this mess with mixed-up contracts," said Ellerbach. "You take care of it," he said, directing the comment to Grimwood but not meeting his eyes. He stalked out of the room.

Grimwood stood. "If you'll excuse me."

And as he headed for the door—hoping that Travis had perhaps not deleted *all* of the earlier versions—he couldn't help but notice the smile that Philip Riva and Elizabeth Owen exchanged.

END OF BOOK 3

*D*ID *you enjoy* The Iron Ring? *If you did, I would be so grateful if you would take a moment to leave a rating and review on your favorite online platform. For inspiration, check out what other satisfied readers have said!*

Thank you!

Matty

AUTHOR'S NOTE

When I began work on Book 4 of the Lizzy Ballard Thrillers, which became *Scare Card*, I had a dilemma; while Lizzy's story would pick up a month or more after her last scene in Book 3: *The Iron Ring*, whatever happened next to Louise Mortensen would happen seconds after we last see her in this book.

That meant that, if I were to present Lizzy and Louise's scenes in chronological order in *Scare Card*, the first several chapters would have to focus on Louise, and I didn't want Lizzy's fans to have to wait that long to re-engage with their protagonist.

My solution was to catch Louise's timeline up with Lizzy's in a novella: *Kill Box Checkmate (Book 3½)*

I had so much fun plumbing Louise's villainous depths in *Kill Box*, and setting the stage for her reappearance in *Scare Card*. If you love villains as much as I do—at least this particular villain—I hope you'll check it out *Kill Box Checkmate (Book 3½)*

In a twisty tale of betrayal and vengeance, a cunning scientist orchestrates her escape from the isolated estate of a sociopathic tycoon. When Louise Mortensen's kidnapper, Theo Viklund, drops dead, she glimpses her chance for freedom—by becoming him.

Joining forces with Viklund's sinister head of security and her hapless lab assistant, Louise makes a chilling pact to conceal her captor's death. Once Louise assumes Viklund's identity, her path to freedom will be ensured ... but first, she must access his biometrically-protected computer accounts.

The key seems out of reach ... until Theo's brother arrives, searching for the truth behind Theo's disappearance. Will he provide Louise the clue she needs to unlock Theo's riches and his secrets?

Louise finds herself navigating a high-stakes web of deception, treachery, and murder. And the closer she gets to claiming absolute power, the deadlier her web becomes.

In this exhilarating thrill ride, a devious antiheroine with a murderous past must unravel a conspiracy of lies to claim a prize worth killing for.

are silenced, and every person who loves her is now a chip someone else is holding.

SCARE CARD is a taut story of loyalty, complicity, and the brutal math of love that asks one unbearable question: how much of what Lizzy does is choice, and how much was decided for her before she could speak? For readers of Stephen King's *Firestarter* who like a cold, calculating villain at the center, Scare Card deals Lizzy into a game where the people she loves are the stakes—and she's about to learn what it costs to be holding the deadliest hand at the table.

Continue Lizzy's adventures in Book 4 of the Lizzy Ballard Thrillers, *Scare Card*!

Join Matty Dalrymple's occasional email newsletter at mattydalrymple.com and receive exclusive subscriber benefits.

ALSO BY MATTY DALRYMPLE

The Lizzy Ballard Thrillers

Rock Paper Scissors (Book 1)

Snakes and Ladders (Book 2)

The Iron Ring (Book 3)

Kill Box Checkmate (Book 3½)

Scare Card (Book 4)

Drawing Dead (Book 5)

The Lizzy Ballard Thrillers Ebook Box Set

The Ann Kinnear Suspense Novels

The Sense of Death (Book 1)

The Sense of Reckoning (Book 2)

The Falcon and the Owl (Book 3)

A Furnace for Your Foe (Book 4)

A Serpent's Tooth (Book 5)

Be with the Dead (Book 6)

The Ann Kinnear Suspense Novels Ebook Box Set - Books 1-3

The Ann Kinnear Suspense Shorts

A Year of Kinnear: 12 Suspense Shorts from the World of Ann Kinnear

All Deaths Endure

Close These Eyes

Ever Thanks

May Violets Spring

Ministers of Grace

More Than a Jest

Our Dancing Days

Sea of Troubles

Stage of Fools

These Hot Days

Wondering Eyes

Write in Water

Non-Fiction

Taking the Short Tack: Creating Income and Connecting with Readers Using Short Fiction with Mark Leslie Lefebvre

The Indy Author's Guide to Podcasting for Authors: Creating Connections, Community, and Income

From Page to Platform: How to Succeed as an Author Speaker with M.L. Ronn

Collaborate to Create: A Guide to Coauthoring Nonfiction with M.L. Ronn

The Podcast Guest Playbook: Turning Conversations into Connections and Community with Mark Leslie Lefebvre

ABOUT THE AUTHOR

Matty Dalrymple is the author of the Lizzy Ballard Thrillers, beginning with *Rock Paper Scissors*; the Ann Kinnear Suspense Novels, beginning with *The Sense of Death*; and the Ann Kinnear Suspense Shorts, including *Close These Eyes*. She is a member of International Thriller Writers and Sisters in Crime. Go to mattydalrymple.com > About to learn more and to sign up for her occasional email newsletter.

Matty also educates and advocates for writers as The Indy Author. She is the host and producer of hundreds of episodes of *The Indy Author Podcast* and has spoken on topics related to writing and publishing at events such as the Writer's Digest annual conference, ALLi SelfPubCon, Author Nation, Authors Guild webinars, International Thriller Writers' CraftFest, and many more. She writes nonfiction books for writers, and her articles have appeared in *Writer's Digest* magazine. She is a Partner Member of the Alliance of Independent Authors. Go to theindyauthor.com > About & Contact for more information about Matty's non-fiction work and to sign up for her weekly email newsletter.

Matty lives with her husband, Wade Walton, and their dogs in Chester County, Pennsylvania, and enjoys vacationing on Mount Desert Island, Maine, and Sedona, Arizona, and these locations provide the settings for her novels.

facebook.com/matty.dalrymple

ACKNOWLEDGMENTS

Many thanks to all the people who generously shared their expertise and advice on various aspects of the story, including Sergeant Rodger Ollis of the Coatesville Police Department; Wade Rogers, PhD, University of Pennsylvania School of Medicine; Linda R. Liotti D.O. (a.k.a. Linda Rawlins); David L. Fried, MD, FACP; Sergeant Tim Klarkowski, Public Information Officer of the Surprise, AZ, Police Department; Jonathan P. Thompson (RiverOfLostSouls.com); KB Inglee; Robert Blake Whitehill; and Daavid Kahn.

Thanks to Jen Blood for taking another of my novels on its shakedown cruise.

Thanks once again to Mary Dalrymple for continuing her role as early reader, and for her unflagging enthusiasm about my authorial endeavors.

And, as always, thanks to my partner in crime, Wade Walton, for his tireless support and encouragement.

Any deviations from strict accuracy—intentional or unintentional—are solely the responsibility of the author.

9 780986 267543